For Mom

You are the one who encouraged my love of books.

I would also like to thank Robin, Diana, and my daughters; Julia and Jojo, who entered the worlds I created and told me to share them with others.

Contents

Title Page
Copyright
Dedication
Chapter One — 1
Chapter Two — 6
Chapter Three — 11
Chapter Four — 19
Chapter Five — 28
Chapter Six — 35
Chapter Seven — 42
Chapter Eight — 50
Chapter Nine — 58
Chapter Ten — 65
Chapter Eleven — 72
Chapter Twelve — 80
Chapter Thirteen — 88
Chapter Fourteen — 96
Chapter Fifteen — 107
Chapter Sixteen — 116
Chapter Seventeen — 124

Chapter Eighteen	131
Chapter Nineteen	141
Chapter Twenty	149
Chapter Twenty-One	159
Chapter Twenty-Two	167
Chapter Twenty-Three	174
Chapter Twenty-Four	182
Chapter Twenty-Five	189
Chapter Twenty-Six	197
Chapter Twenty-Seven	205
Chapter Twenty-Eight	214
Chapter Twenty-Nine	222
Chapter Thirty	230
Chapter Thirty-One	238
Chapter Thirty-Two	246
Chapter Thirty-Three	254
Chapter Thirty-Four	262
Chapter Thirty-Five	271
Chapter Thirty-Six	279
Chapter Thirty-Seven	287
Chapter Thirty-Eight	295
Chapter Thirty-Nine	306
Chapter Forty	314
Chapter Forty-One	323
Chapter Forty-Two	331

Chapter One

Shaking my head, I gaze up at my dad furiously. It isn't fair that I have to go and stay with Uncle John while my parents go out on their yacht for a couple weeks. I am eighteen years old!

"I will be safe here by myself, Dad!" I argue with him for probably the tenth time. "I am an adult and don't need a babysitter anymore! Why won't you trust me?"

Dad reaches out and tenderly strokes my face as he smiles down at me lovingly.

"I do trust you, Jacqueline." He whispers, his voice soft and soothing to my angry tone. "It is the world that I do not trust. Please, just this one last time. Go and stay with Uncle John, just so your mother will be able to relax on our trip? You know how much she worries about you."

My resentment dissipates instantly. I don't want Mom to spend the entire boating trip worried about me and I know she will.

"Ok." I drop my gaze to my bare feet and sigh sadly. Will I never be allowed to grow up?

"That's my Jelly." Dad murmurs to me, pleased with my reply.

His nickname for me never fails to bring a smile to my face. He is the only one that calls me Jelly. I grab my duffel bag off of my bed before getting into my old Dodge Shadow to drive over to Uncle John's house in Seattle.

Uncle John is Dad's business partner in their shipping company and even though he isn't really my uncle he has carried that title ever since I can remember. I pull away from our modest two-bedroom cabin and make my way to the ferry that will take me from our home on Bainbridge Island over to Seattle.

I have always loved the ferry because of the chances you have of seeing whales, dolphins, and all of the other sea life that is in Puget Sound. The ferry is pretty empty since it is the middle of the afternoon and most people take it to and from work in the city. There will be a full ferry, no doubt, on the way back to the island once I go ashore.

Uncle John has a mansion on Lake Washington on the other side of Seattle from where the ferry lets me out at. He lives there alone even though it has five bedrooms, four bathrooms and over six thousand square feet. Not only is he right there on the banks of Lake Washington but he has a clear view of Mount Rainier.

I have been coming to stay with Uncle John forever so one of the five bedrooms is mine. Mom and Dad refuse to spoil me at all, but Uncle John doesn't agree with them so he makes up for it. My bedroom there is full of everything a teenage girl could possibly ask for.

Uncle John is still at work when I arrive but his housekeeper is there when I let myself inside. She gets me a glass of ice tea while I sit out on the dock in the cool October weather.

"There is my Princess!" Uncle John strides across the perfectly manicured lawn towards me with an affectionate smile. "I know you wanted to stay home by yourself, but I cannot tell you that I am disappointed to find you here."

I get to my feet, step into his arms and tip up my face for the kiss he places on my forehead.

"I know." I whisper, giving him a forced smile.

"I wanted to stop at home to let you know that an issue came up at the office forcing me to work late." Uncle John explains to me with a regretful expression. "Helga has an amazing dinner planned for you and I promise to make it up to you tomorrow night. I want you to stay in tonight because there is a storm coming in and it isn't safe for you to take the boat out onto the lake. Promise me?"

"I promise." I nod solemnly. "Will Mom and Dad be alright?"

"Yes. They should be fine." Uncle John reassures me. "They are headed south, away from the storm system."

I spend the evening after dinner studying for a big exam that I have at the college next week and by the time I turn in for the night Uncle John hasn't returned. He takes the next two weeks off of work in order to spend as much time with me as possible. My loneliness always goes away after I spend time with Uncle John.

He takes me to the symphony, ballet, the museums, out on his yacht, and we even just watch movies together sometimes. When I come to stay it as if I am the most important person in his life.

Three weeks later, my parents still have not returned from their trip and I have not heard from them once. Normally, they check in every couple of days. Uncle John tries to reassure me that they are probably fine but I cannot help but worry.

Finally, at the end of the third week, Uncle John takes me down to the police department to file a missing person's report. The search is officially underway for my parents and I return home to the cabin. Uncle John tries to convince me to stay with him but I want to be at the cabin where all of my memories of my parents are.

Weeks turn into months and I throw myself into my studies at the college to keep my mind off of their disappearance. Uncle John checks in with me daily, always pressuring me to come stay with him, but I always refuse. Mom and Dad could return to the cabin any day and I want to be here when they return.

Thanksgiving, Christmas, New Years, and Valentine's Day all come and go with no break in the disappearance of my parents. They were intending on taking the yacht down the coast to California before returning. According to the investigation they never made it to their first stop in Oregon. There was a big storm the night they set sail and it is assumed they went down somewhere along the Washington coast.

Desperation to find my mom and dad's family has me ordering one of the DNA kits online from one of the reputable family tree sites. I order it just a couple weeks into the new year and then wait for the six to eight weeks to get my results. I don't even tell Uncle John because I am afraid that he will try to talk me out of finding my family. Mom and Dad would never talk about their family and I have never met any of them. I am all alone now.

I am sitting in one of my classes on the university campus when Uncle John comes to the door of the classroom. Gathering up my books, I step out into the hallway as my stomach clenches into knots.

They found my parents.

Uncle John confirms my suspicions after we get outside to his car. I am instantly numb as the reality of my situation doesn't sink in right away. Uncle John explains to me that their yacht went down that first night because they didn't make it away from the storm before it hit. I nod my head when he tells me that he will take care of everything for me.

Not trusting me to stay by myself he insists on bringing me back to his house, just for a few days. Too stunned to argue, I silently ride to his house where I shut myself up in my bedroom there. Curling up on the window seat, I gaze out at Lake Washington as the March snowstorm blows in over the water.

I cry silent tears as the reality of my situation finally hits me. I am an orphan. Mom and Dad will never come home.

Uncle John arranges the funeral for me and takes care of everything while allowing me to grieve. I am the only blood relative at the funeral for my parents. The only people that attend are my mother's friends and employees from Dad's shipping company.

Uncle John has them cremated and I fulfill my parent's wishes by sprinkling their ashes together in the waters of Puget Sound close to the cabin.

Chapter Two

I stare at the attorney in shock as he reads my parent's will and I find out that I am actually adopted. Eighteen years old and I never had even the smallest suspicion that they weren't my birth parents.

Being their only living relative, everything goes to me and I have become a very wealthy girl overnight. My mom came from a very wealthy family on the east coast and my father owned his own shipping company.

Not only will I never have to work again due to the profits from the shipping company but my parents were very frugal.

I bite my lip to keep the tears at bay and sign all of the required papers before leaving the attorney's office. At least now, I won't have to worry about hurting my parent's feelings when my DNA results come back.

The thought suddenly hits me that I could discover who my blood relatives are any day now. I sent the kit back with my saliva sample over eight weeks ago and should be getting my results soon.

Mom and Dad went missing six months ago and were just now declared legally dead when their wreckage was discovered.

It will be very strange for me to have access to all of this money because my parents refused to spoil me at all and made me work for everything I got. It has only been in the last couple weeks that I felt brave enough to start driving my mom's car instead of my old beater I bought working at McDonald's.

I sigh sadly as I pull into the driveway of the modest cabin that has been my home for the last eighteen years. The sound of my mother's laughter or my father's joke's will never be heard again. Their death was nearly impossible for me to bear considering that I was homeschooled. I was lucky to have Uncle John there for me.

Six months later it is finally starting to get easier but I don't think I will ever get used to the loneliness. Unlocking the front door and stepping into the family room I realize that everything is mine. I can do things my way because there is no one else here, just me.

Turning on the computer in the study I decide to check my DNA results to see if they are posted yet as well as shop online for a new cell phone, now that there is no one here to tell me I can't have one.

I stare in shock at my results from my DNA test. I have a match that states that the person is my full sibling. My next match says the person could be a great-grandparent, niece, nephew or a great-aunt or uncle. Under these two is a list of first, second, third and fourth cousins that go on for pages.

I open up the profile for my full sibling match and see the name Grayson Devereaux. His profile gives the same birthday as me which would make him my fraternal twin! He lives all the way across the country from my location in Seattle. He is listed as living in New Orleans. As I look over his profile, I see that he has an email listed and I hesitantly send him a message with my name, date of birth and my location.

I turn my attention to the next match on my list and open up the profile page to find a woman by the name of Kyna Trudeau. She is 40 years old and also lives in the New Orleans area. Grayson is listed under her matches as well but I have no idea if this woman is related to my birth mother or father. She also has an email listed so I send her a message as well giving her the same information.

I navigate to the part of my results that shows my genealogical breakdown and am not surprised to see that I am forty percent Scottish; because of my red hair, fifty percent English, and ten percent German. I compare my breakdown to Grayson's and am a little confused to see that he is nearly sixty percent German and the rest split between Scottish and English. Why would our breakdown be so different if we are full siblings?

Turning to Google, I learn that siblings inherit different amounts from each parent and explains why they all look so different from one another. Each child will have a differing amount depending on what they inherit from parents, grandparents and even great-grandparents.

Opening a new tab, I spend some time shopping for a new cell phone and decide on an android instead of an iPhone. I find one that is for sale in a shop downtown and decide to do that so they can set it all up for me.

Once that is done, I log off of the computer and decide to work off some of my anxiety by cleaning the house. There is not much to do since I have been the only one here for the last six months, but with spring arriving there is always extra to be done.

Two weeks later, I have finally received an email back from one of my DNA matches. I am a little disappointed to see that it isn't my brother but instead is the woman. She introduces herself as my maternal great-aunt. My mother was her niece and my maternal grandfather is her older brother. She only tells me that my mother died from complications with my birth. My grandparents thought it best if I was given up for adoption under the circumstances but she would be happy to meet me and be a part of my life.

She tells me that my mother's name was Euphemia Burt and that she will share more with me if I am willing to fly down to New Orleans for a public meeting.

I write her back telling her I would be thrilled to fly down to meet her and will let her know details after I book my flight and hotel. Not sure about how to plan this I call my father's business partner, Uncle John, for advice and he tells me that he will have his assistant make my reservations for me then fax the confirmation to me at the house. I am surprised when Uncle John doesn't react at all to the news of my DNA test and resulting birth family.

An hour later a fax comes through with my flight details, rental car and hotel reservation, all I need to do is show my identification at the airport. I am surprised to see that my flight leaves tomorrow morning and a car will pick me up to bring me to the airport. After emailing the details to my great-aunt I pack what I will need for a long stay, just in case.

I don't have to worry about the cabin because Uncle John promises to have his assistant check in a couple times a week.

After a long hot shower, I gaze at myself in the mirror anxiously. Will I look like my brother or great-aunt? Will my grandparents even agree to meet me? My long red ringlet curls, big blue eyes, and elfin features reflect back at me nervously. I have always wondered why I was so short when both of my parents were at least six feet tall and I am barely five feet. I have always been dainty whereas my mother was a large woman. Will my great-aunt Kyna have pictures of my birth mother? Has she met my brother yet? So many questions.

My hotel reservations are in the Windsor Court Hotel and my lack of experience travelling gives me no idea what kind of hotel it will be. My father traveled because of the shipping company so his business partner, John Van Asselt, has taken care of all of my expenses in addition to transferring all of my dad's credit cards into my name.

I spend a few minutes before bed cleaning out the refrigerator, making sure all the garbage's are empty and the plants are watered. My dishes are all washed and put away, there is no dirty laundry and all of the windows are locked up tight.

Chapter Three

My plane lands in New Orleans in early afternoon and for an April afternoon I am surprised at the heat here. I pick up my rental car and am shocked when I see that Uncle John has reserved an Audi sports car for me. Smiling eagerly after stowing my luggage in the trunk I put the hotel's address into the car's GPS system before pulling out of the lot.

The Audi is an R8 Spyder convertible in yellow and black and I fall in love with it instantly. Its leather interior is as soft as butter and it handles corners like a dream. Uncle John always did try to convince Dad to spoil me a little more so I am not surprised at his choice in cars.

I follow the directions on the car's GPS and soon I am pulling up in front of the luxurious Windsor Court Hotel. I seriously doubt my frugal father would have ever stayed here as I gaze in awe at the building before me. It looks like royalty is right at home in the opulent splendor.

Before I can open my door, a valet does it for me with a welcoming smile while another hotel employee rushes out to grab my luggage. I return the valet's smile with a cool one of my own as I hand him the keys, really attempting to fit into this social class smoothly. I make my way inside the polished interior with my head held high and step up to the desk as if I do this every day.

The older gentleman checks me in efficiently and informs me that the reservation is open ended and when I am ready to check out, they will be pleased to assist. The guy who grabbed my luggage walks ahead of me showing me the way to my room.

I am brought to the top floor and I am stunned to see that I am led into one of the penthouse suites. Not wanting to look as innocent as I feel I refuse to look around in awe while the guy shows me around the rooms. I nod at him slightly, keeping my expression neutral, as he hands me the key card to my room. He smiles at me and my empath abilities allow me to feel his attraction for me. I am unable to stop the blush that rises in my cheeks or keeping myself from gazing down at the floor bashfully. He chuckles at my reaction and makes his way to the door.

"Enjoy your stay in New Orleans Ms. Cassidy." His southern drawl giving me goosebumps. "If you need anything at all please feel free to contact the concierge."

"Thank you." I murmur softly.

Now that he is gone, I wander from room to room looking at the extravagance of my suite and shake my head with a smile as I think of Uncle John finally being able to spoil me. I have called him Uncle John ever since I could remember and he has lovingly lived up to the title.

The windows give a beautiful view of the surrounding city in the bright spring sunshine. The room is done in white, cream, soft blue and dark wood. I have a bedroom with a king-sized bed, separate sitting room, my own private balcony, and a huge bathroom with stand up shower large enough for several people and a sunken marble tub complete with jets. I feel like a princess.

"Uncle John, really?" I ask as soon as he picks up the phone.

"Are you talking about the car or the hotel?" He asks with a laugh.

"Oh, my goodness!" I exclaim. "Both! I am in love with the car and you can fit several families in this hotel suite. What am I supposed to do with all of this room? It is bigger than the whole cabin!"

"Princess, prepare to be spoiled." Uncle John tells me. "I have no children and, god bless him, your father can't stop me anymore."

"I love you Uncle John." My voice breaks slightly.

"I love you too Jac." His voice is emotional as well. "You call me every day and keep me updated on how it is going meeting your birth family, okay?"

"I will." I promise before hanging up.

Too nervous to actually call my great-aunt Kyna, I send her a text message that I am settled in my hotel room and would love to meet for a cup of coffee when she has time. She gets right back to me and suggests we meet at the Café' du Monde as it is a highlight of New Orleans. She says she can be there in a half hour.

I change out of my skirt, blouse and heels into a comfortable pair of skinny jeans and a blue ruffled tank top that matches my eyes with a pair of flip flops. After fluffing my long red ringlets, I put the address of the café into my phone so I won't get lost and head down to the lobby. Not wanting to carry a purse I put my driver's license, credit cards, and key card to the room in my back pocket.

On my way past the desk I collect my car key and decide to walk the half mile to the restaurant. The weather here is gorgeous compared to the still wintery weather in Seattle. I take in the scenery and people as I make my way down the sidewalk.

When I arrive at the restaurant, I do not see a blonde woman who looks like the picture my aunt sent me so I order a café au lait with an order of beignets before taking a seat in a back corner where I can see the door.

A woman looking slightly older than the photo she sent me enters the restaurant but she is not alone. A very tall muscular guy is with her that looks to be between eighteen and twenty years old. He has black hair that is shaved on the sides and in a slightly longer spike on the top. He is tan as if he spends a lot of time in the sun. His eyes look dark from this distance and he has a well-trimmed beard and mustache. He must be well over six feet tall and his muscles are bulging from the tight black t-shirt he is wearing.

My eyes meet great-aunt Kyna's and she smiles at me while saying something to the huge guy with her. He looks over at me and I can feel his curiosity and eagerness all the way over here. I suddenly feel a gentle brush in my thoughts and in shock I slam down a mental wall to keep out the unfamiliar intrusion and see the guy's eyes widen in surprise.

I blush furiously as I realize that he must have psychic abilities just like me. Is he related to me? Standing up I step around the table to greet them anxiously.

"Great-aunt Kyna?" I ask hesitantly. She stands nearly six inches taller than me and has pale blonde hair with green eyes. Her nose is narrow and is slightly too long for her face. Her lips are full but are too wide for her features. She is athletically built with a nice figure.

"Please, Aunt Kyna is fine dear." She says in a warm sincere voice. "You must be Jacqueline."

"Jac is fine." I state softly as I look up the dark-haired guy towering over me intensely.

"Jac, this is your twin brother Grayson Devereaux."

Aunt Kyna introduces us. Taken aback I can only stare up at him silently. I wasn't expecting to meet him since he never responded to my email.

"Why don't you two have a seat while I grab a couple cups of coffee." Aunt Kyna sails away towards the counter, leaving us alone.

I sit down and instantly twist my fingers together nervously and I hear Grayson chuckle as he sits down next to me.

"I'm sorry I didn't see your email." He informs me in a deep southern drawl. "Aunt Kyna called to tell me about you and suggested that I come along to meet you with her. I hope that is okay?"

"Oh yes!" I exclaim. "I wasn't expecting to meet you. I guess I'm just…." I pause not wanting to hurt his feelings as I really wanted time to prepare before meeting him.

"You aren't hurting my feelings." He whispers as he uses his thumb to tip up my chin, forcing me to look at him. I am surprised to see his eyes are a deep dark blue instead of brown like I had earlier thought.

"You are like me." I whisper back emotionally, never having met another psychic like me before. He nods with an affectionate smile.

"You were trying to listen to my thoughts, weren't you?" I ask impressed. He nods once again.

"I'm telepathic. You felt me." He states and it is my turn to nod.

"How long have you known you were adopted?" I ask curiously.

"Not long." He confesses. "My adopted parents told me when I turned eighteen and then helped me to find my birth family. That is how I found Aunt Kyna. You?"

"I found out a couple weeks ago during the reading of my adopted parents will." I tell him. "I don't think they would have ever told me the truth had they not died. I bought the DNA kit online a couple months ago hoping I could find out about the family they never talked about. So, I am guessing that I must have somehow been adopted from down here?"

"Yeah. Our mom grew up here in New Orleans." Grayson explains. "I'm sorry about your adopted parents. Are you all alone now or do you have brothers and sisters up there in Seattle?"

"No siblings. My adopted dad's business partner is like an uncle to me." I share with a sad smile. "I don't see any similarities between us."

"I must take after our father's side of the family." He says and I can feel a brief flash of an intense hatred before it disappears. Aunt Kyna returns to the table and hands Grayson a cup of coffee before sitting down. I wonder at the hatred but do not have an opportunity to ask about it.

"I must warn you that the telling of this will not be easy." Aunt Kyna warns me and when I reach out mentally to Grayson, I can feel the wall he has put up so I can't read him. Wrapping my arms around myself I nod quietly at my aunt for her to continue.

She takes out an envelope and sets a stack of photographs on the table in front of me allowing me some time to look through them. They all feature a tiny red-haired girl who looks like a copy of myself. I see pictures of her from a baby all the way up to about pre-teen age and then the photos just stop. Shouldn't there be more?

"Your mother, Phemie everyone called her, was

abducted one day on her way to school when she was just twelve years old." Aunt Kyna explains at my look of confusion. "She was missing for nearly a month before one day she just showed up on the front porch. She was malnourished and dirty with a haunted look in her eyes that never went away. Poor thing. Your grandfather brought her right to the hospital where she ended up staying for a couple weeks before she was strong enough to come home. Police interviewed her and showed her pictures hoping she could identify her attacker. Finally, she saw a photograph of the monster who kidnapped her. He went to prison just days before we lost her giving birth to the both of you."

"She was just a child." I state in horror.

"Yes." Aunt Kyna agrees. "After everything that happened your grandparents just couldn't keep the both of you. Euphemia was their only child and the trauma of learning what that man did to her was just too much for them. They wanted to forget."

"My father is a pedophile." I whisper to myself brokenly as I rise to my feet, feeling the need to just run away. Grayson takes me in his arms and refuses to let me go when I struggle to free myself. Finally, I relax in his arms and understand the brief flash of hatred he felt when he mentioned he probably looks like our father.

"It's okay, Jac." Grayson whispers to me soothingly. "You're not alone anymore. We have each other, sis."

Grayson finally releases me when he knows I am over the shock of Aunt Kyna's story. I sit back down and shake my head as I realize that I could have accepted anything but this. It sounds like a really bad horror novel.

Aunt Kyna's worry for me washes over me in a flood as does Grayson's.

"I am fine." I reassure them. "It will just take time for me to come to grips with all of it."

Chapter Four

Kyna gets a phone call and has to rush away but hesitates to leave me alone so soon after dropping such a bomb on me.

"Grayson?" Aunt Kyna asks as she rises from the table uncertainly.

"I can stay with her." He tells her with a grin. "Mom and Dad want her to come to dinner tonight and they weren't going to take no for an answer."

"Jac, are you going to be alright?" Aunt Kyna asks me anxiously.

"Yes, Aunt Kyna." I reassure her. "I will be fine. Dinner with Grayson's family sounds like just what I need."

"The photographs are yours to keep." She tells me with a smile.

She rushes out of the restaurant leaving me alone with my newly discovered twin brother.

"Does she know about your gift?" I ask him softly and watch him shake his head.

"I think our gifts may have come from our father's side of the family." Grayson shares thoughtfully as he looks at his watch. "Let's ride back to your hotel so you can grab a jacket. It's supposed to get cold tonight."

Grayson politely pulls out my chair for me and smiles affectionately as we walk out of the restaurant together.

"I walked up here from my hotel." I tell him as we head down the sidewalk.

"Which hotel are you staying at?" He asks curiously as he shortens his steps for me.

"Uncle John put me in the Windsor Court Hotel." I whisper almost shamefully. "It's way too fancy for me. You should see the rental car he reserved for me. It's an Audi R8 Spyder convertible, yellow. He seems to think I need to be spoiled now that my frugal parents are gone."

Grayson whistles appreciatively.

"That car is awesome! They go for over two hundred grand!"

"Please tell me you are kidding." I state, my face paling.

"No, Jac." Grayson insists. "So, what is your house like in Seattle?"

"It is a very modest two-bedroom cabin in the woods." I tell him honestly. "My parents may have had money but they didn't live like they did. I guess now that my father is gone, I am Uncle Johns partner in the shipping company but I am considered a silent partner."

We finish the walk to the hotel in silence, each lost in thought. Grayson is quiet as we take the elevator up to my top floor suite where he once again whistles appreciatively.

"My baby sister is loaded!" He whispers and I laugh.

"I suppose I am." I reply thoughtfully. "Are you sure I am the younger twin?"

"Yep." He confirms. "Aunt Kyna was in the delivery room I guess."

I grab a light jacket and follow Grayson out to the elevator. He is surprised and elated when I hand him the key to the car and insist that he drive us to his house.

Unfortunately for my brother, he doesn't get the chance to see just how fast the car will go as he only lives several blocks away in the garden district. He pulls up in front of a beautiful white two-story house that looks like it belongs in a magazine. It has columns around the entire structure with black shutters on the windows. It has a porch around the first floor and a matching balcony along the second floor. It is absolutely gorgeous.

I hesitate to follow him up to the front door and he stops when he realizes I am not right behind him.

"Don't be nervous sis." He encourages me. "We are just a normal family like everyone else."

I nod and follow him inside the cozy home. The walls are painted in warm earth tones and the floors are polished wood. There are photographs of the family all over everywhere showing how much family means to them.

A beautiful woman with long mahogany colored hair and green eyes steps into the foyer with a loving smile aimed at Grayson. She is tall for a woman but has a curvy feminine figure and gorgeous facial features.

"Mom, this is my baby sister Jacqueline Cassidy. Jac this is my mom, Nicole Devereaux." Grayson introduces us with a happy smile.

"It is nice to meet you." I tell her politely, while inside I am a nervous wreck.

"Welcome to the family Jacqueline!" She gushes warmly before pulling me into a hug. "I am so glad to see that you two hit it off. Grayson was so worried to meet you."

"Mom!" He exclaims in embarrassment.

"Come on into the kitchen so you can meet everyone else." She says as she wraps an arm around my shoulders to walk me down the hallway. Grayson brings up the rear with a sigh, but I can feel his happiness at my presence here.

"Victor look who is here!" Nicole gushes as soon as we step into the kitchen. An older man rises from his place at the table and looks at me curiously. He is several inches shorter than Grayson and must be maybe nine or ten inches taller than my five feet. He has short dark hair that is combed to the side neatly with a full beard that has gone gray. His face is kind and I can feel his relief.

"Dad this is Jacqueline." Grayson introduces us.

"Sir." I whisper uncertainly.

"Please, call me Victor." He smiles at me sincerely.

Before I can quite get over my nervousness of meeting Victor, I find myself staring up into a sexy pair of light brown eyes. The eyes belong to a hot guy with short dark brown hair, full lips, perfect nose, and a light beard. He stands nearly as tall as Grayson and although not as bulky as my brother he is certainly athletic. He looks to be a few years older than me and I definitely have his attention as well.

Grayson chuckles and wraps an arm around me to pull me back into his arms protectively.

"Sis, this is my older brother Lucien." Grayson introduces us. "This is Jac."

I blush at being caught drooling over Grayson's brother and drop my gaze to the floor as I clutch Grayson's arm tightly.

"She's a lot prettier than you are Gray." Lucien states, his husky southern drawl giving me butterflies.

"I would hope so Lucien." Grayson replies with a laugh.

"Give her a tour of the house while I finish up dinner." Nicole states as she gestures us out of the kitchen.

Grayson and Lucien show me just how large their house really is as I see the formal dining room, library, family room, living room, four seasons porch, patio, breakfast nook, the four extra bedrooms and finally Grayson's room.

I walk around his room curious about what it will tell me about my newly found brother. On the walls are posters of some serious bodybuilders and there are books stacked all over about fitness, nutrition as well as running your own business. His bed is a neatly made queen size in black and deep green. He has framed photographs of him and Lucien growing up, his adopted parents, him and his adopted dad, friends from school, and even a few of our mother.

Out of place on the top shelf of his desk is a snow globe of Edinburgh Scotland and without thinking about it I pick it up only to be instantly drawn into an intense vision.

I see my mother and she must be about ten or eleven years old and she is wandering around a locally owned shop that sells souvenir type stuff. She sees the snow globes and excitedly grabs this one to beg her father for it. I can feel his love for her wash over me as he nods his assent to the purchase. My mother clutches the snow globe to her chest ecstatically and can't wait to bring it home to place it on the shelf with her other treasures.

The vision moves forward through time and my mother is lying in bed, pale and gaunt, clutching it once more but this time she is despondent over the fact that her daddy will no longer look at her. Her thoughts turn to the endless days of agony at the hands of her kidnapper. She pictures him in her head and when I see him, I gasp and drop the snow globe as her terror is too much for me to bear.

Lucien snatches up the snow globe before it crashes to the floor and places it back on the desk. Looking up at Grayson I see him watching me thoughtfully and I turn my gaze anxiously to the window at my left.

"Wow. I saw all of that." Grayson states in awe. My eyes fly up to Lucien in fear and he has a thoughtful expression on his face as well.

"I know about Grayson's telepathy." Lucien tells me with a smile. "It would only be natural that you have some abilities of your own."

Grayson pulls me into his arms and strokes my back soothingly until I stop trembling.

"She really suffered." I whisper.

"Did your adopted parents know about your gifts?" Grayson asks curiously.

"No. I tried telling them when I was really little but they just thought I had an overactive imagination. Do your parents know?" I ask.

"No. They are pretty closed minded." Grayson laughs. "Lucien has known since I about five years old. He has always been good at figuring stuff out."

"You don't see things when you touch objects?" I ask.

"As far as I know I am only telepathic." Grayson

shrugs. "I really try to stay out of peoples thoughts because I see it as an invasion of privacy but I seem to have a direct link to yours without even trying."

"Yeah, I know what you mean because I have known every emotion that you have felt since we met at the café with no effort at all." I confess, feeling a little awestruck.

"Can you hear me?" I hear Grayson's voice inside my head.

"Oh my god! I can hear you!" I exclaim excitedly. *"Can I respond to you?"* I think the last statement to my twin eagerly.

"I can hear you just fine." Grayson smiles at me, obviously just as excited about it as I am. "We will have to see if we can still talk to each other when you are at the hotel later."

"Definitely!" I nod at him with a wide smile. "So, are you still in high school? What are you planning on doing with your life?"

"I graduated last year and I have been taking classes at Tulane University. I would ultimately like to own my own fitness center where we have personal trainers, nutrition classes and stuff like that." Grayson replies. "What about you?"

"I was homeschooled my whole life so I finished high school before I turned sixteen." I explain. "I am actually almost done with my bachelors in forensic psychology with a minor in criminology. I have always wanted to be able to use my abilities in my career path. Another thing I have discovered, I am gifted in is I can always tell when someone is lying or telling the truth."

"Wow Lucien, I think you and Jac here have a lot in common." Grayson jokes. I blush and look away from

Lucien's suddenly intense expression.

"I don't understand." I murmur nervously as Grayson's happiness and Lucien's fascination washes over me.

"Lucien, why don't you tell Jac what you do for a living?" Grayson chuckles as he pulls me back against him with his arms wrapped around me comfortingly. Looking up at Lucien, I am instantly caught in the seductive expression in his light brown eyes.

"I am a criminal investigator for the New Orleans police department." Lucien tells me, his southern drawl husky with emotion.

"How old are you?" I blurt without thinking, which just causes me to turn a deeper shade of pink. "I mean, how long have you been with the police department?"

"I am twenty-five." Lucien answers with deep chuckle. "I have been with the department since I graduated high school. I just finished my master's in criminology a few months ago."

A tear trickles down my cheek at the high emotion of the day and all that I feel I gained by traveling down here to New Orleans. I found my twin brother and an aunt who has welcomed me into her life without question and a totally hot guy who shares my love of law enforcement.

"You don't have to cry Jac." Grayson says with a teasing note to his voice. "Lucien isn't that hot. We wouldn't want that to go to his head."

"Stop eavesdropping!" I yell at him, turning in his arms to slam him in the sternum with the flat of my hand making him gasp for breath.

"Wow, for a tiny thing you really pack a punch."

Grayson rubs his chest, impressed with my move.

Chapter Five

Dinner is a warm comfortable meal with everyone catching up on life. I learn that Lucien doesn't live here but instead seems to have his own place a few blocks away. Lucien followed in his father's footsteps because Victor has been a detective with the department for many years. Their mother is an interior designer and for the most part works out of the house.

Nicole won't allow me to help clean up dinner but instead insists that Lucien take me back to the hotel on his way home since Grayson has some studying to do. My stomach does flip flops at the thought of being alone with Lucien at all. I have never liked a guy like this before and because of my abilities have never even been kissed.

"Let me know you got to your room alright." Grayson tells me as he points to his head meaningfully after giving me a tight hug.

"I will." I nod with an eager smile. "It was nice meeting all of you. Thank you so much for dinner. It has been a long time since I had a home cooked meal that wasn't made by me."

"I expect to see you here all the time Jacqueline." Nicole states firmly. "You're family now."

"Grayson was blessed the day that you found him." I state emotionally before hurrying out the door with Lucien following along behind me.

"Do you have a car here too?" I ask as I motion towards my yellow sports car on the curb.

"No." Lucien shakes his head as he walks around my rental with obvious appreciation.

"What is it with guys and sports cars?" I ask with a laugh. "Grayson pretty much reacted the same way when I told him he could drive." I hold out the key to Lucien with a mischievous grin.

Lucien takes the key with a nod and opens the passenger door for me with a flourish.

"How did you end up with this as your rental car?" Lucien asks after we have pulled away from the curb.

"My adopted father's business partner, Uncle John, had his assistant set up all of my travel arrangements and this was the car he picked out for me." I explain.

"So what hotel are you staying at?" He asks.

"The Windsor Court."

"Uncle John like spoiling you?" Lucien laughs as he shakes his head.

"Yes." I nod sincerely. "Now that my very frugal father is gone, he is free to give me whatever he wishes."

"So, what sort of house do you live in up in Seattle?" He wants to know after we get out in front of the hotel.

"A very humble two-bedroom cabin in the middle of the forest." I confess with a grin. "Uncle John has been trying to pick out a house for me in the city but I like the cabin because it is where all of my memories are."

Lucien takes me all the way upstairs to my suite on the top floor and I see him shake his head as he walks around checking out the rooms.

"You are uncomfortable in such luxurious surroundings, aren't you?" Lucien asks perceptively as he stops looking around and turns his attention on me.

"Honestly, yes." I laugh.

"How are you going to go back home to Seattle?" He continues probingly.

I turn away as a tear trickles down my cheek at the thought of leaving all of this behind to go back to my solitary existence. Already, I can feel my heart break at the thought.

Lucien steps up behind me and wraps his arms around my waist flooding me with his attraction for me. I gasp at the feelings rushing through him and grab his forearms tightly.

"I don't think I can Lucien." I whimper as my own attraction surges to the surface. "Am I being naïve to believe I can make a home here?"

"No Jac." He embraces me tighter. "I think Grayson needs you just as much as you need him."

He turns me around and kisses me tenderly. I stiffen in surprise before returning his kiss uncertainly. Lucien raises his head and gazes down at me with an affectionate smile.

"Jac?" Grayson's voice slides through my thoughts.

"Grayson." I whisper out loud.

"Grayson?" Lucien asks in confusion and I point at my head.

"He is checking to make sure I got here alright." I laugh.

"Ah." Lucien nods with a sarcastic chuckle. "Perfect timing brother."

"Yes, I'm here." I reply to Grayson mentally. *"I was showing Lucien the suite."*

"Good." Grayson's reply whispers through my mind. *"Please do me a favor and do not go out after dark. New Orleans can be a dangerous place."*

"I promise. Good night Grayson."

"Good night sis." I can feel the love lacing his tone.

"So, are there any college guys up there in Seattle I need to worry about?" Lucien jokes to ease the tension.

"No." I color even further. "Because of being an empath, I never felt like I had anything in common with anyone. I didn't want to risk them thinking I was a freak."

"You have never dated." Lucien states and I shake my head.

"My parents never would have never let me date when I was a teenager because they were too protective and these last few months since they passed, I guess I never thought about it." I confess in embarrassment.

"Oh darlin'." His husky voice washes over me as he tips up my chin and kisses me lightly. "I couldn't be happier."

I snuggle into his embrace with a happy sigh unable to believe everything that has happened today.

"So, what are you going to do after I leave?" He wants to know after kissing the top of my head.

"I am going to soak in that glorious tub until the water turns cold and then I am going curl up on that uber soft bed and watch a movie." I share with a smile.

"Let me see your phone." He suggests suddenly. I pull it out of my back pocket and hand it to him curiously. He taps away on the screen for several seconds before handing it back.

"What did you do?" I ask, unaccustomed to using cell phones.

"I put in my number, Grayson's, my dad's, and their house number just in case." He states.

"Thanks." I smile at him bashfully.

"Be careful." He admonishes. "New Orleans can be unsafe for someone as innocent as you. Promise me you won't go out after dark?"

"Your brother already lectured me telepathically about the exact same thing not five minutes ago." I inform him saucily. "Apparently, you guys are on the same wavelength."

"Alright. Good night darlin'." Lucien whispers and kisses me tenderly before slipping out the door.

As soon as the door closes behind him, I squeal like a love sick teenager and dance across the suite like a dork. Plopping down on the sofa I look through my contacts on my cell phone with a wide smile. Lucien entered his name as 'My Lucien' and I blush shyly.

I am relaxed and snuggled in the large bed when my phone rings and I look down to see that it is Uncle John.

"Hello."

"Hey Princess." He greets me, his voice soft and affectionate. "How did today go?"

"I not only got to meet my great-aunt Kyna but she brought along my fraternal twin brother Grayson too. She showed me pictures of our mom and told me the tragic story of how she got pregnant with us." I share with him, eager to tell someone else about my day. "My mother was only twelve years old when she was abducted and raped by a pedophile. She was missing for almost a month before returning home. She died after giving birth to us and my grandparents just couldn't see raising us after everything that happened."

"I am so sorry Jac." Uncle John says. "Did you find out anything about who your father is or if they caught him?"

"Yeah. I guess our mother testified not long before we were born and he is in prison." I explain sadly. "I got to meet Grayson's adopted family and they had me for dinner tonight welcoming me with open arms."

"How long until you come home?" He asks with a strange note in his voice.

"I don't know Uncle John." I confess honestly. "I didn't realize that something was always missing from my life until I found Grayson. I don't think I can leave him now that I have found him. To say that we have an unexplained connection doesn't quite sum it up. You had a feeling I wouldn't want to come home, didn't you?" I ask him in surprise.

"I did." He replies, his voice now sad. "I have a confession to make."

"What?" I ask anxiously, afraid I have hurt his feelings by wanting to stay here.

"The car?" He says.

"Yeah?" I probe.

"It's not a rental. I actually bought it for you." He tells me softly.

"Uncle John, that's like a two hundred and fifty-thousand-dollar car!" I exclaim loudly.

"I tried to warn you that I would be spoiling you Princess." He says with a laugh. "Well, I will have my realtor call you tomorrow and help you start looking for a house down there. You find what you want and I will take care of everything else for you."

"I don't need such an expensive car Uncle John." I complain, feeling horrible knowing how much it cost him.

"It would hurt my feelings to have you give it back Jacqueline." He explains seriously. I know when he uses my entire first name, he means it.

"Alright, Uncle John." I give in with a sigh. "I will keep the car."

"Tulane University should be a comfortable switch for school." Uncle John suggests. "They have a great science program so you can finish your master's in forensic psychology."

"I think I will skip summer semester this year and get settled here first and get it set up for me to start at Tulane in the fall." I think out loud.

"That is a good idea. It will be easier for you to concentrate on your studies if you are all settled in before school starts." He approves. "Just fair warning Princess. The houses down there are quite expensive but promise me you won't worry about the cost if you find something you love."

"Yes, Uncle John." I reply sassily. "I will keep you posted. Good night."

"Good night, sleep tight."

Chapter Six

The melodic ring tone of my cell phone rouses me from a deep sleep, and I smile when I see 'My Lucien' on the screen before I answer it.

"Good morning my Lucien." I murmur sleepily as I stretch lazily.

"Mornin' Darlin'." Lucien's sexy southern drawl gives me butterflies. "How did you sleep?"

"Wonderful. You?"

"I slept like a baby." His sensual voice washes over me. "What are your plans for the day?"

"House hunting." I reply as I bite my lip anxiously awaiting his reaction.

"Seriously?" He exclaims and I hear him whoop excitedly. "Grayson will be so excited to hear you are staying."

"Only Grayson?" I tease, surprised to hear the seductive teasing in my own voice.

"I will show you my excitement later this afternoon when I am off work." He promises.

"I can't wait." I confess honestly as I blush bashfully.

"Can I talk you into meeting me for coffee down the street before I go into work?" He asks hopefully.

"I would love to." I leap from bed enthusiastically. "I can be there in twenty minutes."

"It's a date." His husky voice replies before he hangs up.

"Good morning brother." I send telepathically to Grayson softly, afraid of waking him up.

"Morning Jac." Grayson's affectionate voice drifts through my mind. *"You're up early."*

"Lucien wants to meet for a cup of coffee before he goes in to work." I gush excitedly as I rush around getting ready to leave.

"You guys really hit it off. I have never seen Lucien take that much attention away from work before." Grayson tells me.

"Oh." I suddenly wonder if this is alright with my twin. Is it weird that Lucien is my twin's older brother? *"Is this okay with you? Is it too weird?"*

"I am thrilled! I think Lucien needs more in his life than being a criminal investigator." Grayson confesses.

"Does he know who his birth parents are too?" I ask curiously never having thought to ask before.

"Victor and Nicole are his birth parents. They wanted a big family but they miscarried after Lucien was born and then she couldn't have any more children." Grayson explains to me.

"They are wonderful and you are so lucky to have been raised by them." I share with him honestly. *"Will they be alright with Lucien and I?"*

"Why do you think Mom sent Lucien with you last night to escort you back to the hotel instead of me?" Grayson chuckles.

"Oh!" I exclaim in shock.

"What are you doing after your coffee date with my brother?" Grayson wants to know.

"Shopping for a house." I tell him hesitantly and there is a pregnant pause before he speaks again.

"In Seattle?"

"No. I was considering the garden district if I can find something with a large lot that won't cost me a billion dollars." I share bluntly.

"Really? You want to stay?" Grayson asks incredulously.

"Why would I want to leave after I just found you?" I tell him candidly.

"Would you like some help?" He puts out there.

"I would love some. Uncle John is having his realtor call me today and I will let her know what I am looking for. You can come look at them with me and help me pick the perfect place." I reply with a laugh.

At this point I am walking into the Café du Monde down the street from the hotel and I see that Lucien is already there waiting for me right inside the door. He immediately pulls me into his arms and kisses me passionately in front of the whole restaurant before releasing me reluctantly. I blush furiously as I clutch him to keep myself from falling over and hear him chuckle seductively in my ear.

"I missed you." He murmurs softly.

"I missed you too." I confess without looking at him. He tips up my chin and I am instantly lost in his bedroom eyes as he gazes heatedly down at me.

"What kind of coffee to you like?" He asks as he bobs

his head towards the counter.

"The café au lait was good and an order of beignets would be to die for." I smile eagerly at the thought of the powdered goodness. He laughs at my excitement before walking up to the counter.

"Find us a table and I will be right there." He suggests with a twinkle in his eyes.

I choose a table in the back corner where we can have some privacy while we enjoy our breakfast. Lucien sets down our coffee and beignets before sitting down right next to me and kissing me again.

"You are addictive." He whispers.

"Mmm. Yes." I agree and then blush furiously. "I mean so are you."

He strokes a finger lightly across my cheek as he gazes at me intensely.

"So, what are you looking for in a house?" Lucien changes the subject with a sigh. I look out the windows where the sun is just starting to color the horizon in dark purples and pale pinks.

"I would like to be close to everyone and I know that the garden district is a good area but I really need something with privacy. A really large lot would have to be a priority. Hopefully set up so that I can't see the neighbors or the street from the house." I tell him. "Am I asking too much?"

"You are going to pay a lot for something like that but if you are lucky there is just the right piece of property on the market." Lucien tells me. "I am sure you will find something that you can live with and makes you feel at home. It won't be the great north west forest of

Washington but a measure of privacy I am sure."

"Are you working on any exciting cases right now?" I ask him curiously.

"No." He sighs. "Just your normal stuff. Domestic calls, robberies, assaults and stuff like that. Nothing high priority."

"That's a good thing. The high priority ones are usually the most stressful." I point out logically.

"How much longer do think it will take you to complete your master's degree?"

"Well, considering I now have more people in my life to share my time with it will probably take me at least a couple more years." I laugh. "In Seattle that was all I did was study."

I bite into a beignet and moan with pleasure at the yummy pastry. Lucien watches and laughs at my reaction before he pops a whole one in his mouth.

"I am going to take the summer semester off and start at Tulane in the fall. That will give me time to get settled and feel at home before I have to start attending classes." I further explain. "I never dreamed when I got on that plane yesterday that I would not be returning to Seattle."

"Have you told your Uncle yet?" Lucien quirks an eyebrow at me questioningly.

"Yes. He called me last night and he had already guessed before I came down here that I might not want to return. He sounded sad but not surprised and besides Uncle John has a headquarters down here too. It isn't like he couldn't relocate and live down here." I shrug. "It is his realtor that will be showing me and Grayson around."

"So now that you are staying, how long do you get to keep the car?" Lucien wants to know. "That will be a shame to return."

"I don't have to return it." I whisper anxiously.

"What do you mean?" He questions in confusion. "It is a rental isn't it?

"I thought it was. Uncle John probably knew I wouldn't take it if I knew he had just bought it for me." I explain softly.

"It's yours." Lucien says dumbfounded.

"It's mine." I reply in a monotone.

"It's a $250,000 car." He continues in shock.

"That is what I told him but he said if I returned it, it would hurt his feelings." I retort uncomfortably.

"Well. We can't have that can we?" Lucien states firmly. "Come on. I will drive you back to the hotel on my way to work. You didn't drive, did you?"

"No. It is only a half mile."

Lucien drives an older Chevelle that he most likely restored himself. It is red with the white racing stripes on the hood. It is a beautiful car. He politely opens up the passenger door for me before sliding behind the wheel. The muscle car rumble makes me smile when he starts up the engine.

Too soon he is dropping me off in front of the hotel. He leans over and pins me to my seat with a demanding kiss. I kiss him back hesitantly; afraid I am doing it wrong.

"Send me pictures of the houses you look at and I will tell you what I think." He suggests after lifting his head.

"Okay." I breathe.

"Be safe today." I tell him as I slip out of the car.

"I will. Dinner at my parents' house tonight?" He asks with his eyebrow raised questioningly.

"Yes. I will see you there."

Chapter Seven

Curious about my birth father, I turn on my laptop and google Euphemia Burt in the search engine. I choose the first news article about her abduction and see photographs from the trial. There is a large photograph of Seth Pickett, the man convicted of abducting and raping my birth mother. To say that Grayson takes after our father's side of the family is an understatement. Our birth father, Seth, is a beast of a man that towers over everyone else standing next to him. My guess is that he must be close to seven feet tall with massively bulging muscles that Grayson seemed to have inherited. They have the same square face, wider nose, thin lips, and high forehead.

My birth mother must have indeed been terrified to be raped by this monster. Not knowing really anything about sex myself I am stunned that his size alone didn't kill her.

I read through the article where the journalist describes certain parts of the trial that, had I known were in this article, I would not have read. They go into explicit detail about the physical injuries she sustained at his hands over the course of the weeks he kept her captive.

It is my understanding that for a twelve-year-old girl, Euphemia, was a tiny girl anyways. I cannot begin to imagine the horrors she experienced before her freedom.

My cell phone pings and I see that I have an email from the realtor that John said would contact me. Opening up my email on the computer I send her a message back explaining to her in as much detail what exactly I am looking for and that I would dearly love to be out of the hotel I am staying at soon.

Within a half hour she has emailed me back twelve listings across the garden district that meet my parameters in one way or another. I share the listings with Lucien before scrolling through them myself and one particular property reaches out to me as soon as I see it. It reminds me a smaller version of a plantation house on the outside. The entire five block sized property is fenced with a gate at the street. You cannot see any of the neighbors or the street and the high fence provides some noise reducing properties. The house is a comfortable three-bedroom, two bath home with wood and stone floors where the main colors appear to be white, gray, and black. There is an in-ground pool and jacuzzi in the back yard off of the extensive brick patio. The lot size is over seven thousand square feet and I cannot wait to see it in person.

Before I can text Lucien to see which he likes best he shoots me a message telling me he likes the same one that I do. I email the realtor back and let her know which one I am interested in seeing in person, informing her I am available today if possible.

I text Lucien to tell him that I fell in love with the same one and am hoping to get a tour of it today.

"Are you busy? I have found a house that I want to see. If the realtor can show it to me today do you have time to go see it with me?" I ask Grayson anxiously.

"I am taking an exam at the college but I should be done in about an hour and then you can have my help all day." Grayson responds quickly. *"Something is wrong. What's up?"*

"We can talk about it when you get here." I reply evasively.

I research the neighborhood that it is in and it looks like it is a quiet residential area walking distance to shopping and things. My mind keeps returning to the article I read about my birth father and what he did to cause my existence. Remembering feeling Euphemia's emotions when I touched the snow globe is something that I never want to experience again.

My phone pings again and it is my aunt Kyna asking if I am interested in stopping by her house for breakfast. I message her back that I would love to.

"Aunt Kyna invited me to her house for breakfast. I am heading there now." I let Grayson know mentally as I take the elevator downstairs to get my car.

"I will meet you there." His voice runs through my mind softly.

After putting aunt Kyna's address into the GPS I head away from the hotel and into the garden district. When I pull into the driveway of my aunt's house, I see that the homes in this neighborhood look much older and the lots are larger than in Grayson's part of the garden district.

Aunt Kyna opens the door before I can knock and pulls me into a welcoming hug.

"Good morning darling." She greets me happily as she leads me back into her kitchen.

"Good morning." I chuckle as I follow along behind her wondering if she is always this good-natured.

"I hope you haven't had breakfast yet." She says as she stirs something on the stove that smells like sausage gravy. I can smell buttermilk biscuits baking in the oven and my stomach growls loudly.

"I had some beignets a couple hours ago." I laugh at

my loud stomach. "I guess I am starving however."

"Good. I tried calling your brother but he didn't answer. I was going to invite him over for breakfast too." She says as she checks the oven.

"He is at the college taking an exam. He said he would meet me here when he is done." I inform her.

"Oh." She turns to give me a funny look before stirring the scrambled eggs that are cooking slowly on the stove.

"I texted him after you invited me over." I lie to her, feeling guilty. "He was just walking into the classroom. He said it would probably be an hour or so."

"Oh well, that makes sense." She laughs. "Would you like a cup of coffee? Cream and sugar?"

"Yes please." I nod eagerly. My dad always shook his head at me because for as tiny as I am, I can really eat.

"So, tell me how dinner went with Grayson's family." Aunt Kyna says as she tends to the stove.

"His adopted parents are fabulous!" I gush honestly. "Nicole welcomed me to the family immediately and Victor has a very kind face. His brother Lucien is in law enforcement which is what I am getting my masters in."

"I have met them a couple of times." She says. "I liked them instantly as well. They are wholesome, compassionate people."

"I have made a decision." I state, uncertain how she will take it.

"What is that dear?" She says without looking over at me.

"I am buying a house down here." I whisper

hesitantly. "There is nothing left for me in Seattle and I want to be close to Grayson."

She stops tending to the food, turns everything off and turns to me with a shocked expression on her face.

"Are you sure?" She asks and I can feel her fear that I will change my mind. A tear trickles down my face as I feel how important I already am to the woman who is a complete stranger to me.

"Yes, I am sure." I state firmly. "I would love the opportunity to get to know my family here."

"Oh, Jac that makes me so happy!" She exclaims and comes around pulls me into a tight embrace.

Before she releases me, I see an older man with short dark graying hair step into the kitchen as if he is quite comfortable here.

"I'm sorry Kyna." He says. "I didn't realize you would have company this early or I would have called."

"Francis!" Aunt Kyna exclaims suddenly terrified. She releases me and as soon as he sees my face, he drops the cup he is holding and it crashes to the floor where it shatters.

Our eyes meet and I can feel grief so intense it nearly cripples me.

"Aunt Kyna?" I ask her anxiously as I continue to stare at the stranger standing just inside the kitchen.

"What have you done Kyna?" He asks her in a cold voice, his grief still washing over me, nearly drowning me in its greatness.

"This is your granddaughter Jacqueline." Aunt Kyna stands up to him firmly. "I am allowed to have a relationship with her no matter how you feel. This is my house and if you are not comfortable then you can leave."

"I came to tell you that I got a call from the prison. They paroled him." Francis says with rage lacing his tone. Even though he doesn't give the name of who he is talking about I know he is talking about Seth Pickett, my birth father.

The monster has been let loose.

Poor Grayson chooses that moment to walk into the kitchen.

"Get out!" Francis roars at Grayson, his face nearly turning purple his rage is so intense. Flying to my feet I rush right over and put myself protectively in front of my twin. Pushing my grandfather back he stumbles and nearly falls on the floor if it wasn't for Aunt Kyna.

"How dare you allow the spawn of evil in this house Kyna!" Francis screams furiously.

"How dare you! You just threw us away as if we were garbage after the way Phemie loved you. She worshipped the ground you walked on and you dare to judge us after what you have done. She died thinking you didn't love her anymore!"

"You know nothing!" He snarls down at me.

"Don't I?" I rage up at him. "The Edinburgh snow globe you bought for her? After she came home from the hospital, she cried herself to sleep clutching that to her chest praying that her daddy would love her again and talk to her. She died thinking that it was her fault that monster hurt her. She died thinking you blamed her."

"Jac, don't." Grayson tries to pull me from the kitchen.

Francis face pales and he looks down at me as if he has seen a ghost before he looks up at aunt Kyna.

"What did you tell her?" He asks her, his voice broken.

"I haven't had a chance to tell her anything yet!" Aunt Kyna exclaims. "I just met her yesterday!"

Francis sighs and sinks down into a chair at the table where he cradles his head in his hands.

"You look just like her." He says to me after raising his head to gaze at me longingly. "I miss her today just as much as the day that monster took her from us."

"I'm sorry that this happened to your family." I offer him sincerely. "You cannot blame any of this on Grayson just because he looks like his father. Grayson is a loving compassionate man who loves his family very much. Just like you cannot expect me to be just like Euphemia just because I look like her."

"I'm sorry too." Francis tells me. "We just couldn't keep you after losing Phemie. You deserved to be raised by people who loved you and didn't know the situation."

"I understand." I reply with a smile. "What happened was horrible. Grayson and I have an appointment. We will take a raincheck on breakfast Aunt Kyna."

Turning around I practically shove Grayson down the hallway towards the front door. Outside I see he also has a muscle car like his brother Lucien but Grayson's looks like it is a Camaro.

"I will meet you at your house and then we can take my car to go see the house." I tell him without explaining anything else.

"Jac, are you alright?" Grayson grabs my arm forcing

me to look at him.

"He had no right Grayson." I state, fury rushing through me heatedly.

"I look just like him." Grayson tells me. "You can't blame the man for how he reacts to me."

"You are nothing like that monster." I hiss furiously.

"Are you sure?" Grayson asks me softly.

I lean into Grayson's chest and curl into his embrace as he wraps his arms around me.

"Yes." I whisper. "I'm sure."

Chapter Eight

Instead of jumping right into my car to head over to look at the house for sale, Grayson wordlessly pulls me into his kitchen. Nicole looks up at us with a loving smile.

"Oh good. Thank you, Grayson." She says as she gets to her feet. "Are you hungry Jac? Can I make you some breakfast? Did you want some coffee or juice?"

"Thank you, but I'm not hungry right now." I tell her as I wonder why she thanked Grayson for bringing me in here.

"Please, sit down." She says with another loving smile. "There was something I wanted to ask you." Her nervousness is just rolling off of her in waves and I sit down slowly as I wonder what could have possible worked her up into such a state. Grayson sits down next to me and I can feel that he is a little worried too but nothing like Nicole.

"Grayson tells me that you are going to buy a house here in New Orleans so you can stay close and I am just so happy that you will have each other after so many years apart." Nicole says brightly. "I think it is really unnecessary for you to stay in that hotel when we have plenty of room for you right here until you move into your own house. You and Grayson will have so much more time together to get to know one another if you are staying here. Family stays together. Please say you will stay."

I smile at her fondly and now understand why she was so nervous.

"I would hate to impose or become a burden to your family Nicole." I explain reasonably. "The hotel is just down the street and I really don't know how long it will take me to have a house to move into."

"It is not an imposition and you could never be a burden to us sweetheart." Nicole tells me from the heart. "Lucien shared how uncomfortable you are in the hotel and I think you will feel so much more at home here. Please?"

"You seem to have your heart set on me staying." I laugh softly. "I would be honored to stay here with all of you."

"Good." Grayson nods his head and I can feel his excitement over my staying here. "Lucien and I agree that you should stay in his old room."

I blush furiously that he said that right in front of his mother who giggles like a school girl at his suggestion.

"I agree!" She exclaims happily. "It is a perfect idea."

My cell phone pings and it is a text message from the realtor notifying me that she can meet me there in a half hour. I return her message accepting the time to meet.

"That was the realtor. She can meet us there in a half hour." I state nervously.

I open the browser on my phone so that Nicole can see the listing of the house I am going to see and she nods her head approvingly.

"I know where that is." She says. "It was owned by an older couple who ended up in an assisted living facility. Their oldest son is selling the property. I just heard about it a couple days ago, I can't believe it is already listed. If you are interested, I would snatch it up quickly dear because it won't be available for long. I am only an interior designer but I would be willing to go along and give you my professional opinion, if I am not intruding."

"I could really use your help making my decision, thank you." I smile at her with relief.

It is agreed to take Nicole's car since it is a little more spacious than mine. I sit shotgun while Grayson, ever the gentleman, takes the back seat. The gate to the property is open and the realtor is waiting for us next to her car.

I look around at the large nearly two-acre property with an excited smile. The high white fence is lined with trees and bushes all the way around lending more to the feel of privacy. The in-ground pool is pretty large for a three-bedroom house and I am glad there is a small matching jacuzzi as well. There is a lot of lush green lawn surrounding the expansive brick patio and pool area. The two-stall garage is detached and looks more like a carriage house.

Closing my eyes, I can hear a freeway not far from the house but I am sure I will grow to ignore the sound.

"You must be Jacqueline Cassidy." The tall blonde realtor steps up to me with a welcoming smile. "My name is Sarah Waters and your uncle John gave me a call last night to let me know you were shopping in the area. Who is this?" She asks as she looks at Grayson and Nicole.

"My twin brother Grayson and his mother Nicole Devereaux." I introduce them politely and have to bite back a smile as the realtor falters over the fact that it is my twin's mother and not mine. Her face clears excitedly and she turns to Nicole with an expression of awe.

"You are 'the' Nicole Devereaux!" Sarah exclaims. "It is such an honor ma'am to meet you!"

"Thank you, Sarah." Nicole smiles at her warmly. "Show us around and please be honest about your opinions. I would consider myself in your debt if you help this wonderful girl."

"Oh yes ma'am." Sarah gushes like a school girl meeting a celebrity. I look at Grayson with my eyebrows raised and he smiles benevolently.

"Mom is a very good interior designer." Grayson explains along our mental path.

Sarah and Nicole lead the way with the realtor explaining everything to Grayson's mother in a very candid tone. Apparently, Nicole knew exactly what to say to win over the greedy little realtor.

The kitchen, living room, and dining room are one long room with marble floors white walls and floor to ceiling windows letting in a lot of light. The glass doors leading to the brick patio let out here as well.

There is one bedroom on the main floor with its own door leading out to the patio. The bathroom on the first floor has a glass stand up shower with a single vanity and is quite spacious. The master bedroom and third bedroom are on the second floor with the bathroom attached to the master bedroom complete with stand up shower, sunken garden tub and double vanity. All of the bedrooms have a large walk in closet that is easily the size of my entire bedroom at the cabin back in Seattle. The master bedroom has a balcony that spans the whole length of the house and looks down on the pool below. The view from the balcony still appears private due to the tall trees along the fence line leaving you unable to see beyond the property.

There is a room on the first floor that is sort of an alcove that I could easily turn into an office.

The bedrooms are each about twelve feet square, the great room on the first floor is nearly eighteen by sixteen with the little alcove being about nine feet square.

"Before I make my decision, do you think this could be redone in a completely rustic theme?" I ask Nicole anxiously. "The modern look really isn't me and if I am going to be at home here it needs to be more cabin like, at least on the inside. The outside plantation look is beautiful."

"Definitely." Nicole nods professionally as she looks around at the interior critically. "I think putting in a large stone fireplace right in the corner of the living room would really give it the feel you are looking for. We could do a combination throughout of natural wood and stone for the walls and floors. The ceilings are high enough that we can add long wood beams up there. Let me go around and take some pictures so that I have a visual to work with at home. Once I have some ideas then you and I can sit down and decide what you like best."

"You would help me with his?" I ask her in surprise. "Surely you already have other projects going that are taking up your time."

"I have assistants that I can hand those off to." Nicole laughs excitedly. "You are a part of the family now Jac. I would like nothing better than to help you create your safe space right here in New Orleans."

"Grayson?" I ask anxiously.

"I love it. I think after you let Mom remodel it that it will become exactly what you are looking for." He tells me honestly.

"Well, Sarah." I smile brightly at her. "Tell Uncle John I have bought a house. I would like this closed as soon as possible as it sounds like renovations are going to take a little bit of time."

"The buyer will be thrilled." Sarah says with an answering smile. "He just listed this yesterday. I will call your uncle John right away. I can have closing ready in just a couple days and the buyer said the new owner can take possession immediately."

"Wonderful." I nod at the realtor with a happy smile. "Thank you for your time Sarah."

"We will be in touch Ms. Cassidy." Sarah says before hurrying to her car.

We pull out of the driveway ahead of the realtor so she can close up the gate as she leaves.

"We need to talk." Grayson tells me as soon as we are back at his house. "Then we can go check you out of the hotel."

I nod and follow him upstairs to his bedroom where I sit down on his bed wondering why he feels so upset.

"Tell me." He sits down on his desk chair and pulls it up right in front of me where he places his hands on my thighs. I flush and look away from him, not wanting to relive what I read in the newspaper article about our mother.

"I googled our mom." I whisper with a catch in my throat. "I found an article with details about the trial. I read things that I wish I hadn't. If I had known those things were there, I wouldn't have read it. I don't know anything about sex since I was so sheltered, so forgive my ignorance, but he was a beast of a man and she was just a tiny girl. How did he not kill her when he raped her?"

"Just because his body size is enormous doesn't

mean that he is that way everywhere." Grayson tells me.

"Oh." I flush, unable to believe I am having this conversation with my twin brother.

"I know all of the details too." He shares with me sadly. "She was no doubt in constant agony the whole time she was his captive."

"I saw and felt her memories when I held that snow globe." I shudder as I remember. "It was so real it was like I wasn't myself anymore. Her grief over how her father wouldn't even look at her anymore. She wanted to die Grayson. Her daddy was her whole life and she didn't think he loved her anymore."

"That's really why you got so angry with him today." Grayson nods his head as he understands.

"You are my other half Grayson." I tell him as tears pour down my cheeks. "I can't allow him to hurt you like that."

A tear falls down his face as he pulls me onto his lap where I sob like I haven't since I was a little girl.

"If it weren't for finding my family, I would almost say I would have been better off not knowing any of this." I hiccup from the extremity of my weeping.

"What are you guys doing?" Lucien states as he sails through the bedroom doorway only to stop with uncertainty when he sees me on Grayson's lap with a tear-streaked face.

"Darlin' are you alright?" He asks and I can feel his need to comfort me. "What happened?"

"She met our esteemed grandfather Francis." Grayson tells him as he stands up to hand me over to his brother. Grayson fills in Lucien about the confrontation at our aunt's house this morning.

I gratefully cuddle into Lucien's chest as I continue to hiccup from the effort of my sobs. He strokes my back and kisses the top of my head as he holds me tightly.

Chapter Nine

"I just heard about Seth at the station today." Lucien states, his grip on me tightening slightly as I feel his fear and anger. "Did Mom talk to you about staying here instead of at the hotel?"

"Yes." I whisper my response. "Grayson and I were just getting ready to go and collect my things there."

"Let's go do that now then." Lucien stands up and sets me on my feet gently. "Are you alright darlin'?"

"Yeah." I nod after my soft reply.

"We are going to head up to the hotel and get Jac all checked out, Mom." Lucien says as we pop into kitchen to see Nicole pouring over interior design samples for my house with her laptop open. "Did you need us to stop at the store for anything?"

"Thank you, sweetheart but I think we are all set for now." She replies, obviously distracted. "Oh, your aunt Kyna called. She was very sorry that your breakfast was ruined this morning so I invited her over for dinner tonight to make up for it."

"Thanks Mom!" Grayson exclaims gladly.

Unfortunately, we are unable to take my car since there are three of us and my car only seats two. Lucien heads towards his red Chevelle SS explaining that at least his trunk is clean.

"You do realize it is only one o'clock and it's Friday

afternoon." Grayson taunts from the back seat. "Lucien, what are you doing away from the precinct?"

"I have so much vacation time built up that I figured I would take a long weekend for once." He shrugs as he pulls out into traffic.

The hotel is busy since it is Friday afternoon and the lobby is full of people as we step onto the elevator taking us up to my suite. Lucien and I are holding hands as we step into the living room and I am stunned to see Uncle John standing there looking out the window.

"Uncle John!" I exclaim and when he turns, I throw myself into his arms with a squeal of delight.

"Princess!" He swings me up and embraces me tightly. "I missed you."

"I missed you too! What are you doing here?" I ask after he sets me on my feet.

"I have business, so I figured I would stop and check on you." He tells me affectionately. "So, tell me who these fine gentlemen are."

"This is my twin brother Grayson Devereaux." I introduce him after stepping up to my brother's side. "That is his older adopted brother Lucien Devereaux. This is John Van Asselt, my adopted father's business partner in Delta Logistics."

"You own Delta Logistics?" Lucien asks in surprise.

"Well, technically Jac here does too." Uncle John explains. "She is a forty-five percent shareholder on the board."

"I'm really just a silent partner." I flush at Uncle John's statement.

"You know of the company then?" Uncle John asks Lucien.

"I do." Lucien replies respectfully. "They are the largest shipping company running down to the gulf. Your ships are seen in every port in the world."

"Yes, we are." Uncle John accepts the praise gracefully. "Through lots of hard work, son."

Uncle John looks quite short compared to the Devereaux brothers. He only stands about five foot nine and even though he towers over me he is five or so inches shorter than Lucien. Uncle John's dark graying hair is combed back off of his forehead, his eyes are an icy blue in an oval face with a well-trimmed beard. He has a slim build, but the expensive suits and his demeanor makes him feel slightly intimidating.

"Are you staying here in the hotel?" I ask Uncle John curiously.

"Just for tonight and then I thought you and I could go stay at the house." He replies as he looks at me lovingly. "The staff is preparing it for us."

"Oh." I drop my gaze to the carpet uncomfortably and wring my hands anxiously. "I am here to check out of the hotel Uncle John. Grayson's adopted mother has invited me to stay with them until the house is ready for me to move into."

"Well, now you won't have to do that Princess." Uncle John states confidently. "Now that I am here, I am sure you will be more comfortable to stay with me."

I can feel everyone's emotions swirling around me like a storm. Uncle John is displeased, Grayson is worried, and Lucien is suspicious.

"I'm sorry that my decision has upset you Uncle John but I have already given Nicole my word that I would come and stay with them." I explain to him firmly.

Uncle John takes a deep breath and pauses for several seconds before continuing.

"Now Jacqueline." Uncle John says.

"I don't want to hurt your feelings but I am an adult and capable of making my own decisions. I am grateful that you came to check in on me to make sure that I am alright but I am doing just fine on my own. I don't need you to babysit me anymore Uncle John. Please, let me grow up." I plead with him.

"I really think we should discuss this in private, don't you think that would be best?" He pushes further and I can feel his determination to win me over to his side.

"No!" I shout furiously. "I don't think that would be best Uncle John! Grayson is my twin brother. You cannot understand the connection I have with him so no; I don't need to have this discussion with you in private. If you cannot respect my wishes then maybe I need to take care of the purchase of the house myself. Mr. Sorenson will be most happy to help me with this if you insist on this course of action."

I instantly feel him close down and his emotions are suddenly carefully blank and I cannot tell what he is feeling.

"As you wish Princess." He relents gracefully. "I only thought to protect you. The realtor, Ms. Waters has assured me that the seller has accepted our offer and I will transfer payment in full from your shares immediately. Ms. Waters will be in contact with you to have you sign the papers and give you the deed to the house. She said she should only need the weekend to have everything ready for you Monday morning."

He steps over to the side table next to the sofa and hands me a large envelope. Inside I find a set of keys and some paperwork for the security codes on the gate as well as the house.

"Ms. Waters thought you should have this so your interior designer could have this weekend to begin planning her remodel." Uncle John explains. "I just came from the property and Ms. Waters shared with me your plans for the remodel and I think it will be just what you want when it is complete."

"The house will be completely paid for?" I ask him in surprise. "Isn't the house listed at over two million dollars? I have that much money just lying around in the company for this in addition to the cost of car?"

"Of course, you do." Uncle John smiles at me affectionately. "I don't want you to have to worry about a house payment while you are still in college. I paid for the car myself as a gift. Remember, Princess? Now, I have a dinner meeting with some potential clients and have to clean up after my flight."

Uncle John heads for the door and I can feel his disappointment in me just radiating off of him.

"Uncle John?" I whisper uncertainly. He turns around and gazes at me silently while I battle with my guilt over the way I spoke to him. Smiling lovingly, he steps back and wraps me in his arms tightly before kissing my forehead.

"I will always love you Jac. No matter how much we don't see eye to eye. You will always be my girl." He whispers. "See that you take good care of her." Uncle John says to my brother coolly.

"Yes sir." Grayson replies with a respectful nod as I watch Uncle John stride from the hotel suite.

"Hey." Lucien takes me in his arms as soon as the door closes. "You did the right thing. He's a big boy and can handle allowing you to grow up and be an adult. It's alright that you don't allow him to coddle you forever."

"I hurt his feelings." I moan remorsefully.

"He hurt your feelings." Lucien states bluntly. "You just reminded him that how you feel is just as important and that you don't like having yours ignored. It is healthy for you to stand up for yourself. You both hugged and bonded before he left."

"You're right." I nod at his logic and know he is telling me the truth. Uncle John has always loved to spoil me but he has also always been very protective, just like my adopted dad was.

Lucien tips up my face and kisses me tenderly.

I pack up what few things I took out of my suitcases, put my laptop back in its case and I am ready to check out.

"Are you alright with me sleeping in your old room?" I ask Lucien anxiously as we take the elevator down to the lobby.

"Darlin', I wouldn't want you sleeping in any other bed but mine." He smiles down at me wickedly.

"Oh." I reply as my face turns a deep shade of pink at his blunt statement.

"Brother in the elevator!" Grayson states with disgust lacing his tone. "Wait until you're alone."

Lucien chuckles as he kisses my cheek softly.

"You're my girl now." Lucien whispers in my ear so only I can hear.

"Yes, yes I am." I agree as I reach up and stroke his face lightly.

Chapter Ten

After the high emotions of the last couple days I am completely exhausted and head for the stairs so I can rest a bit before dinner.

"Jac! I have some ideas if you want to look them over." Nicole calls from the kitchen.

I step into the room with a wan smile on my face and sigh as I step towards the table.

"Mom, I think Jac needs to lie down for a little bit before dinner." Lucien comes to my rescue. "She has had a pretty stressful day already."

"Of course." Nicole gazes at me with concern. "Is there anything I can do for you sweetie?"

"Do you have any chamomile tea?" I ask curiously, remembering how my adopted mom would make some whenever I was upset.

"I do. I will get it steeping and then send it up with Lucien." She tells me with a smile.

"Thank you, Nicole." I smile back at her tiredly.

Lucien leads me up to his bedroom at the end of the hallway and I am surprised at how neat everything is.

"It is so organized." I state as I look around curiously.

"Just the way I like it." Lucien replies with a huff. "Grayson's room drives me crazy."

Lucien's bed is a king size four poster that is

made out of logs. It is definitely a rustic style that I can appreciate. It looks absolutely massive. The comforter actually looks like it is made from red and black flannel and I find myself smiling with approval.

"Why didn't you bring the bed with you when you moved?" I ask him as I stroke the softness of the flannel with a sigh. "It's fabulous."

"I have a similar one at my place only it's more of a medieval canopy style than just a four-poster bed." He explains. "There are times I have to sleep during the day and my bed at home has thick velvet bed hangings to keep out the light."

"Oh! I can't wait to see it!" I exclaim eagerly because of my love of history.

"Darlin', not as much as me." Lucien's husky drawl washes over me giving me butterflies.

Blushing, as I always seem to do in his presence, I look away from him.

Feeling uncharacteristically bold, I turn in his arms and pull his head down to kiss him before I lose my nerve. I bashfully dance my tongue against his. He growls down deep in his chest as he picks me up and lies me beneath him on the bed. Lucien kisses me until I arch up attempting to feel the same desire for him as he obviously feels for me.

He kisses down my neck to the curve of my shoulder deepening his kiss there.

"Please." I beg although I am really not sure for what.

"I am going to regret going any further darlin'." His husky voice washes over my neck as he nuzzles me tenderly. I hide my face in the curve of his neck in shame at how easily I threw myself at him.

After several seconds, he lifts his head and looks down at me his face changing to concern when he sees the uncertainty on mine.

"Jac?" He asks.

"I'm sorry." I whimper. "I'm just so confused. This is so new to me and unfamiliar. You are a grown experienced man who has probably been with lots of gorgeous sophisticated women compared to me. We just met yesterday and I am already throwing myself at you. That is not how a good girl behaves. I can hear my mother's voice now...."

Lucien kisses me deeply effectively ceasing my babbling.

"You are a good girl darlin'." He reassures me with a warm smile as he strokes my cheek tenderly. "I don't want to be with anyone else but you Jacqueline Cassidy. We have the rest of our lives to get to know one another and I am not trying to rush you I just can't help touching you and kissing you. I will not let this go too far until I am certain you are ready."

"I was afraid you didn't feel the same way." I confess, afraid to believe the adoration I feel coming from Lucien.

He leans down and kisses me so tenderly and filled with emotion that my eyes tear up.

"Now, before we are rudely interrupted by someone I am going to run down and grab your chamomile tea." He kisses my forehead before sliding from the bed.

A couple hours later I tiptoe downstairs and follow Lucien's voice to the library where he is talking with his dad and I stop when I hear my birth father's name.

"Everyone knows that Pickett is guilty of more than

just Euphemia Burt." Lucien's furious voice washes over me. "He is just smart enough that he didn't get caught until his last victim got away somehow. I have studied the case files after Grayson discovered who his birth parents were. There were fifteen other girls in the surrounding areas that went missing never to seen again during the seven years before Euphemia disappeared. They were all between eleven and thirteen years old, all tiny for their age, all beautiful girls, all from middle class to wealthy families."

"Nothing could be proven, son." Victor sighs in frustration. "The detectives on the case continued to try and pin any of those on him while he was in prison and they couldn't find a trace of evidence."

"I have a really bad feeling about his release and finding Jac." Lucien shares with his dad. "Euphemia was eight months pregnant with twins when she testified. Pickett knows he has at least one child."

"You should let them know you heard them, sis." Grayson's voice drifts across my thoughts.

Feeling guilty I step into the library with red cheeks and my eyes pinned to the floor.

"I'm sorry." I apologize to the two of them. "I woke up and followed the sound of Lucien's voice and then I heard you talking about my birth father. I shouldn't have stood there listening."

"Come here darlin'." Lucien says in a soft voice. I step closer, feeling like a naughty child that deserves to be punished.

"I didn't mean to be rude." I confess, terrified to look at Victor.

Lucien pulls me onto his lap and wraps me into his arms comfortingly.

"I probably would have done the same thing Jac." Lucien tells me calmly. I don't feel that he is disappointed in me and neither is Victor. "We were talking with the door open so it's not like it was a private conversation."

"I didn't remember that about Phemie being pregnant during the trial." I shudder at the thought. "Do you think there is a chance he will come looking for us?"

"You are safe here Jacqueline." Victor tells me, his voice confident. "Don't be surprised if we don't let you go anywhere alone for a while."

"Trust me, I don't want to." I shake my head and cuddle into Lucien's embrace so I feel safer. "I was thinking about my house. I like that it's completely surrounded by a high fence with a gate at the street, but I would like the security system completely upgraded and wanted your thoughts on a dog?"

"I know the perfect guy to do the security system and I might just know the dog that would be a good fit for you." Victor says to me before turning his attention to Lucien. "Do you remember the wolf that Anderson tried getting into the program a couple years ago but was turned down?"

"Yeah. Everyone thought he was out of his mind for wanting to trust a wild wolf pup. Why?" Lucien asks.

"The wolf ended up being privately trained by an ex-military and given to a young girl who needed protection." Victor explains. "The girl was just killed by the man they were protecting her from and they don't know what to do with Rune. They say he is despondent over the girl's death and they are afraid he won't recover because he refuses to eat. I will give the guy a call back right now. Maybe we can go and see Rune tomorrow; introduce him to Jac."

"A wolf? Is that safe?" I ask anxiously.

"He was found so young he had to be bottle fed to survive." Victor says. "He is still a wild animal but has never once acted untrustworthy. My friend says that Rune and the girl were inseparable."

"Okay." I nod.

"Aunt Kyna is in the kitchen going over remodel ideas for your house with Mom." Lucien tells me.

"Oh!" I exclaim, leaping off of his lap anxiously. "Why didn't you wake me up?"

"They were enjoying themselves all alone just fine." Lucien laughs as he follows me to the kitchen.

"Jac!" Aunt Kyna stands up and rushes over to hug me tightly as soon as I walk into the kitchen. "I am so sorry about this morning."

"I understand how he feels Aunt Kyna." I state honestly after she releases me from her loving hug. "It is logical that he feels the way that he does."

"Nicole has worked out some wonderful ideas about your new house." Aunt Kyna hurries back around the table and sits back down.

Nicole needs no further prompting and immediately launches into a professional discourse on her tentative plans for my new home. She has picked out the wood that will be for all the walls throughout, both downstairs and upstairs. It is a lighter color with beautiful wood grain. She wants to do natural stones for the floors even though it will be expensive and a little time consuming but it will offset the wood walls so nicely. She has the fireplace picked out and it will be made of stones nearly identical to the ones on the floors. The cabinets in the kitchen will be a slightly darker wood grain than the walls for slight contrast with gray appliances that match the stone floors. She has tentatively chosen all of the furniture I will need and I have to admit I picked the right person for this job because I absolutely love all of her ideas.

"I wouldn't change a thing." I tell her with an affectionate smile. "I will contact my attorney Mr. Sorenson and have him give you a call so that you will have funds to draw from. Before you try to say that you won't allow me to pay you, just let me say that is the one sure way I will not let you do this. I must be allowed to pay my own way. If you hadn't thought of it already, I think this will make the perfect article for one of those home magazines. Let's hire a journalist do follow you through the process. I can imagine it will be good for business. A sort of before and after masterpiece."

I can feel Lucien's happiness at my reaction to his mother's work.

"Yeah Mom, let Jac pay you." Grayson laughs as he comes in the door. "She owns Delta Logistics."

Nicole looks up at me in stunned surprise.

"Your adopted father was that William Cassidy?" She asks.

"Yes." I nod as I hold back my emotions, talking about him makes me miss him.

Chapter Eleven

Nicole managed to make a huge pot roast while she was working on my remodel at the same time. Lucien, Grayson, and even Victor helped to peel all of the potatoes while I took my nap. Seeing firsthand how well this family pulls together for each other is heartwarming.

"Do you mind if I ask you some questions about my birth mother's childhood?" I ask Aunt Kyna as we are all gathered around the table eating dinner in the formal dining room. "How close were you in age because it looks like you are a lot younger than Francis."

"I was eight years older than your mom." Aunt Kyna tells me. "I lived with Francis then because our parents had both passed. I was in love." She laughs as she remembers. "She was such a beautiful happy baby. She never fussed, threw fits or cried unless she really had a reason. She was the princess of the house. As she grew up her and I would play together so we became friends as well as her being my niece. She really was Daddy's girl. Francis doted on her and would move heaven and earth for his little princess. He would buy her little gifts and she treasured each and every one of them. The snow globe you spoke of was bought for her when they took a trip to Scotland when she was eleven."

Aunt Kyna pauses for a second and wipes a tear from her cheek before she takes a small jewelry box from her pocket and slides it across the table towards me. I stare at it, terrified to open it in front of all these people who are not aware of my ability to have visions. Lucien, who is sitting right next to me, perceptively reaches over and opens up the jewelry box for me so I can see what is inside without touching it.

Lying there on the velvet is a necklace with the pendant 'Daddy's Girl'. I want to show I am grateful for the gift but my gut is telling me I cannot touch this in front of all of these people.

"Aunt Kyna I don't know if I can accept this." I tell her truthfully. "Francis gave this to you to give me, didn't he?" I can feel from her internal reaction to my question that he did. I sigh as I gaze at it, feeling a tear coursing down my cheek.

"Why would he give this to me?" I ask her.

"He wanted to be able to give you something that was important to Phemie." Aunt Kyna says, her voice trembling with her own emotion.

"This wasn't just important to my mother." I tell her. "He is giving it to me because it was also important to him. After she died, he carried this necklace with him, everywhere didn't he? It was his last connection to her and he couldn't let it go."

"How did you know that?" She asks me in surprise.

"Because of the grief on his face when he saw me in your kitchen this morning." I whisper through my tears. "He was looking at a ghost. If you look at the pendant the edges of it are nearly worn off it has been handled so much. The jewelry box almost has no velvet left on it."

"Here Gray." Lucien hands his brother the jewelry box. "Keep this for Jac until she is ready?"

Grayson places the jewelry box on his lap out of sight

and I can feel myself relax now that I don't have to touch it anymore.

"Thank you Aunt Kyna." I tell her in a heartfelt whisper. "It means the world to me to have that necklace of my mothers."

Conversation thankfully turns to lighter subjects and I am grateful to not be the center of attention. I am unable to stop thinking about the necklace as everyone talks around me about daily things.

I would stake my fortune that the reason the necklace was so important to Francis was because it was the last thing he gave her and she was wearing it when she went missing. For that reason alone, I cannot touch it.

Nicole still doesn't allow me to help clean up after dinner so I retreat to Lucien's room to be alone for a little while. I am unaccustomed to being around so many people all the time and since I arrived the only time I am alone is when I sleep.

I wander around Lucien's room looking at things he kept from his childhood and smiling over the boy who grew into a man. After some time of examining nearly everything in his room I find a girl's necklace hung over a high school picture of his class. I am staring at it curiously when Lucien comes in behind me.

"Go ahead." He encourages me.

"It's a girl's necklace." I state obviously.

"It is." He agrees.

Hesitantly, and only due to his prodding, I reach out and grasp the necklace in my fingers. I see a beautiful blonde girl with a ready smile who is looking at someone excitedly. Then she is gazing down at this same necklace that has just been placed around her neck. She is full of teenage romance and thinks she is the luckiest girl in school.

The vision changes to a hospital room and her head hurts so badly she is sobbing uncontrollably.

The vision changes once more to a cemetery with a younger Lucien standing at the grave side trying not to cry as the minister is talking about a young life taken too soon.

I let it go with a sigh of regret. The girl was a good person, full of happiness and light.

"She was your high school sweetheart." I state sadly.

"She was." Lucien says softly. "I was the quarterback of the football team and she was the captain of the cheerleading squad. Brain tumor at sixteen."

"Did you love her?" I ask curiously as I look up at him to see his expression. He smiles at me sadly.

"No." He shakes his head. "She was a nice girl and we were close friends but I didn't love her like that."

"She loved you like that." I state and his expression changes to surprise.

"She never told me." He sighs. "We dated and went to school dances and everyone thought we were the perfect couple, but I guess I stayed with her just because everyone expected me to. Looking back on it as an adult, I only felt for her what a guy would feel for his sister."

"Did you date anyone seriously after her?" I ask.

"Nope." He shakes his head. "Her death was a big blow to me. I might not have loved her romantically but losing her was almost more than I could bear. I dropped out of football, my grades dropped, and my parents had to put me into counseling. It was after I started feeling better that I decided to follow in Dad's footsteps and not go to college for football."

"Did you sleep with her?" I ask as I look away from his nervously.

"Yes." He answers softly and then suddenly his bare feet are in my line of vision right before he tips up my chin. "The way we feel when we kiss each other? With Tiffany it was fumbling, discomfort and relief that it was over before I embarrassed myself."

"You are too gorgeous for a dork like me." I confess with a goofy smile.

"I believe the words you thought when we first looked at each other were 'the sexiest pair of light brown eyes I have ever seen' were what was told to me." Lucien smiles at me mischievously. "I think I also heard you described me as being 'hot' and were embarrassed at being caught drooling over Grayson's brother."

"I'm killing him." I laugh as I punch Lucien in the arm. "I will officially be an only child."

"Brothers have to stick together you know." Lucien whispers before he claims my lips beneath his almost roughly.

"You keep questioning the validity of my feelings for you darlin'." Lucien lifts his head and looks down into my bashful gaze as he pants.

"I'm afraid." I confess as I run my finger across his well-trimmed beard.

"I'm not good enough for your innocence Jac." Lucien tells me, and I feel that he truly thinks this is accurate. "You have more compassion than anyone I have ever met. You are always putting other's feelings ahead of your own and you desperately want to believe that there is good in everyone. I have been tainted by my job as an investigator."

I stretch up on my toes and pull him down do I can tenderly kiss him.

"Alright." I whisper against his lips. "We will agree that we are good enough for the other. Deal?"

"Deal." He murmurs huskily before kissing me again. "Your twin would like to know if you are interested in watching movies downstairs tonight?"

"That sounds fun." I nod with a smile. "Is food part of the deal?"

Lucien throws his head back and laughs at my question.

"I have never seen anyone as tiny as you think about food as much as you do." He states with an indulgent smile. "I'm sure Mom has something scrumptious planned for dessert."

"Yum, dessert." I giggle as I saunter saucily ahead of him into the hallway.

I sit on the sectional in the living room between Grayson and Lucien and I am surprised to see their parents join us for the movies.

"We can stop and see Rune right after breakfast." Victor states. "They are relieved that we are interested and pray that Rune takes to Jac."

"I can't wait to meet him." I smile at Victor eagerly. "Thank you for thinking of him and setting it up."

"You are quite welcome honey." Victor returns my

smile warmly.

Grayson puts on Frozen 2 and I am a little surprised until I see Nicole's joyful expression. I loved watching the first movie but honestly hadn't really thought to watch the second one.

I have just as much fun watching Nicole because of her facial expressions and her emotions as I do seeing it myself. Grayson and Lucien both know what I am doing but keep it to themselves.

As soon as the movie is over Nicole happily returns to the kitchen for the dessert. I follow her into the kitchen and my stomach grumbles loudly when she pulls hot fudge cake from the oven.

"Oh, my goodness." I breath in awe. "May I have a double please?"

"Yes, you may." She laughs at my reaction. "Ice cream and whipped cream too?"

"Oh, my yes." I lick my lips hungrily.

"Do you think you can wait until we give the guys theirs first?" She questions me with a mischievous glint in her eyes.

"I suppose I won't wither away in just a couple minutes, but just in case we should hurry." I reply with mock seriousness.

She doubles over because she laughs so hard at my sense of humor.

"Oh Jac!" She wipes the tears from her eyes she laughed so much. She hands me two big bowls to hand out to the guys and follows me with two more.

"I have yours dear." She tells me and has me sit back

down between her boys before she hands me an enormous bowl of hot fudge cake with ice cream and whipped topping.

"She's the tiniest one here and she got the biggest helping!" Grayson exclaims, pretending he is hurt.

"She earned it after making me laugh so hard." Nicole states airily. "Our Jac is a funny girl when she relaxes herself."

I smile to myself hearing her call me 'our Jac' and smile at Lucien when he gives me an 'I told you so look'.

Nicole sits back down several minutes later with her own bowl and Grayson starts the movie 'John Wick 3'.

I practically inhale my dessert and then sigh with pleasure at just how delicious it was. Hot fudge cake is one of my favorite desserts. Nicole gathers all of the empty bowls before returning to the movie.

I never got to watch movies as a family before. My parents weren't really into movies so if I watched something it was alone. I envy my brother having been able to grow up this way.

After John Wick, Victor and Nicole excuse themselves and go to bed leaving the three of us alone to watch Avengers; Endgame.

Grayson raids the kitchen for potato chips, French onion dip, Doritos, pretzels, pop, trail mix, and mini chocolate bars. I manage to eat so much more that I get really sleepy and I know that I fall asleep because I am lying against Grayson only remembering flashes of the movie.

Chapter Twelve

It is Lucien, Victor, and I that are going to go check out the wolf, Rune, after breakfast. Grayson has a workout planned with a potential business associate that he cannot cancel so he won't be coming along.

"Did you forget something on the windshield of your car Jac?" Victor asks as we get close to where all the cars are parked in the driveway.

"No." I reply. "Why?"

"There is something propped on the windshield of your car." Victor tells me as he walks over there to check it out.

Lucien and I follow behind him quickly, only when we get up there and I see what it my face pales. It looks like my copy of the book 'Bridge to Terabithia' that I read like a hundred times when I was little. One day the book just disappeared from my bedside table. I wrote my name in marker on the front cover of the book. JAC

There it sits on the windshield of my new car. How did it show up here after like ten years?

Victor picks it up and plucks a sheet of paper shoved inside the cover, reads it, and looks up at me as he radiates fear, a lot of it. I shake my head at him and begin to back up towards the house, not wanting to go anywhere anymore.

Lucien steps behind me and wraps his arms around me stopping me from escaping.

"I need you to touch it and tell me who left it here darlin'." Lucien whispers to me so only I can hear.

"I don't want to." I shake my head irrationally.

"You need to read the note." Victor says as he looks at Lucien.

"Come on Jac." Lucien encourages me as he walks me up to his dad.

Lucien looks over and read the note, tenses and I am instantly flooded by his rage. So powerful I cringe and whimper.

"I'm sorry darlin'." Lucien whispers to me. "I need you to help me."

I straighten up and stare anxiously at the book that was once my prize possession. My childish penmanship evident above the title of the book. I am trembling so much Lucien has to support me as I take the book and note from Victor. I keep my expression carefully blank as I see an older version of Seth Pickett writing the note. 'From Daddy SP' and placing the book on my car. I can feel his eagerness to get me alone because I am his, only his.

"It was my book when I was a little girl." I tell Victor in a monotone as I hand it back to him. "That is my writing on the cover. The book disappeared from my room when I was nine years old."

Lucien turns me around and cradles me in his arms while I tremble and cry.

"It was Seth." I whimper softly. "I watched him write the note and place it on the car. He wants to get me alone because he thinks I am his and only his."

"I need to call this in and get them to process the scene but we can't miss having her meet Rune." Victor tells

Lucien. "You take her over to Ted's on River Road. If she bonds with that wolf at all you bring him home."

"Yes sir." Lucien helps me into the passenger seat of his car and within seconds we are speeding away from the city.

"Did you spend the night last night?" I ask him curiously. "You still looked sleep rumpled when I came down for breakfast."

"I did." He confesses. "Dad and I think it is a good idea under the circumstances that I stay."

"I am in your room." I state the obvious. "Surely, you will sleep better in your own bed."

"I will sleep better knowing that you are safe." Lucien points out the obvious. "I like knowing you are safe in my bed."

"I'm scared Lucien." I confess as my voice trembles. "What if…."

"Don't Jac!" Lucien explodes furiously. "You are *my girl!* I will not allow him to touch a hair on your head."

"Lucien, did Grayson tell you he thinks our abilities come from him?" I ask bluntly. "What if Seth is telepathic or something stronger? What then? He has an advantage! Maybe that is why he got away with kidnapping and murdering so many little girls!"

"Grayson said you felt him try to read your thoughts when you met at the café." Lucien says. "Did you feel that at all by your car just now?" I pause and think about it for a second.

"No." I shake my head.

We are quiet the rest of the drive out to the

plantation where the wolf is. Lucien opens my door for me when we pull up in front of the spacious plantation house. An older man with a military hair cut bounces down the steps to greet us with a smile.

"Where's your dad, Lucien?" Ted asks curiously. "I was just on the phone with him a half hour ago."

Lucien explains what happened with the book on my car and Ted is suddenly all business.

"Let's introduce these two then." Ted says as he leads us into a barn where a beautiful black wolf lies. His outer guard hairs are snowy white giving him a very unique appearance. He doesn't even lift his head at our entrance and I do not see his ears move either.

I reach out to him mentally and feel his grief for his lost girl. He remembers feeling her die. He stirs as he feels my presence in his head and I attempt to send him something, anything but I think all I manage to do is share my fear of Seth with him.

I can feel I have gotten the wolf curious and he raises his head and looks at me. His eyes are a very pale color and look almost white. His muzzle is almost pure white along the sides with a black streak along the top. His ears are lined with black fur while the hair inside is white.

He is beautiful and I can feel his intelligence as he watches me hopefully. Opening the gate to the stall he is in, Ted moves to stop me, but Lucien grabs his hand and shakes his head.

"Let her. It's ok." Lucien whispers.

I step into the stall and approach him slowly all the while sharing myself with the wolf telepathically. Squatting down next to him I hold out my hand for him to smell and am pleased when Rune gets to his feet. He stretches before he steps right up to me, nose to nose and breathes in my scent.

I feel his acceptance of me just seconds before he licks and nibbles on the underside of my chin.

"That is amazing." Ted exclaims as he watches our interaction. "He just accepted her into his pack. He has completely ignored the tons of people I have brought through here. Many people were willing to take him to guard all kinds of young girls but he wanted nothing to do with any of them. Two minutes with her and he is back to his old self."

"They connected." Lucien says. "Rune just needed someone he could connect with, like the girl he lost."

"Thank you." Ted replies. "You are doing me a favor by taking him knowing he is going to be happy with Jac."

"What do you think, Rune?" I ask the wolf as I communicate with him mentally. "Do you want to go home with me?"

Rune bounds towards the gate to the stall with a fervent bark. As we walk back to the car Ted explains how we care for Rune. What he eats, how much exercise he needs and says that Victor knows how to get a hold of him should anything arise.

Ted loads several boxes of Rune's stuff into the trunk of the car for us; mostly the meat he that he feeds to Rune.

"Why is Rune so big?" I ask Ted curiously. "The wolves I have seen are all lanky and sort of skinny. Rune is like the bodybuilder of wolves."

"He is a Mackenzie Valley Wolf." Ted laughs at me good naturedly. "They are the largest wolves in the world weighing in close to two hundred pounds. They are more filled out than their lankier cousins. Trust me, he eats enough to keep that wolfish figure."

"How old is Rune?" I continue, wanting to know as much about my new friend as possible. "I heard he was found when he was just a tiny pup."

"Rune will be two in June so he isn't even fully grown yet." Ted explains. "Yeah, he was only about three weeks old when he was discovered. His mother had been caught in a trap and he was the only surviving pup in her litter. I sent Victor a video to watch. Rune only responds to Gaelic commands. The girl he protected was fluent in Scots Gaelic. He seems to understand English too but his training was done in Gaelic."

Rune is walking around Lucien's car sniffing it thoroughly when we step up. Lucien steps towards Rune to open up the door for him but Rune lowers his head and growls at him. Before Ted can step in, I walk over to Rune sharing with him that Lucien is not a threat.

"Trust me and promise me you won't laugh." I whisper to Lucien as I pull him down to squat in front of Rune. The wolf cocks his to the side as he watches me kneel down in front of Lucien show submission to him by using my nose to tap Lucien under the chin. At the same time, I nuzzle Lucien's neck while sharing with Rune mentally that Lucien is my mate and as such, he is my alpha, thereby he is also Rune's alpha.

Rune whines uncertainly until I use my nose to tap under Lucien's chin again several more times. The wolf lies down and crawls to us slowly before rolling over to show Lucien his stomach submissively. I hear Ted gasp as he watches this quietly.

"Now, reach down and rub his stomach to show him that you accept him and then move up to his face and stroke him there too." I instruct Lucien as I still connect with Rune mentally.

Lucien strokes Rune gently and as soon as he is done petting the wolf's face Rune leaps to his feet to lick and nibble on Lucien's chin.

"You told Rune that Lucien was your alpha." Ted whispers in awe. "How did you do that? You formed your own pack with Lucien being the alpha."

"I need Rune to trust Lucien implicitly." I explain to Ted. "Rune accepts Lucien as his alpha because Rune accepts Lucien as my mate."

"The way you nuzzled Lucien's neck." Ted nods thoughtfully.

Lucien continues to pet Rune and scratch his ears affectionately.

"Thank you, Ted." I state with a smile. "I promise Rune will be in good hands. Am I supposed to pay you?" I ask as the thought suddenly occurs to me that maybe a payment was already promised.

"No." Ted shakes his head soberly. "You saved Rune's life. That is payment enough."

Lucien opens the door for the wolf and this time Rune happily jumps into the back seat where he lies down with a groan.

"Alpha huh?" Lucien murmurs after we are heading back towards home and I can feel his desire growing.

"Lucien." I breath, my voice suddenly husky. I had intended to sound chastising but it didn't come out that way.

"You just remember who your alpha is darlin'." He

reaches over and squeezes my thigh tenderly.

"Duly noted, my mate." I whisper sassily. Lucien chuckles deeply.

Chapter Thirteen

Lucien is forced to park the car in front of the house because the driveway in the back of the house is crowded with police officers. I am a little nervous about letting Rune out of the car because it isn't like he has a leash or anything and I am not sure how he is going to react to all of the people.

"Lucien, what about Rune?" I ask anxiously before we get out of the car. "He isn't going to attack anyone is he?"

"No Jac." Lucien reassures me as he lets Rune out of the car. "He will attack only if he thinks you are in danger. It is how he was trained. He will ignore all of those people until they get too close or seem threatening."

True to his word, as soon as Rune gets out of the car, he positions himself between me and all of the people he sees in the back yard. The wolf raises his head and scents the wind and when I connect with him mentally, I can feel that he is cataloguing all of the different people back there.

Victor comes around to the front of the house and as soon as Rune sees him the wolf's body language becomes defensive. As soon as Victor gets within six feet of me Rune growls low in his throat and lowers his head threateningly.

"Rune." I whisper and place my hand soothingly on his neck. The wolf sits down at my side but continues to watch Victor. I step around Rune and walk right up to Victor being careful to share my affection with Lucien's father with my wolf. Giving Victor an affectionate hug and kissing his cheek I show that the older man is part of our family too.

"Kneel down with me." I instruct Victor. After we are both squatting down, I mentally call Rune over to us to meet Victor. Rune doesn't submit to Victor but he nudges his hand and licks it once.

"Good boy." I stroke Rune affectionately.

"What did you just do?" Victor asks curiously.

"Told Rune that you are family." I shrug. "Now you won't have to keep your distance from me because you aren't a threat."

"Good idea." Victor agrees as he reaches out and strokes Runes ears softly. "He's beautiful and huge."

"Have they found anything back there?" Lucien asks as he gestures to my car in the driveway.

"Nope." Victor shakes his head in disappointment. "Seth wiped everything down and left nothing behind not even a hair."

"Let's put Jac's car inside the garage." Lucien suggests.

"My thoughts too." Victor says. "Her car will fit right next to your mother's."

"Can you help me carry in Rune's boxes of meat?" Lucien asks his dad. "There is a couple of them."

"Sure. I believe Nicole was making room in the small fridge in the pantry for Rune's meat." Victor says as they grab the two large boxes out of the trunk.

Victor and Lucien put Rune's meat into the extra fridge while I introduce my wolf to Nicole and Grayson. After that is done Nicole helps me find a large water bowl for Rune as well as a bowl large enough to feed him his raw meat in twice a day.

I fill Rune's bowl with meat hoping he will eat now that he is with me but when I walk out of the four seasons room where we have placed his food and water dish he whines, following me instead.

"What Rune?" I ask him as I squat down in front of him in concern. "It's ok for you to eat." I tell him out loud as I encourage him mentally at the same time. I can feel his agitation when I try to leave the room again thinking he should eat in privacy so I sit down right next to his food bowl. When he realizes I am not leaving him he finally inhales his food quickly.

"Why are you sitting on the floor?" Grayson asks as he pokes his head out onto the porch.

"Rune won't eat when I leave the room." I share thoughtfully. "I think he is afraid something will happen to me like his other girl."

"Poor guy." Grayson says as he squats down to scratch Rune's ears. "Don't worry boy, between all of us I am sure we can keep your girl safe."

"I still can't believe how huge he is." I trace Rune's massive paw softly. "I didn't know wolves got so big."

"We need to talk to Mom and Dad." Grayson says quietly. "Lucien and I think it is time to convince them of the reality of our abilities because Seth probably has them too. We need to have Dad believe us because it will help with the investigation."

"How are we going to do that?" I ask incredulously.

"Let Lucien and I do most of the talking." Grayson says with a smile. "Come on."

Grayson helps me to my feet before Rune and I follow him into the formal dining room. Lucien has already gathered his parents at the table is just talking about the happenings this morning with my car.

Terrified, I sit in between Grayson and Lucien as I need both of their encouragement right now. Rune places himself at my feet right under the table with a sigh of contentment.

"Remember when Grayson was five and him and I tried to convince you that he could hear what people were thinking?" Lucien starts the discussion lightheartedly. "You guys told us that he just paid close attention and had a wild imagination. The times he was spot on you said he was just lucky."

"Yep." Victor agrees with an indulgent smile. "You both grew out of such childish fantasies too, didn't you?"

"Did we, Dad?" Grayson asks, his tone dead serious.

"Why are you boys bringing this up now?" Victor asks tightly. "We don't have time for such foolishness right now. It is imperative that we pull together to protect Jac."

"That's exactly why we are bringing this up." Lucien states emphatically. "Convincing the both of you that this really exists will potentially save Jac's life."

"It wasn't important before this to try and convince you guys that I have special gifts." Grayson explains. "So, we just let you guys be ignorant."

"Now you are going to say that since Jac is your twin sister she also has these special gifts?" Victor's voice raises as his emotions start to get the better of him.

"Yes." Grayson replies softly. "This has nothing to do with all of the quacks you have seen in your years on the force, Dad. Yes, there are a lot of people out there who pretend to have gifts so they can cheat people. There are also people out there who are evil who have these abilities and use it to hurt innocent people. Jac and I didn't get this ability from Euphemia or her family. We got it from Seth."

"So, if you are telepathic what can Jac do?" Nicole asks softly as she quietly watches her men argue amongst themselves.

"I am what is called an empath." I reply softly. "I feel the emotions of others. With this ability I am able to tell when someone is lying. I see things when I touch objects and I just learned today that I am able to communicate with Rune with our thoughts."

Nicole chews her lower lip anxiously and I can feel her desire to believe us.

"Victor." Nicole whispers as she places her hand on his arm.

"Test us." I challenge them. "Surely we can prove it to you somehow."

Victor sighs and shakes his head after looking deeply at his wife.

Grayson starts repeating the weird random thoughts that are shooting through his dad's head and after several minutes of this Victor holds up his hand.

"Okay." He looks at Grayson and me studiously.

Nicole leaps from the table and disappears quickly with a look of determination. She returns seconds later holding a small shoe box that she sets down on the table in front me.

"Nicky don't." Victor's voice reflects the grief he is feeling. I keep my hands on my lap as they gaze at each other intently.

"No one else knows this but us Victor." Nicole says firmly.

Victor nods his permission and I slowly open up the shoe box to find a pink handmade baby quilt folded inside. My stomach clenches as I know the grief I am about to share with these two wonderful people.

"I don't need to do this." I whisper, my voice already breaking with the thought. "This is private."

"Please Jac." Nicole whispers as a tear already trickles down her cheek.

With a sigh I reach into the box and place my hand on the beautiful baby blanket. I am taken back to see a much younger Nicole eagerly working on this quilt by hand. She rubs her swollen abdomen with a loving smile as she feels the baby kick. I can't stop the smile as I too felt the baby move. The vision moves forward and Nicole is driving somewhere and someone plows into her side of the car. By the time she makes it to the hospital it is too late to save the baby. Victor makes it to the hospital in time to watch his wife give birth to their premature daughter.

The doctor quickly examines the baby and shakes his head sadly at them.

"Say your goodbyes." The doctor says. "There is nothing we can do."

Victor wraps their daughter in the quilt and hands her to Nicole before climbing up into the bed with his wife.

"Isabelle Victoria Devereaux." Nicole murmurs down to their daughter. "You be sure to tell Grandma hi when you get up there."

I have whispered everything I have seen and felt

during the whole vision so that everyone at the table has a ringside seat to the greatest pain this wonderful couple has experienced. Nicole is crying quietly as she listens to me remember her most painful moment. Victor is stoic but his heart is breaking all over again as he watches the pain on his beloved's face.

I draw my hand back and realize when a tear falls on my arm that I too am crying.

"Why was this necessary?" Victor asks tightly.

"Because Jac saw Seth write the note and place the book on her car!" Lucien exclaims furiously. "Jac felt Seth's desire to have her to himself because he believes she belongs to him alone! Why do you think I forced her to hold the book and note out there Dad?"

"I don't believe this." Victor states firmly and rises from the table to leave the room.

"Victor." I say his name softly. "I did mention that I can tell when someone is lying?"

"Dad, we have no intention of embarrassing you in front of the guys at the precinct." Grayson says after no doubt pulling the information from his father's thoughts. "This stays between the family only. We need you in on this so we can talk to you about things that we discover."

"You are the one with all the cop experience." Lucien brings up. "We will need to share everything with you so we can keep Jac safe."

Victor's cell phone goes off and after listening to the person on the other end for several minutes he mumbles something before hanging up. He is radiating rage to such an extent that it scares me causing Rune to get to his feet anxiously, growling menacingly at my heightened emotions.

"Dad?" Lucien asks after Victor stays silent for several seconds.

"An eleven-year-old girl was just reported missing just a few blocks from here." Victor explains tightly. "Susie Banks. Red hair, blue eyes, and tiny for her age. Her and her mother were placing flowers on some graves when the girl just disappeared."

"I want to help." I stand up anxiously, feeling like this is all my fault.

"This isn't your fault, Jac!" Grayson leaps to his feet furiously. "The last thing you should do is put yourself in danger when that is probably what Seth wants!"

"I might get a vision that tells me where he is taking her!" I shout furiously. "Our father has that innocent little girl Grayson! I saw Phemie's memories of her time with Seth. I know what he is going to do to Suzie and I will not just sit here safely while he destroys another life!"

Rune paces anxiously at my feet whining due to the chaos he can sense from everyone. Squatting down I send my wolf reassurance mentally that I am alright.

"She's right Grayson." Lucien says with a sigh of resignation. "Jac is key to helping us find her before he hurts her."

"Lucien is right, son." Victor agrees with Lucien. "The cemetery is packed full of law enforcement and FBI there is no way Seth can get his hands on Jac."

Grayson shakes his head furiously and says nothing more even though I know he vehemently disagrees.

"Stay with your mother." Victor tells Grayson. "We will take the SUV. Bring Rune."

Chapter Fourteen

St. Louis Cemetery number one is crawling with law enforcement when Victor parks the SUV as close as he can get. Rune stays right at my side on hyperalert because of all the people.

I stay close to Victor and Lucien as we make our way over to where a young mother is trying desperately not to sob more as officers are questioning her. I listen closely to her answer questions and when she says where her daughter was standing, I have Lucien and Victor walk me over there so I can take a look.

I lightly touch headstones and crypts as we pass by and try to focus my thoughts on Seth and only Seth. The stones are full of information from tons of people over the years but I am really endeavoring to limit my readings to just him.

About fifteen feet from where the girl disappeared, I find where Seth stood and watched the mother and child. He placed his hand on a crypt and as he watched the tiny girl, I can feel his excitement. Looking around from this vantage point I try to guess which way he would have taken the girl to get her out of the cemetery unseen.

Following my instincts, I walk slowly towards the edge of the cemetery where there are trees to hide in. I touch all of the crypts along the way and can tell I am going in the right direction. Right at the edge of the trees Seth struggled briefly with the girl and I can feel his agitation as he puts her in a light choke hold until she passes out.

Hoping something of the little girl's fell during the struggle I get down on my hands and knees and search the tall grass in a near panic. A dainty little silver bracelet has been ground down in the grass and I almost miss it before my fingers brush up against a larger charm of a butterfly.

I see the mother talking to another person placing flowers at a crypt while the little girl's attention is drawn to the large man who is holding a small little cage with a butterfly in it. Seth is drawing the girl away from her mother with the promise that he has another butterfly the little girl can keep. She trustingly walks just far enough away from her mother, putting several crypts between them so Seth can grab her swiftly.

Looking down at the ground I see the path that Seth took through the trees and when I place my hand on one of the trunks for balance I see Seth picturing him and the little girl at a place with butterflies, beetles, bees, spiders and there are other people there.

I have shared my vision with Lucien and Victor the entire time, keeping up a running dialogue so they don't miss anything.

"Bugs?" I ask, knowing it is a clue Seth has left but I don't know the area well enough.

"The Audubon Insectarium." Victor states.

Right before we turn away from the trees, I see the crushed butterfly cage lying on the ground.
"Look!" I point at it, not wanting to touch it.

Lucien scoops it up and we carry it back to the spot where the mother is being interviewed. I give the bracelet to Victor and he steps up to the mother. When he shows it to her and asks if it belongs to her daughter the poor woman nods her head and breaks down in sobs once more.

Victor steps up to a man who is ordering most of the law enforcement around and has a quiet conversation with him before we head back to the SUV with about thirty other police officers bringing up the rear.

"We are going to check out the insectarium and see if Susie is really there. Sergeant Curtis is sending back up." Victor explains.

All entrances and exits are quietly guarded as Victor speaks to the person in charge at the insectarium so more people can be on the alert for Seth and Susie. No one is allowed in or out until we are finished searching. Rune always at my side.

I stay close to Lucien and Victor and they quickly and efficiently search around the butterflies first and see Susie standing by herself searching the crowd anxiously. As soon as the little girl sees me her face brightens hopefully and she begins waving frantically.

"Jacqueline Cassidy!" The little girl yells my name and I feel all color drain from my face.

She is holding an envelope when we step up to her. She refuses to speak to anyone but me and gets very afraid when Victor attempts to keep her away from me.

"Please." Susie begs. "I can only see my mom again if I talk to her!" She points at me emphatically.

Victor motions me forward and I kneel down in front of her, my anxiety sky high.

"Are you Susie Banks?" I ask the little girl softly and she nods that she is.

"He made me promise to give this only to you." Susie hands me the envelope. I don't want to touch it but I really have no choice.

I get no reading from touching it at all which really makes me nervous. Opening it up I see there is a note addressed to me.

'My dearest Jacqueline,

I knew you would make me proud.

Daddy

"I did exactly what he wanted me to do." I exclaim after stepping away from Susie. "He was testing me."

"Why would he do that?" Victor asks in frustration.

"I don't know, but this is just the beginning." I tell him honestly.

"You said yourself he was excited watching the little girl." Victor points out. "Why didn't he take her somewhere private and do what he wanted to most? Why lead us here to this public place for her to be found safely?"

"Because he wants me more." I tell him as I wrap my arms around myself protectively.

Victor and Lucien read the note and I can feel their helpless rage that we fell into Seth's little game.

Several of the officers take Susie into their custody so they can deliver her down to the station where she will meet her mother and give a statement.

"Do you have any idea what he would have done if you had not come along and found her yourself?" Lucien asks.

"He would have hurt the next girl." I state with certainty. "He is testing my abilities and he feels a sense of pride because I got this gift from him. Phemie was daddy's girl to Francis and Seth wants me to be his daddy's girl. I would like to know how he managed to get his hands on a book that disappeared from my bedroom in Washington state while he was in prison here in Louisiana."

"Let's get you home." Victor states firmly as he looks around the insectarium on high alert.

Lucien, Victor, and Rune guard me closely as we make our way back to the SUV. The officers are no longer at the house when we pull into the driveway and my car is nowhere to be seen so Grayson must have put it in the garage.

Nicole is anxiously pacing when we get inside and hugs me fiercely with a sigh of relief.

"Let's lose ourselves in my remodel." I suggest to Nicole. "We could use a fun topic to take our minds off of things."

"Oh yes!" She exclaims. "That sounds perfect."

"Good." Victor nods his head wholeheartedly. "I was planning on taking Lucien over to Jac's new place so we could go over the new security system. Why don't the two of you come along so you can discuss your ideas there."

Grayson arrives at home before we leave so we decide to take two separate vehicles the few blocks over to my new house. Apparently, Victor already called the people who are supposed to install my security system and they are all gathered by the gate waiting. Victor opens the gate and we all file in until there are a half a dozen vehicles on my property.

As soon as Rune is let out of the car, he instantly starts to run around the property checking everything out. I give him his time to get used to the place and become familiar with it before calling him inside the house with Nicole and I. He does the same thing inside the house, rushing around exploring until he is satisfied.

Nicole shows me what she wants to do with each room with examples that she has on her tablet. There is going to be a lot of natural stonework in the house and I have to admit that I really love the idea instead of just woodwork, like my cabin back in Seattle has. The fireplace in the corner of the living room will be a large eyepiece that adds just the right amount of rustic charm. The ceilings on the first floor are really quite high for a house with a second story so Nicole will have plenty of room to put in some wooden beams up there.

The bathrooms she planned on replacing the glass shower stalls with a more natural stone shower, giving it an outdoor feel to it. She wants all of the floors to be natural stones with soft throw rugs for comfort and added color. Due to the privacy of my property I won't need to have curtains necessarily so Nicole has suggested indoor wooden shutters instead. I can close these when I want privacy plus, they will be added protection during hurricane season.

I agree eagerly with all of Nicole's ideas and give her the green light to begin. My attorney, Mr. Sorenson has already contacted her to give her instructions on the line of credit that has been extended to her for the remodel. Nicole is immediately on the phone hiring her best workers to begin construction.

Outside, Lucien, Victor, Grayson, and the security personnel are gathered on the patio by the pool discussing the best plan for my property.

"I think we should tear down a portion of the fence with the gate." Victor tells me.

"Why would we do that?" I ask him curiously.

"I want to make room for a guard booth to be put up just outside the gate but the way yours is set up there isn't any room for it." He explains. "If we remove a portion of the fence, we can put the new fence up in such a way that the gate will be placed further inside the property, giving room for the security booth. The new gate will be a necessity anyway. That one is too dated."

"What else do you have planned besides the new gate and fence?" I ask, having a feeling that Victor is just getting started.

"I want to put up cameras with motion detectors on poles throughout the property that will not be impeded by the trees. The trees and bushes will have to be trimmed away from the fence just slightly in order for the infrared motion sensors that will be placed there." Victor tells me. "I want to place solar panels on the roof in order for the security system to use that for its power supply. This way if the power to the house goes out or is cut on purpose the security system will still run to keep you safe. There will always be a guard in the booth that monitors the camera's and sensors."

"I had no idea that residential homes could have this kind of a security system." I confess in awe.

"I think it is a good idea for Grayson to live here with you." Victor suggests. "Not only will it keep you safe but it is a good way for the two of you to make up for lost time."

"I would love that." I nod my head with a smile before Grayson can say a word.

I can feel my twin's pleasure at my quick agreement to living together. Lucien's relief is also there, easy for me to pick up on without even looking at him.

"I am glad that my new house is so close to you guys." I tell Victor sincerely.

"I am too Jac." Victor hugs me and kisses my

forehead affectionately. "Nicole and I couldn't be happier to add a daughter to the family." His voice cracks with emotion for a second.

"While I am thinking about it." I bring up anxiously. "All of the men that will be doing the security work and remodel work will be screened thoroughly? I would hate to find out after the fact that they somehow were reporting to Seth."

"Of course." Victor nods firmly. "I personally know the men that will be putting in the security system as does Nicole with her work crew. She uses the same people for all of her projects over the years."

"There is a man at the gate demanding entrance." One of the security guys steps over, obviously irritated. "He says he is the owner's uncle and is really being rude."

"Check his identification and if he is indeed John Van Asselt then please allow him inside." I instruct firmly.

About a minute later, another car enters the property and parks behind all of the other ones and Uncle John steps out just radiating anger.

Instead of running to him and throwing myself into his arms like I normally would I stay where I am surrounded by Victor, Lucien, Grayson, Rune and the many security guys. He steps up to our group confidently with a smile that hides his true feelings.

"I have been calling Princess." Uncle John states in a calm voice.

I pat my back pockets for my phone and when I don't find it, I realize I left it in Lucien's bedroom on the bedside table.

"I'm sorry. I left it on the bedside table back at the

house." I reply, keeping my tone purposefully light. "I'm still not used to carrying it around yet."

"What is all this?" Uncle John asks as he motions towards all of the security personnel prepping my property for the new system.

"I am having the security system replaced." I inform him coolly.

"That is a wonderful idea, but I could have handled that for you." He persists in his earlier conversation.

"I am handling it just fine Uncle John." I state, my tone becoming icy. "What can I help you with?"

Lucien steps up to me and possessively puts his arms around me and kisses the top of my head. Idly, I stroke his arm as I watch a brief flash of fury cross uncle John's face before he stamps it down so I can't even feel the emotion.

Rune's growl tells uncle John that he has stepped too close to me as the wolf lowers his head and takes a step closer to him.

"You got a dog too?" Uncle John asks, his fury slipping through his control as he takes a couple steps back.

"I have always wanted one but Mom was allergic." I reply simply. "What do you want Uncle John? I have a lot that I am handling right now with the security system and the remodel needing my approvals."

"I wanted to see if you would like to go out to dinner." He smiles warmly, the earlier rage just disappeared as if were never there. "Just the two of us."

"I will have to take a raincheck." I reply as I wonder at his ability to hide his emotions so well. "If I hope to move in soon, I really need to get these projects going."

"Do you think it wise to move in here all by yourself?" Uncle John persists, keeping his tone soft.

"Oh, I didn't tell you?" I ask as I think to test him a little further just to see if he is really willing to let me grow up at all. Let's see how he reacts to my little white lie.

"Lucien and I are seeing one another and I have asked him to move in." I share in an innocent naïve tone of voice. "I will feel so much safer being able to sleep next to him every night."

To everyone's credit, no one denies the truth of my little lie, but I can feel Lucien tense behind me slightly. I am really not surprised as I watch Uncle John's face turn red and then nearly purple as he struggles to contain his mounting fury at my statement.

Rune positions himself directly in front of Lucien and I and even presses himself back against my legs slightly as he growls at Uncle John once more threateningly.

"I will not allow you to throw your innocence away on a......" Uncle John doesn't finish his thought but instead steps towards me purposely. I mentally command Rune to not attack but to instead lie at my feet. The wolf grudgingly lies down but continues to growl which gets much louder when Uncle John reaches to grab me.

Lucien grabs Uncle John's wrist in his hand, preventing him from seizing me while Rune growls, snarls and whines to be released. I calm my wolf commanding him to stay where he is.

"Mr. Sorenson will be in contact to see to my affairs Mr. Van Asselt." I state softly. "Please see yourself out. We have nothing further to discuss."

John snatches his wrist away from Lucien and stalks

back to his car furiously. He leaves the property but I know this isn't done because he will continue to try and change my mind. I needed John to be happy for me about Lucien. It was probably unfair of me to lead him to believe that Lucien and I were already having sex but I needed to push for a sincere reaction from him because he was really trying to hide himself from me.

The security guys get to work leaving me alone with the Devereaux's. I sigh sadly as I squeeze Lucien's arm tightly.

"Why did you let him think that we were having sex darlin'?" Lucien asks, his voice tense.

"Because her Uncle John was trying to hide how he truly felt from her." Grayson pipes up. "He was thinking all kinds of things and none of them were good. He was okay with her having a relationship with me because we would only spend so much time together being siblings but he is against her being with you. You have the power to take his princess away from him. He cannot allow such a thing to happen. You were pushing his buttons weren't you Jac?"

"I was. I kept feeling fleeting glimpses of rage that he managed to just make disappear. I had a feeling he wouldn't be happy about you so I added the sleeping together thing because I knew he wouldn't be able to hide that true reaction from me." I agree with Grayson's take on the situation.

Chapter Fifteen

Nicole manages to get her crew ready to begin with promises of double time for the entire project. I watch as what little bit of demolition begins on the house's interior in order to prepare for the remodel phase while the guys outside begin work on the fence.

Victor wants the portion of the fence torn down, replaced and the new gate up before the weekend is over to keep as many people off my property as possible. Once Victor and Nicole are certain that the work can continue without their presence, we all leave to go back home.

The last thing I want to do is pretend to be happy around everyone after my confrontation with Uncle John. I really want to hide away in Lucien's room alone with Rune so I can feel sorry for myself, honestly.

Uncle John has been a stable happy part of my life and I can't remember a time when he wasn't there. Am I ready to leave him behind?

As soon as I head for the stairs Grayson stops me gently.

"No sis." He shakes his head as he leads me into the formal dining room. "Mom is going to order in some Cajun for dinner and Saturday's are always family game night. The last thing you need to do is go up there and feel sorry for yourself because John was a jerk."

Lucien takes Rune out to the four seasons porch to feed him while Grayson and I set the table for the takeout food. I am pleased that Rune manages to eat with Lucien there. I hope that means the wolf is feeling more comfortable here and less anxious.

There is a huge serving of chicken and andouille gumbo that is served over rice, crawfish etouffee, and seafood alfredo pasta. It all smells a bit on the spicy side but my love of food has my stomach growling fiercely as the aromas take over the dining room.

I am a little nervous about trying the crawfish as they look a bit on the strange side but Grayson puts a portion of the etouffee on my plate with a challenging grin.

"Bet you're too scared to try it." My brother states as he raises his eyebrow at me.

"How do I get it out of its shell?" I ask curiously. Lucien shows me just how easy it is and I am surprised by how much I love the taste. Soon, my plate is overflowing with all three of the entrees and I am moaning with delight at the spicy food.

"How do you stay so tiny?" Nicole asks with a laugh. "I have to count calories to stay this trim and you just get to eat whatever you wish."

"High metabolism." I smile eagerly as I help myself to more of the seafood pasta.

After the dinner dishes are cleared off of the table Grayson gets out a deck of cards called Monopoly Deal.

"I thought Monopoly was a board game?" I question in surprise.

"Oh, the card game is so much more fun and cutthroat." He replies with a wicked smile. Nicole joins us after throwing the dirty dishes in the dishwasher and then Grayson deals out the cards.

I find the game to be an awesome way really let your inner wicked self out as you steal properties, force people to pay you so much they have nothing left, and then when they recuperate you do it again.

Everyone seems to have a turn winning the game and there is a lot of good-natured yelling going around the table.

After several hands of Monopoly Deal Victor gets out a Euchre deck and the complicated game of strategy is taught to me slowly with Lucien whispering to me every step of the way.

Several hours later finds me yawning tiredly after a long exhausting day. Everyone seems more relaxed after an evening of games at the dining room table. Lucien and Grayson both walk outside with me and Rune so the wolf can go to the bathroom before going to bed.

I am still amazed at how comfortable the temperatures are here in mid-April compared to Seattle. Rune keeps me in sight while he sniffs around the yard and to my surprise does his business at the very edge of the backyard. Taking the plastic bag out of my pocket I clean up his mess and put it in the trash before all of us head back inside.

After a long hot shower, I climb into the awesome bed in Lucien's room and smile when Rune decides his place is on the bed next to me.

The sun is high in the sky when I finally open my eyes the next morning and I groan when I roll over and see that it is after ten o'clock. Not bothering to change out of my leggings and tank top Rune follows me eagerly downstairs, no doubt he has to go outside.

The house is quiet as I make my way to the back

door to go outside with Rune. I can hear Nicole talking to someone softly from the kitchen but don't hear anyone else. I wonder if everyone is still sleeping? Maybe this is normal for a Sunday morning in the Devereaux household.

After Rune has done his business, I fill his bowl with meat, watch him inhale it quickly before he follows me into the kitchen where I pour a much-needed cup of coffee. Nicole is on a conference call with her work crew at my house checking on their progress and giving advice for problems that have arisen overnight.

I am surprised as I listen in to learn that her work crew was there all night. Sitting down at the table with my cup of coffee, Rune at my feet, I sip the delicious brew as I listen to what was accomplished last night.

A lot of the drywall had to be removed in order for the wood walls to be put up as well as the flooring coming up down to the subfloor. The crew is working room by room and since the great room is the biggest that is what they are tackling first. The old kitchen cupboards and appliances were removed to make room for all of the new. They have started putting up the new walls already and a company that specializes in the fireplace have begun putting that up as well.

Nicole assures me after her conference call that they should be done with the remodel in just a couple weeks since they are working around the clock. I am eager to see my house now that the work is underway.

Even though it is a Sunday I call my attorney, Mr. Sorenson, and explain my last couple conversations with Uncle John. I ask that Mr. Sorenson please have my rightful shares of the company profits placed into a bank account that be opened here in New Orleans. Mr. Sorenson understands that all further contact with John will be through him only. My attorney assures me that he will be auditing Delta Logistics to be certain that I am indeed getting my fair share of my father's company. I also inform him that I will be needing to purchase a vehicle and return the sports car John bought for me because it just isn't practical. Mr. Sorenson tells me to have the dealership I plan to purchase the car from call him so he can take care of the financial end.

"Buying a car?" Lucien asks as he sits next to me at the table. "What about the Audi?"

"It isn't practical now that I have Rune." I shrug. "I like it but I definitely don't need two cars."

"Darlin' you don't need to worry about not being able to afford it." Lucien points out. "It is perfectly fine for you to have a car you use as for enjoyment only. Dad, Grayson, and I can take you to buy another vehicle, that isn't a problem. If you like the Audi, then let's go get you another one, maybe an SUV where you can transport Rune in the back."

"Okay." I nod at his logic. "It can't hurt to go look and I confess I really do like the Audi."

"I don't know what you have for car insurance on the sports car, but it might be a good idea that you get your own policy instead of assuming John is taking care of it." Lucien points out as well. "You will need insurance on the house as well so we can help you find your own agent right here in New Orleans."

"I asked Mr. Sorenson to open up a bank account for me here in New Orleans so he can transfer my profits from Delta Logistics into it. I think after my last couple conversations with Uncle John I need to take care of my own interests." I explain with a sad sigh. "My attorney said he was going to have Delta Logistics audited to be sure I am truly getting what is mine by rights."

"You never told me that your adopted parents had a daughter of their own." Lucien states after refilling his coffee.

"They didn't." I shake my head. "They never said anything about another child. I never saw pictures or any memorabilia of any kind leading me to believe there was. Are you certain?"

"Wilhelmina Marie Cassidy." Lucien states as he flips through his phone before showing me a newspaper article that was dated just a year before my birth. It shows a picture of my adopted parents begging for the safe return of their little girl. The article says that ten-year-old Wilhelmina disappeared while at the park playing with school mates one afternoon while her nanny was there watching her.

"I have never heard about this." I whisper in shock. "What happened?"

"She was never found." Lucien says. "It remains a cold case to this day. No trace of her was ever found."

"That might explain why they were so overprotective with me." I think out loud. "I was never allowed to go to school and my dad was even against me taking any of my college classes on campus. I had to throw a fit to be able to work at the local McDonald's so I could have my own money."

"I have also been digging into Pickett." Lucien says. "He was raised by a single mother with no father listed on the birth certificate. His mother was a cocktail waitress and get this; she disappeared shortly after Pickett turned eighteen. She is considered a cold case as well. Pickett was expelled by three different public schools because of reports from female students that he was inappropriate. He finally just stopped going to school. There are several records of domestic calls made to their house before his mother disappeared. The officer's reports state that the mother had multiple bruising that she claimed came from one-night stands. The officer's suspected that they came from the son due to his violent behavior when they arrived at the home. Neighbors were always the ones that called in to the police, never the mother."

"Did you get any sleep last night?" I ask him, noticing now that he is wearing the same clothes and they aren't rumpled at all.

"Nope." He shakes his head with a yawn. "I had work to do. The more background I do on Pickett the easier it will be to find him before he gets his hands on you."

"Why were you researching my adopted parents?" I prompt him curiously.

"Why did a Washington couple adopt a baby from New Orleans?" Lucien asks as he raises his eyebrow questioningly.

"Maybe Phemie knew she was going to give us up?" I suggest.

"I don't think so. There are no records of her contacting any of the adoption agencies at that time." Lucien shakes his head. "Your adoption was completed just a couple hours after you were born. There are no records that your adopted father was even down here on business during Phemie's pregnancy at all. He had no way of knowing about you. Someone was keeping tabs on her and when they found out she died giving birth you were snatched up immediately. I think whoever set up your adoption somehow knew Pickett or were following the trial."

My face pales at the thought that I was given to my adopted parents by someone who knew Pickett personally.

"I checked Pickett's prison record and he received a package during the same time period that your book went missing." Lucien says as he watches my facial expression carefully.

"Who sent it to him?" I ask, not really wanting to know.

"Delta Logistics." Lucien whispers. "I have been unable to trace who sent it from the company. Pickett received mail from Delta Logistics several times over the years he was incarcerated. It was the only mail he ever received."

"Someone at Delta Logistics knows Pickett personally and they are probably the person who found me for William and Zacari." I state, stunned.

"That is what I am thinking." Lucien says. "Your company is so massive there is just no way to narrow it down. You never told me that your adopted parents were murdered. I thought they were caught in a storm or something?"

"They weren't murdered." I shake my head, this all becoming too much.

"I read the report." Lucien says. "Their bodies were found inside the cabin when the yacht was recovered. They had their throats cut before the yacht was sunk. Detectives think it was done in such a way that they would never be found."

"Uncle John refused to let the police speak to me." I state as I remember back to when the yacht was found. "He told me that he would handle everything for me, like he always does. I am sure he was just protecting me from knowing something unnecessary."

"I think it is necessary for the daughter to be aware that her parents had been murdered." Lucien tells me honestly.

"This is all so much to take in." I murmur as Victor and Grayson join us at the kitchen table.

"I told Lucien it is best for you to know what we know as we find it out." Victor explains to me seriously. "I think you have spent your whole life being kept in the dark. Some people might think that is being protective but I am a firm believer in knowledge is power."

"My whole life was based on a lie." I state emotionally. "Have you tried looking into John yet?" I ask pointedly. "I hate to be the one to say it, but he would have the most to gain from my parents' death. He was originally from New Orleans and only moved to Seattle when William's company merged with his. Maybe he is the connection with my adoption."

"We have both looked into John, but so far we are coming up emptyhanded." Victor shares honestly.

Chapter Sixteen

Grayson, Lucien, Rune, and I head down to the dealership while Victor and Nicole head over to my house to check on the construction progress. Victor wants to be sure that the new gate is up and operational before tomorrow morning.

The Audi dealership is pretty quiet for a Sunday morning. The salesman has a problem with Rune until Lucien flashes his badge and explains that the dog is there for my protection. I inform the salesman that Rune won't be allowed inside the vehicles until after I have paid for it and he is satisfied with that.

Lucien asks to see their SQ5 models and the salesman smiles charmingly as he leads us over to a whole row of them in different colors. He explains to both Grayson and Lucien in guy talk about this particular model and within minutes Lucien states that he wants Grayson to take it for a test drive. Grayson agrees knowing that Lucien is staying behind to protect me just in case.

I walk past all of the colors that are available for this model and decide that black is probably best. I am tempted to go with the red but I think I like the understated black better.

Grayson gives the thumbs up when he comes back. The salesman straightens his tie nervously after exiting the car because Grayson tested just how fast the car would reach eighty miles per hour on the highway. Lucien and Grayson whisper together for several minutes before looking at me questioningly. I nod my agreement since I trust their judgement and we all step inside to sign papers and call my attorney.

Mr. Sorenson talks to the salesman on the phone and sets up the full payment for the car including all of the insurance, title fees and everything else involved. It is agreed that I can take the car with me today after the salesman puts the temporary plate in the rear window. He even lets me take a black model that has no miles on it at all. I appreciate that, considering I get psychic readings off of objects that other people have touched.

Lucien rides with me in the new car while Grayson drives Lucien's car. It is agreed that we will meet over at my place so we can check on the remodel while their parents are still there. I have to admit I like this Audi just as much as my sports car. It has pretty much the same bells and whistles as the other car and handles just as nicely.

There is a huge construction dumpster in the driveway when we pull through the new gate of my house that is full of building materials. The new guard booth outside the gate is up and looks like they are working on placing all of the monitors inside for the cameras. Victor has explained that once I move in there will be a guard inside the booth at all times guarding and screening all visitors as well as watching the camera feed.

I am amazed when I step inside the house and see that the great room walls have been replaced with wood and the difference is just astounding. I love it instantly. They are putting the finishing touches on the kitchen cupboards while the new appliances are installed. The fireplace will take a couple more days but there is a lot involved with its installation. They can only start laying the stone floors once all of the other work is done, so that will be last.

The workers that were putting up the walls have moved on to the other three rooms on the first floor; the office alcove, Grayson's bedroom, and bathroom, to remove all of the drywall in preparation for the wood.

I am truly impressed with how quickly construction is coming along.

Outside, Victor is helping the guys from the security system test all of the cameras that have been set up on poles around the perimeter of the property. They apparently are set up to rotate on a schedule but are also set up to capture movement as well. There are enough cameras to be able to capture the entire yard just in case someone tries to scale the fence and somehow manages to sneak past the motion lights on the fence itself.

Victor comes over and checks out the new car and nods his approval before taking the time to explain my new security system to me. I will be grateful to have Grayson in the house with me to depend on.

Nicole encourages me to take Grayson and Lucien to some furniture stores to pick out what I want in the house instead of leaving it to her. This way it will feel more like mine. I agree with her and decide to leave Rune here with Victor and Nicole so I don't have to leave him in the heat of the car.

Lucien says that we should start at the Ashley Furniture store first because of the quality of their products. Once there, I look around the showroom but don't find anything that begs me to buy it so I ask to look through their catalogue instead.

I insist that Grayson have a new bedroom set as well arguing that it is always a good idea to leave a functioning bedroom with his parents just in case. As Lucien and I pour over the catalogue I finally find a bedroom set that I just love. The bed is a king size canopy that looks like it is made of large logs. The bedside tables and dressers also look handmade of logs and bark as well.

Lucien agrees with my choice and once that room of furniture is ordered I move on to the living room, dining room, and office.

With the walls being a pale wood grain, I choose a dark brown leather for the sofa, loveseat and recliner. The end tables and coffee tables I choose more log like look to match the rustic theme throughout.

I find a beautiful dining room table and chairs that appears to be hand carved from a large tree. It is definitely a unique piece of furniture and I fall in love instantly.

I follow the same theme in both the bathrooms finding handmade cabinets to place the towels and things in.

For my office I find a gorgeous desk that follows the same handmade theme as the rest of my furniture as well as four tall bookshelves.

The patio furniture I choose a more antique setting to go along with the plantation look of the outside of the house.

Once all of the furniture has been chosen, I call Mr. Sorenson to set up payment with the furniture store while I set up the delivery. While I am on the phone with my attorney, I ask him to hire a moving company to pack up the cabin in order to send me everything down here to New Orleans. My adopted mother, Zacari, made quilts by hand and I have chests of them up in the cabin that I want to use here in my new house.

Lucien talks me into turning the third bedroom into a workout room. I agree that it is a good idea to have some workout equipment and maybe line the floor in those gym mats too. I turn that project over to him while his mom helps me turn all of the utilities into my name. I have never had to pay my own bills like this before so I really have no idea how it works. Gas, electric, water and sewer, garbage removal, internet, cable or satellite television and then there is the pool. Do I hire a pool company to come and care for it because I sure don't know how to?

After Nicole and I have taken care of that she encourages me to go buy everyday items that I will need for the house; garbage cans, dish drainer, towels, wash cloths, linens for the beds, dishes, pots and pans, silverware and so on.

Grayson and Lucien offer to stay at my house with Rune while Nicole takes me to the mall where we can shop at some of the department stores. Thankfully I have my credit cards with me today.

Nicole takes Victor's SUV and tells me to take my own that we have plenty of room to haul everything back here after we are done.

Excitement takes hold as soon as we are inside the first department store and I start choosing items that I fall in love with. I absolutely love that I don't have to worry about what my frugal parents would have insisted on. The department store offers to set aside all of my purchases for me and have them delivered to my address this afternoon so I don't have to worry about multiple trips to my car.

I never realized just how fun it would be to shop for mundane things like a coffee pot or a set of cast iron frying pans. Considering my house has a large pool with two acres I make sure I buy several sets of dishes, silverware, and glasses so that if I decide to throw a party there will be enough.

Nicole walks along with me smiling the entire time at my eager expression as I go absolutely crazy outfitting my new home.

Three department stores later, all of them delivering my purchases for me, Nicole and I make our way to the grocery store since my fridge is installed. I have a large walk in pantry behind the kitchen by the laundry room and I might as well stock up on food for the people working so diligently.

My adopted mother taught me how to cook from a young age so I am already familiar with the staples I will need to stock up on in order to cook meals. Even something this mundane I find myself enjoying while Nicole reminds me of the items I would have forgotten. My pantry, fridge and freezer will be well stocked by the time we get back to my house.

Grayson, Lucien, Victor and Nicole all help bring in the groceries and everyone even helps to put it all away. My department store purchases have already begun arriving and just to keep the house clear for construction Victor has had them place everything in my two-stall garage so I can sort it from there.

I take the time to find the coffee pot and bring it in the house to set up on the kitchen counter. I brew a pot and set out the disposable coffee cups along with cream and sugar so that the workers will have it available them all the time. I set out the coffee and filters next to it for easy access. The fridge is full of bottled water, soda, yogurt cups, cheese sticks, lunch meat, cheese slices, different juice bottles, and many other items making it easy for them to just grab and eat.

After that is all done to my satisfaction, I take the time to draw out the dimensions of the house on some notebook paper. I intend on using it to determine where I am going to put the furniture in the dining room, living room and my bedroom. I make sure to draw in where all of the windows and doorways are in each room, making notes on how long each wall, window, and doorway are.

I sit back and watch the workers inside the house and contemplate just how much money I spent today. My Audi SUV easily cost me sixty thousand dollars all by itself and that doesn't count the thousands I spent just in the department stores and the hundreds at the grocery store. I easily spent fifty thousand picking furniture out of the catalogue as well. I sigh as I picture the heart attack my adopted father would have had if he had known.

"Electronics." Grayson comes up to me with a raised eyebrow.

"What about them?" I ask as he sits down in a folding chair across from me.

"Did Mom bring you to pick out televisions, computers, stereos or any of that stuff for the house?" Grayson points out logically.

"My attorney is having the cabin in Seattle packed up for me and shipped to your parent's house." I explain to him. "There is a television, computer and stereo in my parent's things."

"Sis, come on now." Grayson protests. "How old are they? Be honest."

"I don't know." I reply with a shrug. "I was probably seven or eight when we got the television. My dad replaced the desktop maybe three or four years ago and I have no idea about the stereo."

"My turn to take you to the store." Grayson says firmly. "They now have smart televisions or android televisions and really cool Bluetooth sound systems that go along with them."

"Grayson! Do you know how much money I spent today?" I argue with him, starting to get a stomach ache from the stress.

"You admitted yourself that you have so much money now you won't ever be able to spend it all and besides these are purchases you won't make again for a really long time." Grayson argues back logically.

"Alright." I sigh grudgingly. "Let's go."

Grayson drives my SUV to a big box electronics store and eagerly pulls me inside. Our first stop is the televisions, of course. I am impressed that Grayson has picked the best wall to place the television and knows just what size will work best for the room. I allow him to pick out the television, speaker system, and the stereo system as well. While those items are being delivered to the front of the store, I walk over to the computer section to get myself a new desktop and laptop computer with printer, fax and sound system too.

I allow the salesman to explain the differences between them before I choose a desktop with large dual monitors, a printer that also serves as a fax machine and copier as well as a top of the line set of speakers. The laptop I want something lightweight, touch screen, fast, with lots of memory. I of course will need to wait for the cable guy to come and install everything bringing with him the modem to connect to the internet with.

Grayson is satisfied by the time everything is paid for and loaded into the SUV.

Chapter Seventeen

Nicole finally relents after I beg for several minutes straight to allow me to make dinner for everyone. Grayson's whole family has accepted me as one of their own really without question and the least I can do is cook them a homemade meal to show my appreciation for all they have done.

I find enough sirloin steak in the freezer, egg noodles, gravy mix in the pantry and fresh mushrooms and sour cream in the fridge so I decide to make a big pot of beef stroganoff. Once I get started on the meal prep slicing mushrooms, onions, and steak I find that I have missed cooking for other people.

Once I get the beef stroganoff simmering on low, I dig through the large freezer and am pleased to find some cheesy garlic bread to go along with my dinner. There seems to be enough fresh vegetables in the fridge to make a nice salad as well.

I set the table and have dinner strategically placed before calling everyone in to the dining room. Nicole looks impressed and the guys eagerly dig in after sitting down to the table. They all agree, around mouthfuls of stroganoff, that it is the best they have ever had. It makes me feel good to be able to give back even just a little bit.

Nicole insists on cleaning up dinner so I retire upstairs to take a long hot bath and relax in Lucien's bedroom quietly with Rune. It has been a long chaotic weekend and I am exhausted both physically and emotionally. Being that I am an empath, I have always felt overloaded by processing everyone's emotions on a regular basis. My adopted parents really did me a favor by homeschooling me away from other people. I never realized how peaceful my life in Seattle was until I moved down here to New Orleans.

I hope that Grayson's family doesn't take my need to be alone personally.

It is nearly noon when I finally open my eyes and see that all of the curtains in the bedroom have been closed against the bright spring sunshine. Rune is no longer on the bed with me and I can only guess that someone fed him and let him outside for me.

Lucien and Victor are both gone to work and Nicole is in the kitchen on her laptop when I walk into the room.

"Coffee Jac?" Nicole asks after looking up at me with an affectionate smile.

"Yes, please." I yawn widely. "Where are Grayson and Rune?"

"Grayson wanted to go for a jog so he thought Rune could use the exercise and brought him along." She explains as she sets a fresh steaming mug of coffee in front of me with cream and sugar.

"Thank you." I state making happy noises in my throat from the aroma of the hot beverage.

"Do you have any plans for the day?" Nicole asks, turning her attention back to the laptop.

"I thought I should probably drive over to Tulane University and get signed up for fall classes." I sigh. "I only have a few classes to finish up my bachelor's degree and then I can get started on my masters."

"I will be heading over to your house to check on the

construction." She informs me. "They got a lot done last night. The fireplace is done so now they are going to lay the stone on the main floor. Construction will stop long enough for the floors to set and then they will get started upstairs. I have a catering company delivering meals to the house three times a day so no one has to worry about eating."

"It sounds like the house will be ready for me to move in pretty soon." I exclaim.

"Yes. My best guess is that it may be done in two weeks. The stone floors will take the longest." Nicole returns with a smile. "You plan on bringing Grayson with you to the college, don't you?"

"Yes." I nod with an answering smile. "He can show me around as well, saving me time from wandering around lost."

I sip my coffee while Nicole continues to work quietly on her laptop until Grayson sweeps in with Rune from his run. Rune greets me excitedly, obviously having loved the jog with Grayson.

"Did he give you any trouble?" I ask curiously as I scratch the wolf's ears.

"Nope." Grayson shakes his head. "He was all about the exercise."

"Did you want to come with me to Tulane so I can get signed up for my fall classes?" I ask him.

"Yeah." He nods. "Let me take a quick shower and then we will head over. I need to sign up for my classes too."

Grayson insists that we go out for lunch first since he just got done working out and I readily agree as I haven't even had breakfast yet. We stop at a locally owned diner that specializes in po'boys and I watch Grayson inhale two of them along with a huge side of shrimp. I manage to eat my po'boy and a side of French fries without a problem and drink all of my soda. With our hunger taken care of we head over to the university and I am quite taken with the main building. It reminds me of English castles I have seen pictures of. The campus is quite sprawling and is much larger than I expected.

Switching my classes from Seattle to Tulane is much easier than I thought it would be and within a couple hours I have signed up for all of my fall classes. I will be ready to start on my master's degree in winter semester after Christmas.

Grayson gives me a tour of the campus and shows me where all of the classes are held and anything else I might need the location of. Half of my fall classes are online so I will only have to come to the college for a couple.

To my surprise, Grayson stops at a local flower shop and picks up a small bouquet of carnations. He doesn't say anything to me just quietly drives to a large cemetery in the garden district where he parks in the lot.

I walk with him and wonder what we are doing because I can't get a reading off of him. Due to the little girl being abducted from a cemetery recently, I stay close to Grayson anxiously.

I am speechless when he stops in front of the Burt family crypt. Using a key off of his keyring he opens up the locked door and escorts me inside. Our birth mother's coffin is in the middle of the room and Grayson steps up to it to place the carnations on top.

Before Grayson can say anything, the door opens behind us and Aunt Kyna enters with her own flowers in hand.

"Grayson! Jac!" Aunt Kyna smiles at us happily. "I was going to call you both after I dropped these flowers off for Phemie. I would like to have you both for dinner tomorrow night. Your grandparents have finally agreed that it is time to meet the both of you."

I look up at Grayson, because after seeing the way Francis treated him the decision should ultimately be his. He is looking down at me questioningly and I shrug at him, not wanting the decision to be mine. I don't want to feel responsible for more emotional pain for my twin.

"We would love to Aunt Kyna." Grayson sighs reluctantly.

"I have had a long talk with Francis and he promises to be on his best behavior." Aunt Kyna assures us. "Your grandmother, Millicent, is most anxious to have the opportunity to finally meet the two of you."

"Are you sure this is a good idea?" I ask aunt Kyna honestly. "I look just like Phemie and my appearance will no doubt just cause them more pain."

"I think they need this in order to finally let go of the past and truly move on." Aunt Kyna nods her head firmly.

"Did you want us to bring something?" I ask, forcing a smile for her benefit.

"No, dear." She shakes her head. "Just yourselves."

Grayson mumbles an excuse to get us out of the crypt and on our way which aunt Kyna accepts without comment.

Instead of taking me back to his house, Grayson stops at a mall with a grin.

"What are we doing here?" I ask, wondering why a guy would want to walk through a mall on a Monday afternoon.

"You need to update your wardrobe for the climate here." Grayson states with a shrug. "Seattle's summers are much different than ours down here and knowing your adopted parents like I do you haven't been allowed to just go nuts for clothes, ever."

"Didn't I spend enough money over the weekend?" I protest.

"You were the one who said you now have more money than you could ever spend." He replies logically. "Besides, what's the point of having all of that wealth if you don't allow yourself to enjoy life. I don't know any girls who don't like shopping for clothes."

"Fine." I huff, although inside I am starting to feel excited to just buy things just because I think it is cute.

Grayson actually has an opinion on some of the clothes I pick and I find that I like his ideas. I have always wanted to wear more dresses and skirts than jeans or shorts so I indulge that craving for the first time in my life.

Grayson carries all of my purchases and when it becomes apparent that I am not picking out jewelry, sunglasses or other accessories he starts picking out things for me. By the time we leave the mall his back seat is overflowing with bags. Not only did I buy a whole new wardrobe, but I also got jewelry, sunglasses, cell phone cases, watches, nail polish, shoes, perfume, toiletries like lotions, hair ties, and so many other things that I never really thought to buy before.

Grayson helps me carry it all upstairs to Lucien's room where it takes me an hour to put it all away.

It is dinner time when I come back downstairs and I pause at the serious air in the dining room. Victor and

Lucien both appear upset when they see me walk into the room and give each other a resigned look.

"Something happened." I state as I sit down next to Lucien.

"Another little girl went missing in the early morning hours." Victor tells me somberly. "Eleven-year-old Annie Wilson took the family dog outside to go the bathroom at seven this morning and was not seen again."

"Did she drop anything during the struggle?" I ask, hoping maybe I can touch the object and help somehow.

"No." Lucien shakes his head.

Victor hands me Annie's file and I open it to find a tiny girl with black hair and bright blue eyes. My chest tightens with agony over what the poor girl has no doubt experienced all day with Seth.

"I want to help." I whisper as I stare at Annie's picture sadly. "I felt what Phemie went through and knowing the same horrors are happening to this innocent little girl…."

"I understand your desire to help." Victor tells me softly. "We have to be careful because you are Seth's daughter. To the public it would appear you might have a conflict of interest in this case."

"Have you searched Seth's home?" I ask.

"The judge won't give us a warrant until we find more proof that we suspect Seth." Lucien shares with a frustrated sigh. "We can't find anything that ties him to the girl's yard this morning."

"If you will excuse me." I whisper as I rise from the table. "I'm not hungry. I think I will just go up to my room."

Chapter Eighteen

I find myself restless and bored. No one is home by the time I make it downstairs the next morning so I have a cup of coffee and let Rune outside. I can't go over to my house because they are working on the floors and no other work can be done at the same time. Nicole already arranged for food to be catered to the flooring installers so there is nothing for me to do over there. I have no homework to do and it is not safe for me to even go for a run with Rune.

I set up my laptop in the breakfast nook where there are plenty of windows to let in the sunshine and proceed to research Annie Wilson. The reporters have interviewed family and friends of the little girl and she is known for being outspoken with no fear. She loves her family and friends and would do anything to protect those she loves. Many of her friends stated that she came to their defense at school to the point where she was sent home for fighting the bigger boys. She sounds like Phemie. My birth mother was the only girl to survive Seth Pickett. Maybe Annie will too.

I want to help this little girl so she can come home safely but I don't know how to do that without putting myself in danger as well. Shaking my head, I shut down my laptop and decide to get dressed to go out. Annie needs someone to help her and the only way I can do that is to go out.

I roll my hair into a bun on the top of my head so I can wear a hat with sunglasses to help hide my identity. I choose a plain pair of blue jeans, sweatshirt, and tennis shoes so perhaps I can pass for a young boy. I borrow a baseball cap from Lucien's room and a pair of his sunglasses because all of mine are definitely girly.

Rune is unhappy that I am leaving him home but I cannot have him along with me and take the chance that his presence will give away my identity.

Annie lives right next to a park so I pull into their lot and begin to wander through the part closest to her house. There are several very large trees lining the sidewalk directly across the street from Annie's house and to me it looks like the perfect place to hide while watching her.

Now that I am here, I hesitate before placing my hand on the tree because I am terrified of what I am going to see. Taking a deep breath, I finally place my palm on the bark and I instantly feel Seth's excitement as he watches Annie exit the house with her dog.

I can feel Seth's anxiety as he plays a recording of tiny puppies whining and barking on his cell phone, hoping to attract the little girl's attention. Sure enough, Annie's head lifts as I continue to watch the vision with trepidation. She leaves her golden retriever inside her fenced yard while she hurries across the street.

Seth pulls the little girl back against him in a choke hold until she stops struggling. At his feet is a large duffel bag that he slips her inside of, zips it closed and strides away from the tree with no one the wiser.

The vision ends and I am left shaken with no more clues as to where he may have taken her. Sliding to the ground I allow the tears free reign as I am careful to not touch the tree again.

"Excuse me." A deep voice interrupts my tears. "Are you alright?"

I look up into a startling pair of bright blue eyes set in a very Italian looking face. He looks like he is in his mid-twenties and I can see his badge attached to his belt.

Oh no! I wasn't supposed to be seen here!

"Yes." I reply softly as I scramble to my feet quickly and try to hurry away.

"Wait!" He exclaims and gently grabs my wrist, effectively stopping me from fleeing. "What are you doing here? Why are you crying?"

"I was just walking through the park." I state, keeping my eyes on the ground in front of me. "I needed to get some air."

"Come on now." He says disbelievingly. "I don't believe in coincidences. A young girl dressed as a boy complete with a ballcap and sunglasses to hide her identity across from a crime scene?"

"What crime scene?" I whisper as I try pull my arm free to no avail, my sunglasses falling to the ground.

He grabs my chin between two fingers and forces me to look up at him. He is quite tall, at least six feet with broad shoulders, big biceps, and large hands. His face is square with a roman nose, hooded brow, curved lips and a well-trimmed beard. His expression is one of concern as he gazes into my face intently. I am unable to get any readings from him at all and I don't know if that frightens me or relaxes me.

My baseball cap falls off my head and my hair tie actually snaps causing my long red curls to tumble down to my waist.

"You're Seth Pickett's daughter." He whispers. "I thought you looked familiar. That's why you are here!"

"Please." I whimper, still trying to squirm free. "I just wanted to try and help."

"Does Vic know you are here?" He asks. My face pales. I hadn't thought that I would be caught here in the park by someone who knew Victor or Lucien.

"I should go." I state softly. "Please let me go."

He finally releases me but backs me up against a tree, thankfully not the one I got the vision from, and blocks me in with is arms.

"I'm detective Zander Cody, sex crimes unit." He introduces himself. "This is my investigation so I don't need to inform Vic or Lucien that I saw you here. I know who you are, Jacqueline Cassidy. You led police officers to Suzie Banks at the insectarium where Pickett left her for you to find. You are here because you want your...... *gift*....to save Annie."

My face pales even further at his declaration. He knows about my abilities?

Seeing my reaction to his words Zander smiles down at me with satisfaction.

"No one believes in those kinds of things." I whisper and shrug my shoulders as I look away from him anxiously.

"Pickett did." Zander whispers back to me. "He had his cellmate convinced he was telepathic."

Grayson was right! We do get our psychic abilities from our father.

"Tell me what you saw when you touched the tree Jacqueline." Zander insists as he grasps my chin gently, forcing me to look at him again.

"I don't know what you're talking about officer

Cody." I reply as my lower lip trembles, my anxiety skyrocketing due to the fact that I can't even tell if Zander is telling me the truth or not. Why don't my gifts work on him?

"Oh, I think you do." He continues. "Help me save her Jacqueline. Help me bring Annie home to her parents."

"He stood by that tree." I nod to the next tree. "He watched her come outside with her dog. He played a recording of puppies crying on his phone to draw her over here. As soon as she started walking around the tree, he grabbed her and put her in a choke hold until she went limp. He stuffed her into a large duffel bag that was on the ground at his feet before he simply walked away. He knew she lived here. He knew she would most likely be the one to bring the dog outside."

"See?" Zander murmurs as he nuzzles my cheek softly. "Was that so hard? You couldn't see where he was planning on taking her?"

"No. I only felt his excitement for her when she stepped outside." I confess. "Please let me go. I did as you asked."

Zander sighs and steps back from me. I run across the park as if the demons of hell were on my tail, not even bending over to pick up the baseball cap I dropped.

"You just buy a whole new wardrobe of girly clothes and you go out looking like that?" Grayson asks me as I try to sneak upstairs without being seen.

"I didn't want to be recognized." I confess honestly. "I felt cooped up and thought if I went out like this there was less chance anyone would know it was me."

I keep a mental wall up in case Grayson doesn't believe me and tries to read my thoughts. His face registers surprise when he tries to do just that and feels my mental block.

"Are you alright?" He persists. "You look upset."

"I just wish I could help that little girl get home to her family safely." I tell him honestly. "I am the only other person alive who knows what it feels like to be that man's captive. I am going to go shower and get ready for dinner with our grandparents."

I am careful to keep my thoughts centered on safe subjects, refusing to dwell on my afternoon at all, lest Grayson sees what truly happened.

I take my time getting ready, wanting to look perfect when I meet my grandmother. My hair falls down my back in ringlet curls, my makeup is in light earth tones, and I am wearing a blue summer dress that brings out the color of my eyes with heeled sandals making me look just a tiny bit taller.

Grayson is pacing the foyer waiting for me when I come down the steps. Lucien and Victor are not home from work yet when my brother and I head over to our aunt Kyna's house.

I force myself to lead the way into aunt Kyna's house in order to protect Grayson from our grandfather, just in case. I step into the formal dining room and the first person I see is an older woman with auburn hair with a facial structure similar to mine. Her eyes are brown whereas mine are blue. She gasps when she sees me and her hand instantly goes to her chest.

She crosses the room to me without hesitation and pulls me into her arms as she struggles to control her emotions. Without conscious thought I return her embrace tightly and feel my own tears wetting her blouse because her hug feels like I have come home.

She pulls back and gazes down at me with love shining in her deep brown eyes as she strokes my cheek softly. Looking up at Grayson, she releases me and steps right up to him too, pulling him in to a loving embrace with no hesitation or judgement on her face.

She steps back from Grayson and wipes the tears from her cheeks as she colors slightly in embarrassment.

"I have wondered about the two of you since the day you were born." She confesses. "I hope you understand why we gave you up for adoption. We truly wanted you both to be raised by people who didn't know what happened to your mother."

"We understand." I tell her with a smile. "Grayson has wonderful parents and mine were as well."

"Were?" She asks me curiously.

"Mine died in a boating accident six months ago." I share with her. "I just recently moved down here from Seattle after finding Grayson on a DNA family tree site."

"I'm so sorry." Millicent says sincerely.

"Let's all sit down and eat." Aunt Kyna states as she sets the last dish on the table.

I see I get to try another New Orleans favorite because aunt Kyna has made a big pot of jambalaya. My stomach tightens anxiously at the thought of eating after my afternoon at the park but I force myself to breath slowly to try and relax enough to eat. Grayson will be suspicious if I don't eat at least a little bit. There is also a big pan of cornbread that smells like aunt Kyna may have put hot peppers in.

I manage to eat a partial bowl of the delicious

jambalaya and a small piece of cornbread. The hot peppers in the cornbread add just the right amount of heat.

Our grandfather has been quiet thus far and I can feel the shame he is feeling after the way he has treated Grayson.

"So, Grayson." Francis says hesitantly. "What do you plan on doing after high school?"

"I am already taking classes at Tulane in nutrition and fitness." Grayson answers. "I would ultimately like to own my own fitness center where we teach people how to eat healthier and get into shape. More from a medical standpoint than a bodybuilding one. I should have my associates done by next spring and will be able to start on my bachelors."

"What about you, Jacqueline?" Francis asks with a smile.

"My adopted parents homeschooled me so I was able to finish high school before my sixteenth birthday. I continued my online classes to complete my associate's degree shortly after that. I will be done with my bachelors by Christmas this year. I am hoping to complete my master's degree in forensic psychology with my minor in criminology in just another two years." I share proudly. "I am not sure at this point if I want to work for the police department or the FBI. I guess somewhere along completing my master's I might have a better idea."

"What made you choose that?" My grandmother Millicent wants to know.

"I have been told I am very perceptive at reading people and wanted to be able to use that in a career." I shrug. "I always loved watching criminal minds, the CSI's, NCIS, and all of those other crime shows that show the science part of it."

"You never knew about Euphemia growing up?" Aunt Kyna questions curiously.

"No. It does seem like quite a coincidence now though." I nod thoughtfully. "I guess that just makes me want to succeed even more so I can help return people to their families."

"The little girls are starting to disappear again." Francis sighs sadly. "That little red head they found the same day, but the one that went missing yesterday morning hasn't been found yet."

"My father and brother are working the case." Grayson states. "Hopefully, now that they know who they are looking for they will catch him."

"I am not feeling well." I communicate with Grayson telepathically. *"Can we make an excuse to leave early please?"*

I am not lying to my brother because I truly feel a killer headache starting and it is making me nauseous.

"Aunt Kyna?" Grayson asks. "Do you have a piece of paper and a pen? Jac and I would like to leave our phone numbers. Jac isn't feeling well and I should really take her home."

"I will give Millicent and Francis your numbers." Aunt Kyna says as everyone suddenly looks at me with concern.

"What's wrong?" Millicent asks anxiously.

"I'm getting a really bad headache and it's giving me a stomach ache." I explain. "I think I just need to try and catch up on my sleep."

"Would you like to take some of the jambalaya and

cornbread home?" Aunt Kyna asks. "There is too much for me to finish up."

"I would love that." I nod eagerly. "It tastes fantastic and I would love the chance to enjoy it better when my headache goes away."

Aunt Kyna laughs as she sails out of the room to bowl up some of the dinner for us. We all stand up and head towards the foyer where my grandmother pulls me into another tight embrace. I hug her back fiercely and fight back the tears that are threatening once more. She feels so much like home when she hugs me, I don't ever want to let her go.

"I would love for the two of us to get together for coffee or something." I whisper so only she can hear me.

"I would love that Jac." She whispers back before kissing me on the cheek. She wipes away her own tears as she steps back to let Francis hug me too. His grief is nearly too much for me as he holds me for several long seconds before letting me go.

"You are both welcome at our home." Francis says, his voice thick with emotion. "Any time."

Chapter Nineteen

Victor and Lucien are still at work when Grayson and I walk into the kitchen to find Nicole eating a solitary dinner.

"You're home early!" She exclaims. "Did something happen?"

"No, nothing happened." Grayson smiles at his mom reassuringly. "Jac is getting a bad headache and wanted to come home."

I place the jambalaya in the fridge and the cornbread on the counter.

"I'm going to soak in the tub before turning in for the night." I state softly, holding my aching head. "Grayson, do you mind taking care of Rune for me tonight? Feed him and let him out before putting him in my room with me?"

"Sure, sis." He nods as he watches me leave the room.

The long hot soak in the tub helps relax me enough that my headache is nearly gone and Rune is anxiously waiting in my bedroom for me when I step in. I slip into the soft bed after putting on a nightgown and my wolf jumps up on the bed with a happy sigh. I stroke his ears with his head on my lap.

Lucien pokes his head into the room several minutes later and steps in when he sees that I am still awake.

"How was work?" I ask, too afraid to ask for details about the missing girl.

"The missing little girl turned up in a park this afternoon." Lucien tells me with frustrated sigh.

"How is she?" I ask, terrified to think about the torture she was put through.

"She was raped repeatedly while blindfolded." Lucien sits on the edge of the bed and shakes his head. "She said she crossed the street into the park across from her house because she heard a puppy crying. Someone grabbed her from behind and choked her until she fell asleep. She never saw him or heard him speak. She thinks she was held in a basement because the walls felt like cold concrete, but she never saw anything. He kept her tied and blindfolded the entire time."

"Could she hear anything to give any clues as to where he was holding her?" I ask hopefully.

"No." Lucien replies. "She heard what sounded like a fan kick on every once in a while, but nothing else; no birds, animals, cars, trains. Nothing."

"Physically, is she going to be alright?" I raise my eyebrow questioningly.

"The doctors are hopeful. They are intending on keeping her for a few days." Lucien shares with me. "She is pretty dehydrated and doesn't appear to have been fed while she was gone. There were no fluids, no hair, no DNA on her entire body or clothes. He made sure to wash her thoroughly and wore a condom."

"At least she was found." I bring up the positive. "Phemie was the only girl out of what, fifteen pubescent girls, that was seen alive after she went missing during that time period? Something is different. If he took the time to wash her then he meant to let her go. Why?"

"We have all given our thoughts on exactly that."

Lucien says. "Something is different in his life this time around versus before prison. It makes no sense why he would let her go. The fact that the others were never found is why he got away with-it last time."

"I hope parents will keep a closer eye on girls matching his preferences." I state.

"I was hoping you and I could go out for dinner tomorrow night." Lucien suggests hopefully. "Spend some time getting to know each other better. Maybe somewhere romantic? Grayson told me about all the new clothes he made you buy, maybe there is something pretty you would want to wear."

"I would like that." I blush pink and look away from him bashfully, making him chuckle. He leans over, lifts my chin with his thumb and kisses me tenderly.

"Sleep well darlin'." He nuzzles my neck giving me goosebumps.

I am up extra early the next morning due to how early I went to sleep. Rune is anxious to go outside so I let him out into the fenced back yard and watch him from the door. After he comes back inside, I feed him before I head into the kitchen to make a pot of coffee.

Lucien finds me in the breakfast nook watching the sun rise through the windows as I sip my coffee. He sits down next to me after kissing me softly with a seductive smile.

"How is your headache?" He asks.

"Better." I nod with a smile.

My phone pings and I grimace when I see a text message from uncle John.

"Meet me for coffee this morning?"

"Where and when?" I text back.

"The hotel restaurant in an hour?" Uncle John messages me again.

"Fine."

"What's up?" Lucien asks curiously.

"Uncle John wants to meet for coffee at the hotel restaurant in an hour." I sigh. "What is he going to pressure me for this time?"

"Don't let him." Lucien states simply. "You are going to be nineteen soon and are your own woman, not a child anymore. After being raised by overprotective parents you are more than ready to fly all on your own. Have you heard from your attorney about Delta Logistics' audit?"

"No. As large as the company is it will no doubt take some time." I explain. "Why?"

"I know I have only met him briefly, but something about him just rubs me the wrong way." Lucien confesses. "I will be honest because I don't want to hide anything from you. I seriously question his motives with you."

"I will be careful I promise." I reply sincerely. "He can't ground me to my bedroom or anything. The only thing he can do is try to convince me that I should let him control my life because he has more experience and my best interests at heart."

"Alright." Lucien rises from the table. "Text me how it goes with famous uncle John. I will be home early tonight and our reservation is for seven."

"Where are we going?" I ask mischievously, knowing he won't want to tell me. Lucien shakes his head.

"How will I know what to wear?" I persist with an innocent expression on my face.

"Nice try darlin'." Lucien chuckles. "Wear something formal and if you don't have anything formal then go buy something because I will be wearing a tux."

"Oh alright." I pout as he walks out of the room.

I sigh as I take my coffee cup back into the kitchen where I rinse it before loading it into the dishwasher and heading upstairs to get ready for my meeting with uncle John. Looking through my closet I decide on a white, lace and silk, short sleeved dress that goes to mid-thigh. I leave my hair loose and wear a new necklace, bracelet and earrings with dainty white sandals. The necklace is a long silver necklace with a Celtic knot pendant and the bracelet is matching as are the earrings.

I grimace as I look down at my fingernails. I really should go get a mani-pedi today in preparation for my date with Lucien. I have never had one but I am sure Nicole knows where I can go.

Nicole is in the kitchen pouring a cup of coffee when I step in and she turns to smile at me.

"You are up and ready to go early this morning." She says. "You look lovely. Where are you off to?"

"My uncle John wants to meet for coffee up at the Windsor." I explain with a long-suffering sigh. "Do you know where I could go to get a mani-pedi?"

"Oh, yes!" She exclaims as she sends me the name and address of a salon to my cell phone. "Tell Tiffany that I sent you and she will take good care of you. If you wanted to get your hair trimmed as well, she is the only one I would trust with that sweetheart."

"Thank you, Nicole." I smile at her gratefully. "I have been meaning to get my hair trimmed and styled for a while now, I have just been too busy."

I decide to take my yellow sports car since it is just me and since the weather is so warm, I put the top down so I can feel the wind in my hair. The drive to the hotel is short and only takes me a couple minutes.

John is already waiting for me politely in the lobby when I step into the hotel.

"You look beautiful Jacqueline." Uncle John kisses my cheek affectionately as he holds out his arm to me. I lightly place my hand in the curve of his elbow and allow him to lead me into the restaurant.

The hostess leads us to a table by the windows where I can see out onto the street. When the waitress appears, I order only a cup of English tea as my stomach has tightened with anxiety. John settles for a cup of coffee even though I know he intended on having breakfast with me.

"I don't want to sound rude, but why did you call me here?" I ask pointedly, done with the civilities.

"Well. Right down to business?" John states. "Alright. I just wanted to check in and see how you are doing?"

"I am doing well, thank you." I reply coolly. "My house should be remodeled in a couple weeks so I can move in and I am all signed up for my fall classes at Tulane University. How is business? You aren't planning on returning to Seattle any time soon?"

"We are being audited." He says crisply, his tone offended. "No doubt you don't trust me and think I am capable of cheating you."

"I am looking out for my own best interests." I point out logically. "You have been drilling that into my head for years now. Why didn't you tell me that my parents had been murdered? You allowed me to believe they were just lost at sea!" I soften my voice so only he can hear my rage. "Don't you dare tell me that you were protecting me."

"I see your police friends have been digging into your past." He replies, his voice sounding like a stranger all of a sudden. "What is the point in doing that?"

"When my birth father left me a gift from my childhood on my car a few days ago, they felt it necessary to look into my background." I inform him furiously, keeping my voice to a whisper. "I wanted to know how a book from my bedroom in Seattle ended up in a prison cell of my birth father all the way across the country. Every piece of mail my birth father ever received was sent from Delta Logistics and you want to know why I am having the company audited."

"Surely, you don't suspect me Jacqueline." John protests his innocence.

"Who should I suspect *Uncle John?*" I stress angrily. "You want me without friends or connections too, just like my adopted parents did. You will only be happy if you are the only person I depend on."

"That's not true Jacqueline." He further protests. "I encouraged you to find your brother."

"Then had a complete meltdown when you discovered I was dating someone." I point out. "Is it just Lucien you have a problem with or is it all men? Would you ever allow me to get married and have a family of my own or are you the only man allowed in my life?"

"Please. You are blowing this all out of proportion."

John states logically.

"I think it best if we don't contact one another." I rise from my chair, leaving my tea untouched. "If you need me to know something you can go through my attorney, Mr. Sorenson. Good day Mr. Van Asselt."

I leave him sitting at the table with his mouth hanging open in shock and I feel a giant weight lifted off of my shoulders after being brutally honest with him. This isn't the end with him because he doesn't ever give up easily.

Chapter Twenty

It's still too early to shop for my dress or to get my mani-pedi done so I decide to stop at the Café du Monde for some beignets. I can't go all day without eating and after unloading a lot of pent up stress about John I am feeling much better.

I am surprised at how busy this place is this early in the morning as I step inside the café. I choose a table right in the midst of the busy café where I will most likely be safe being around so many people. A waitress takes my order and promptly returns with my pastries and coffee.

I have just taken a sip of my café au lait when detective Zander Cody sits down at my table with me.

"You are even sexier in that dress." He murmurs softly so only I can hear him.

"What do you want detective Cody?" I ask him rudely as I raise my eyebrow at him sardonically.

"Do you really want me to answer that question sweetheart?" His deep voice is seductively husky. His blue eyes darken slightly and he just oozes sex appeal.

Unfortunately, I am unable to stop myself from blushing at his boldness and I can see from his expression this only gives him encouragement.

"I'm not interested detective Cody." I state firmly as I force myself to stare at him coldly. "I'm seeing someone."

"Oh, I know." His husky voice washes over me, making me distinctly uncomfortable. "Let me see if I have this correctly. You are just starting to date your twin brother's brother. Hmmm……That sounds just a little incestuous. Are you sure you don't want to rethink that relationship?"

"Lucien and I are not related as well you know." I whisper heatedly as I flush in embarrassment.

"Oh, but it is one of those gray areas that I would stay away from if I were you Jacqueline." He persists with a mischievous grin. "So. I am sure you heard that Annie Wilson was found. Any thoughts on why he is suddenly releasing them? Surely you know that all the other girls from before his prison stint were never found, except for your mother."

"I think you have to figure out what is different in his life." I shrug. "He enjoys what he does to them but I didn't feel any violence from him that led me to believe he wanted them dead. He thinks he loves them."

"Someone from your company, Delta Logistics, has been keeping in contact with dear old dad while he was in prison. It was the only mail he ever received." He says as he watches my expression carefully for my reaction.

"You aren't going to surprise me detective." I smile at him, faking confidence. "I am well aware of that fact already and I am looking into it."

Zander grabs one of my beignets and bites into it with a grin, getting powdered sugar on his beard. Wanting to portray that I am as comfortable as he is, I take one myself and bite into it daintily, not dropping any powdered sugar onto myself.

"You never told the Devereaux's about your little trip to the park across from Annie's house, did you?" Zander asks perceptively and I blush my answer which makes him chuckle as he gets to his feet. "Be careful, little one, we wouldn't want Lucien finding out you are keeping me a secret." Zander whispers into my ear as he leans down close to me from behind my chair.

Before I can respond Zander strolls from the café whistling happily.

Do I confess my trip to the park? The last thing I need I another person trying to control me and as much as I like Lucien that is exactly what he would do. Unfortunately, Zander has me exactly where he wants me because I cannot confess that I know him to any of the Devereaux family.

Despite my fear of him, because I cannot read him at all with my gift, I find myself attracted to Zander. I would never confess such a thing to his arrogant ego, but it is yet another secret I must keep.

I people watch while I manage to eat a couple more beignets and finish my coffee. The salon must be open by now so I decide to drive over and see if I can be squeezed into their schedule last minute. I can always go shopping for my dress while I am waiting for my appointment.

I am surprised when I step into the salon that Nicole has already called ahead and Tiffany takes me right back. She starts with my hair and listens to my idea for my hair cut and then offers some suggestions of her own.

After shampooing and conditioning my long waist length curls she takes it from one length and rounds out the ends so that the front of my hair will be shorter than the back. She adds a lot of layers so that my hair will curl up easier and gives me some longer bangs after cutting in my new side part.

I look in the mirror when she is done and I love the new me. My hair still falls to my waist but it is styled in a very fashionable way and I definitely look older than before.

She gives me a French manicure and I love the natural look to my long natural nails. I choose a rose color for my pedicure and I fall in love as they pamper my feet. It is so relaxing.

Tiffany helps me choose a good shampoo and conditioner to use at home as well as some products to comb through after washing it to keep it from frizzing.

It is well after noon when I finally make it to the mall to shop for my dress. I fall in love with the first dress the salesgirl shows me. It is a blue that matches my eyes, strapless with a high waist that flares to mid-thigh. It is silk with tulle over the skirt and swirls around my legs beautifully. She helps me find matching heels and a clutch as well.

Now that Grayson isn't shopping with me, I take the time to go to Victoria's Secret so I can update my under things without my nosy brother making me uncomfortable. I allow the girl there to size me for a bra so that I actually buy some that fit correctly.

For the first time in my life I buy all matching bra and panty sets as well as some more sexy lingerie, just in case. I am nearly nineteen years old and have never had anything sexy to wear to bed because I never needed it. I have the girls in the store help me pick out a few strapless bras that fit right, giving me lift without being uncomfortable. The last thing I want to do is feel the need to keep pulling it up all night long.

I make it back to the Devereaux house in just enough time to retreat to my bedroom before Lucien comes home from work. He is standing at the bottom of the stairs waiting for me when I descend to the foyer slowly.

His approval and desire wash over me as I step down the staircase. Nicole and Victor are standing off to the side watching me as well, proudly, as if I were their daughter too.

"Have fun." Nicole says as Lucien whisks me out to his car.

Lucien takes me to a restaurant called Muriel's that, when we enter, I see is French. The interior is done in dark red and gold with tall windows, antique French dining sets and chandeliers. I am quite impressed.

Lucien orders for both of us. Shrimp and goat cheese crepes, bayoubaisse, which is a gumbo with shrimp, mussels, crab and seafood meatballs in a tomato broth with orzo pasta and andouille sausage. He orders us a gorgonzola cheesecake for dessert.

Lucien orders a single malt scotch while I get a sparkling water.

"You got your hair and nails done today." Lucien states as he gazes at me heatedly. "The new hairstyle becomes you."

"Thank you. It was fun to be pampered." I confess with a laugh. "Your mom suggested I go to her beautician and Tiffany was awesome."

"What sorts of things did you do up in Seattle for fun?" He asks curiously after taking a sip of his drink.

"I did a lot of hiking. We actually lived on an island outside of Seattle. Bainbridge Island. We lived on the northern part of the island and it was just a short walk from the cabin to Puget Sound. I spent a lot of time on the beach. My favorite thing to do was just hike to the water and watch the whales, dolphins, orcas, boats. There are a lot of beautiful places to hike around the island too. Nature is peaceful for me." I share with a smile as I remember.

"Did you ever learn how to sail or how to handle a yacht by yourself?" He asks.

"Eventually." I nod as I remember how much I had to argue and beg and plead. "They were so overprotective that they thought I should just be happy going out on their boat, but I finally got to have my own small boat."

"How big is small?" Lucien asks with a laugh.

"I had an older thirty-foot cruiser with a small cabin that slept four." I explain. "It was small enough for me to handle on my own as long as I promised to never take it out in questionable weather."

"Do you still have that boat?" He wants to know.

"Yep. It's docked close to the cabin, why?" I cock my head curious.

"Well, we have lake Pontchartrain north of New Orleans and it is a great lake to go boating on. There is also a marina that you can dock the boat at close to the Gulf of Mexico." He shrugs. "You should have the boat brought down here. It would be great for you to relax on and get away from the chaos of the city."

"What about you?" I ask him. "What do you do to unwind and relax?"

"I enjoy a good hike, although down here it is best to do that in early spring or late fall when it isn't so humid. I like to stay active so I like anything physical. I started that wall climbing at the gym. Swimming, running, hiking, working on my car, helping Dad with projects around the house, lifting weights, shooting hoops or playing football with Gray."

Our food arrives and we chat further while we enjoy

the scrumptious meal. I am really starting to love the local food here. So many spices and flavors in everything.

After stuffing myself on cheesecake, I excuse myself to use the ladies' room. I ate way too much but everything was just so good I couldn't bring myself to stop.

The restroom is empty when I walk in, but when I step out of the stall to wash my hands, I see a massively huge man blocking the exit. Instantly terrified, I look up at him wondering what he is doing in here and see that he looks like an older version of Grayson.

Oh my gosh, it's Seth Pickett!

I shake my head and try backing away from him but he grabs me quickly, slapping a meaty hand over my mouth.

"Seth Pickett has me in the ladies' room at Muriel's!" I send telepathically to Grayson. *"Call Lucien!"*

"Please let me go." I attempt to communicate with my birth father mentally, praying it works and he won't hurt me.

"You shouldn't have called for help." Seth's gravelly voice slips through my thoughts. *"I won't hurt you, my daughter, I only wanted us to meet."*

Before I can reply to him telepathically, he puts me in a choke hold.

"Please, don't." I beg to my birth father fruitlessly as my struggles are in vain and I feel myself losing consciousness.

"Choke hold." I manage to whisper to Grayson mentally before darkness claims me.

By the time I wake, I find myself cradled on Lucien's lap in the restaurant which is full of police officers and empty of patrons. Grayson is sitting next to Lucien and I with a thunderous expression on his face.

"Thank you." I whisper as I try to desperately clear my blurry vision. I am now regretting how much food I ate as nausea suddenly overwhelms me.

"How do you feel?" Grayson asks as Lucien strokes my cheek tenderly.

"Nauseous." I croak. "How long was I unconscious?"

"Not long." Lucien whispers. "Grayson, go get Dad and detective Cody so she can tell us just once what happened in there."

Hearing detective Cody's name makes me instantly tense as I wonder if I should just confess that I already know him. After this I think it is probably a bad idea to confess to seeking out the crime scene alone. The Devereaux men will never let me alone as it is.

"How are you feeling Jac?" Victor asks as he leans over and strokes my cheek affectionately. "You had us scared for a minute there."

"A little nauseous and I'm having a hard time clearing my vision, it's a bit blurry." I offer honestly.

"This is detective Zander Cody." Victor introduces me to detective Cody politely. "He is heading up the investigation into Seth and the missing girls. Detective Cody this is Jacqueline Cassidy."

"It's nice to meet you Jacqueline." Zander greets me politely without missing a beat. "Can you tell us what happened in the ladies' room?"

I pull Lucien's arm around me tighter before I look up at Zander anxiously, being careful to keep my thoughts on the task at hand.

"I was coming out of the stall to wash my hands and he was standing there. I didn't recognize him at first. When I realized who he was I tried backing away to the somewhat safety of the stall. Before I could scream, he had grabbed me and put his hand over my mouth so I couldn't scream. He told me he wasn't going to hurt me just that he wanted us to meet. Something must have spooked him because he put me in a choke hold until I went limp." I explain, including as many details as I dare, leaving out the telepathic communication of course.

"How was he dressed?" Detective Cody questions me professionally. "Did you notice any odd smells?"

"He looked like the bus boys or kitchen staff!" I exclaim suddenly. "His hand smelled like soap as if he just got done washing them."

"How long have you had the reservation here?" Detective Cody asks curiously. I shake my head uncertainly as I wasn't the one who made it.

"Last night." Lucien answers. "I didn't want to make dinner reservations while the Wilson girl was still missing."

Detective Cody and Victor both look thoughtful at that piece of information.

"He wasn't wearing gloves?" Victor asks.

"No." I shake my head.

"How long after she was in the bathroom did you go and check on her?" Detective Cody asks Lucien.

"I knew she wouldn't take long and after the book

he left on her car I didn't want to take any chances." He states. "I walked back there after about four minutes. Jack doesn't chat much with strangers and I didn't see any other women go back there after she did so I figured she was in there alone. She was just lying on the floor and none of the restaurant staff noticed anyone out of the ordinary."

"You can go ahead and take her home Lucien." Detective Cody says dismissively before handing me his card. "If you remember anything, anything at all please call me."

"Will I need to go to the hospital to get checked out after he knocked me out?" I ask curiously.

"No, I don't think so." Detective Cody says matter-of-factly. "You weren't unconscious very long and you are only feeling nauseous. If you start throwing up violently, I would go in, but I think you will be fine."

Lucien stands with me cradled in his arms and heads for the exit with Grayson following along behind us carrying my clutch.

Nicole has to fuss over me as soon as we walk in the door. She insists that Lucien place me on the sofa in the living room so she can make me a cup of herbal tea to soothe my nausea.

Lucien sits on the recliner with me on his lap, refusing to let me go even for an instant but that is okay because I feel safe on his lap. A couple minutes later, Nicole brings me a cup of tea that I sip slowly, relieved when it lessens my nausea.

Chapter Twenty-One

The next several days drag by slowly as I am basically grounded to the Devereaux house for my safety. Grayson and Nicole are my constant companions while Victor and Lucien work every day, even the weekend.

I try to keep myself busy reading and watching television but I just can't concentrate on either one. I am restless and since I am not allowed to go anywhere alone that is of course the one thing that I want to do desperately.

I use the time to my benefit instead and practice trying to hear everyone else's actual thoughts instead of just emotions. By the time Monday rolls around I am able to catch a word here or there but have suffered extreme headaches for my trouble.

Knowing this will be a good thing for me to do I continue to practice even though my head hurts so badly I want to cry. I haven't even told Grayson what I am trying to do because I am afraid that he will tell me it is hopeless to expand my abilities.

Nicole announces Tuesday morning that the floors are completed over at my new house and that her and Grayson can take me over there to check it out. Anxious to go anywhere else, I readily agree and within minutes we are all squeezed into my SUV with Rune in the back.

I expect the house to still look like a construction zone when I walk in but I am pleasantly surprised to see that the main floor is ready to live in. All of my furniture is set up, the kitchen, dining room, living room, bathroom, and Grayson's room. Valances are on the windows, placemats are on the dining table, throw rug in front of the sofa, television mounted on the living room wall, and all of the small kitchen appliances unpacked and set up.

I feel instantly at home here and couldn't be happier with the job that Nicole's crew did on my new house. My office space on the main floor has been completed as well. Someone has placed my desk where I can look out the windows and even set up my computer and printer for me.

I climb the stairs to the second floor and see that the floors up here are done as well. The workers are finishing up the walls and ceilings up here. Once they are done with that, they will take the time to set up all the second-floor furniture so I can finally move in.

Out in the garage I find all of the boxes have arrived from the cabin in Seattle and I happily have Grayson help me carry in the chest with my handmade quilts.

Nicole helps me lie them all out so I can decide which one I want to use in my bedroom upstairs. I finally settle on one that has light pink, rose, light olive green, and cream-colored rectangles with tiny flowers throughout for my bedroom. This gives me all of those colors to use as accents throughout the room. This is also the last quilt my adopted mother made before she went missing. She made it for me special for when I finally got my first apartment. I can still feel her love for me when I touch it.

Nicole helps me hang all of them out on the clothes line I insisted her construction workers put up for me outside behind the house. This way they can air out before I pack them away in the chest to use for guests.

Eager to use my new kitchen, I dig out everything I will need to make a big pot of chili to put in the crockpot for the workers. I send Grayson to the grocery store to pick up several bags of corn chips, shredded cheese, fresh cilantro, sour cream, and a couple jars of pickled jalapeno peppers.

It doesn't take me long to whip it together and throw it in the commercial size crockpot I bought and now it just needs to simmer for a few hours. It should be ready for them for a late lunch or early dinner.

I set out disposable bowls and plastic spoons so they can just throw the mess away when they are done eating.

Before we head back to the Devereaux house I take a picture of my quilt so that I can use it to find curtains, throw pillows and other color accents for my bedroom.

Grayson takes a couple minutes to show me that the television in the living room has access to all of the cameras set up around the property. He shows me how to access the cameras and how to scroll through them. The ones at the gate are accessible in here as well which I love. It made me nervous that I had to depend on a security guard to view all of the footage.

He also shows me that I can open the gate from inside the house with the security panel set on the wall by the front door. I also have access to all of this from my cell phone. If I am away from the house, I can use my phone to see camera footage too.

Now that the house is nearing completion of the remodel, I am so excited to move in to my own house.

Nicole has managed to find me a company, that she knows personally, that will come and take care of the pool on a weekly basis. She tells me that her and Victor already talked to the owner and insists that the same person come every week, just for security purposes.

On the radio in the car we hear the devastating news that another little girl has just gone missing from a school field trip to the Marigny Opera House. Bobbi De La Fontaine is a twelve-year-old with brown hair and green eyes. Anyone with any information is asked to call the toll-free number.

My positive mood is dashed with the traumatic news and a tear trickles down my face at my helplessness. I so want to help bring her home before she gets hurt.

Victor and Lucien do not come home but instead are busy working the missing child case. I spend the rest of the day up in my bedroom where I am focusing on reaching the thoughts of my birth father, Seth Pickett. If I can reach him mentally maybe I can figure out where he is holding the girl. The only thing I manage to do however is give myself a migraine.

Nicole gives me something for the pain and I have no choice but to lie down.

Unfortunately, I sleep until the next morning and my headache is thankfully gone. I need to somehow sneak out to the opera house to see if I can get a vision off of anything there. Maybe this time I will see something that will help find Seth's hideout.

The opera house is on the other side of the French quarter about six miles from here. Nicole has an emergency at my house with the remodel and that leaves me alone in the house with Grayson, who is currently lifting weights in his bedroom.

I dress in the same clothes I wore before when I went to the park across from the other missing girls house and put my hair up under a baseball cap. I breathe a sigh of relief when I manage to drive away from the house without being discovered.

Minutes later finds me at the opera house where

I smoothly lie to the girl there that I am interested in hosting a private seminar here for my employees at Delta Logistics. She allows me to walk around by myself since there is nothing on their calendar for today. With a map in hand I wander around the large building as I touch things that other people make contact with hoping to find the right one.

It takes me a long time and when I look at my watch, I see I have already been slowly walking around for over an hour.

"I somehow knew I would find you here today." Detective Cody steps up to me with a seductive smile. "Giving up already?" He asks as I lean against a wall looking defeated.

"No, I am not giving up." I retort sharply. "I can't just ask where the girl went missing now can I?"

"You can ask me." Zander whispers as he leans over me closely. Unfortunately, his nearness affects me in ways I am not ready to even confess to myself. Using the flat of my hand I slam him in the sternum as hard as I can.

"Oof!" Zander exclaims without backing up, chuckles breathlessly and then place his hands on either side of me, blocking me in. "You're a feisty little thing, aren't you? You can't hide your reaction to me, ya know."

"I don't know what you're talking about." I deny hotly. "Back off Zander!"

"Has anyone ever told you that you don't lie very well?" He chuckles once more. "Your heart is racing, your pupils are dilated, and your nipples are hard."

I flush with shame as he hit the nail right on the head and I lower my head breaking eye contact with him.

"Bobbi was taken back by the stage." Zander whispers into my ear before he backs up a couple steps. "Come on."

Zander strolls towards the stage, whistling softly, as I stare after him with roiling emotions. How can I feel this way for another guy when I like Lucien so much?

Pushing away from the wall, I hurry after him. I step through the curtains to the backstage area and see Zander looking around with frustration.

"The teacher was standing on the stage and they all had their backs to the curtains when Bobbi was grabbed from back here." Zander explains to me softly. "Everyone has been on high alert with the other two girls being taken recently so the teacher said she only turned her back for maybe ten to twenty seconds."

I walk around the backstage area slowly and find the door leading outside. Stepping up to it I get a vision of Seth picking the lock as he pictures Bobbi in here waiting for him.

"He knows Bobbi will be here." I state softly as Zander watches me closely. "He picked the lock to get in."

I turn and look towards the curtains around the stage and really see no other object that he would have touched except for the curtains. Walking up to the curtains I start at one end and grab each curtain until I find the one where he was standing.

I concentrate on his thoughts and feel him breath slowly to keep himself calm as he peeks through the curtains to the children on the stage. A flash of poured concrete walls, no windows, and a bare full-size mattress on the cement floor crosses Seth's mind before it disappears.

I continue to watch the vision unfold as Seth takes the opportunity to quietly grab Bobbi who is standing much too close to the curtain a short distance from the other kids. He uses the signature choke hold on her, stuffs her in the same duffel bag and out the back door he goes. I get one more brief flash of trees and grass before I get a quick view of a metal ladder set against a poured concrete wall.

I explain all of this to Zander and watch him get excited about my description of the poured concrete walls, bed, and ladder.

"It sounds like a bunker." He states as he paces back and forth while he thinks about my vision. "His parole lists his address as an apartment in the French quarter so if he is walking through the woods to get to this bunker it must be on property of someone he knows."

"Is that even a possibility here where we are under sea level?" I ask curiously.

"Military grade bunkers could be put in the ocean and withstand the pressure without leaking." Zander explains. "Years ago, wealthy people were having them placed on their property so they would have somewhere to go in case our country was attacked. Many of them would be safe to stay in for months at a time."

"Maybe you need to take some time to find out what you can about Seth's mother. She was a cocktail waitress who raised him alone." I suggest. "Just because his father isn't listed on paper anywhere doesn't mean that Seth hasn't discovered family from his father we don't know about. What about people who worked with her years ago? Maybe they have important information they don't even realize is significant. One of them may know who she had an affair with."

"Are you planning on coming to work with us once you are done with college, little one?" Zander's seductive whisper washes over me as he backs me into the wall slowly. Reaching up, he removes my baseball cap and watches in fascination as my hair tumbles around my shoulders.

"Don't!" I state as I try to push him away futilely.

He gently yet firmly takes my chin between two fingers and holds me still while he lowers his head and kisses me passionately. I try to keep my lips closed against him but he just pulls on my chin until I open to him. He becomes demanding in his possession and I can't stop my heart from racing or my blood from boiling in response to him.

He lifts his head and gazes down at me heatedly as he struggles to regulate his breathing. I am also panting and flushing a deep crimson at the shame and guilt washing over me.

"I'm with Lucien." I whisper. "I don't want you."

"Oh, I beg to differ, baby." He nuzzles my neck, giving me goosebumps. "You are fighting it, but you definitely want me just as much as I want you. Our secret is safe for now Jacqueline."

Zander steps away from me and points towards the curtains.

"Run home to Lucien while I let you." He murmurs huskily.

Chapter Twenty-Two

I am stunned to walk in the door at the Devereaux house and Grayson is not there asking where I was. I sigh with relief as I take Rune outside into the back yard while I sit on a patio chair.

Rune lays at my feet, content to just be with me.

After about an hour in the sunshine I retreat inside lest I get sunburned and head upstairs to change my clothes. I put on another one of my new summer dresses, this one is a peach colored cotton with a tight bodice and full skirt that falls to my knees. Leaving my feet bare I pad downstairs to see if Nicole needs any help preparing dinner.

I hear voices coming from the formal dining room and I am stunned speechless to find Zander sitting there with Victor and Lucien. Scurrying into the kitchen without being seen I keep myself busy helping Nicole finish her fried chicken, mashed potatoes, corn on the cob, buttermilk biscuits, and dinner salad.

She hurries upstairs to change her clothes while I finish up in the kitchen. Grayson finally makes an appearance and sniffs the air appreciatively.

"I love mom's fried chicken." He exclaims with a wide smile.

"Hey. Will you set the table while I get all the food ready for the dining room?" I ask Grayson, using any excuse that I can to avoid the formal dining room as long as possible.

"Sure." He shrugs. "Do you know if detective Cody is staying to eat?"

"I don't, but your mom may have already invited him knowing her." I point out logically.

By the time Nicole makes it back downstairs, Grayson and I have set the table and everyone is just waiting on her. To my misfortune, Nicole did indeed ask Zander to stay for dinner and it takes all of my effort to not be anxious.

Lucien gets to his feet as soon as I step into the dining room and politely pulls out the chair next to him for me to sit in. He leans over and kisses me on the forehead before he takes his chair once more. I can feel the tension in the room from whatever the guys were talking about, but the rule of no shop talk at the table seems to be honored tonight.

"I thought I would save the wonderful news to announce at the dinner table." Nicole states eagerly. "My crew finished Jac's house this afternoon and she is free to move in whenever she wishes. Grayson was over there this afternoon helping to put together some of the upstairs furniture."

"My house is all done?" I ask, dumbfounded. I didn't expect it to be completed for at least a few more days.

"Yes, my dear." Nicole gushes enthusiastically as the bowls of food are passed around the table and everyone digs in. "I wanted to surprise you. Lord knows, we need all the good news we can get lately."

"It will definitely be quiet around here with only Nicole and I living here." Victor states gruffly. "Rune will love having two acres to run free on. I had the crew install a dog door for him so he can come and go as he pleases."

"Yeah, I thought I would be living with you guys until I got married." Grayson laughs.

"Have you called your attorney about having the yacht moved down here yet?" Lucien asks curiously.

"Yes. He said it should arrive in just a few days." I reply with an eager smile as I had completely forgotten about my yacht. "I found an open slip at Island Marinas. Taking it out onto the gulf would be fantastic."

"Have you thought about scuba diving?" Lucien asks between bites.

"Oh." I state uncertainly. "No, not really."

"Why not?" Zander asks from across the table, seemingly truly interested in our conversation.

"I like boating, but I have always been extra careful to make sure I don't have to end up in the water." I confess.

"You don't know how to swim?" Nicole asks in surprise.

"I know how to swim." I hedge. "I enjoy swimming in a pool, I just have a hard time swimming in anything else."

"Come on, sis." Grayson pushes. "Why?"

"I was in Puget Sound swimming with my adopted father when I was nine years old." I begin, feeling anxious just talking about it. "A pod of Orcas joined us and for some reason one of them separated me from my dad. It nudged me towards the shore while my dad was swimming out deeper. I was terrified it was going to eat me. I remember crying and slapping it on the nose but it didn't stop until I was close enough to nearly stand up. I have never gone swimming, except in a pool, again."

"You know, Orcas have been known to steer a human swimmer away from danger." Zander says thoughtfully. "I have read of several instances where they kept humans away from sharks that were swimming nearby. Perhaps that orca was only protecting you."

"How do you know that I could have been in danger?" I ask, failing to keep my voice polite.

"I am an avid scuba diver and I have dived in Puget Sound on a number of occasions. Great Whites are known for passing through there. They don't normally linger, but sharks that attack humans are known to be in those waters." Zander tells me softly, ignoring the sharp tone in my voice. "Even though an orca is carnivorous they seem to protect us more than attack us."

"I have never scuba dived before." Lucien states as he looks at Zander eagerly. "Maybe, if it's not an imposition, you could teach Jac and I this summer?"

I watch with horror as Zander's facial expression shows the joy he is truly feeling at this horrible idea.

"It's not an imposition." Zander nods his head as he seems to think about the idea. "I would love to teach you guys how to dive. I happen to have a boat at Island Marina as well that we can take into the gulf."

I turn my attention to my dinner and attempt to make it look like I ate something as my stomach tightens up nervously. Just the thought of being forced to spend time with Zander makes me afraid.

Zander shares tips about scuba diving with Lucien while the latter asks pointed questions. They seem to be getting along fantastically!

Nicole has made apple crisp for dessert and I help her hand it out to everyone, still warm with ice cream. I shake my head when she tries to give me some and I stay in the kitchen to clean up dinner instead.

Luckily, no one seems to notice my absence as Lucien and Zander seem to have really hit it off and are talking non-stop.

Victor brings his bowl into the kitchen and I take the opportunity to ask him questions I have been dying to ask.

"Any news on Bobbi?" I take his bowl and look at him hopefully. I desperately want to hear that she has been found alive, like the last girl. Victor's expression mirrors his anger and I can feel the answer before he even utters the words.

"Scuba divers found her in the gulf." Victor tells me softly, his voice anguished. "She hadn't been in the water very long. Her throat had been slashed and the medical examiner says she wasn't sexually assaulted."

"I don't understand." I shake my head in disbelief. "Why would he kill her before he got to do what he truly wanted to with her?"

"She wasn't the only remains the scuba divers found." He continues. "Bobbi was found in a duffel bag weighed down with stones as was the fifteen other duffel bags found in the same area."

"The other missing girls from years ago." I murmur in shock.

"We think so." He nods. "The medical examiner will need time to process that many remains."

"He needs to be caught." I wipe away a tear angrily.

"We are doing our best." Victor tells me. "Detective Cody is good. He has been working cases like this his entire career."

"You guys must be exhausted." I look up at Victor perceptively. "Have you slept since she went missing?"

"We are, but that is how our jobs work unfortunately." He explains as he shakes his head in the negative.

I take Rune out into the backyard after he eats, now that I am finished cleaning up the kitchen. I sit down on the patio and wonder if I will be at my own house this time tomorrow. Rune will love having the extra space to run and I will be more comfortable with the extra security.

Lucien, Grayson, and Zander join me on the patio. Lucien and Zander are both drinking beer and still talking about scuba diving.

"You're upset." Grayson says telepathically.

"I have never been comfortable around strangers." I return on our mental path, being partially honest.

"Zander makes you uncomfortable." Grayson persists telepathically, perceptive as always.

"I learned to be uncomfortable around guys. I never dated in Seattle even though I got asked out a lot once I started working at McDonalds. Honestly, I think the reason I am giving Lucien a chance is because he is your brother." I share with my twin candidly. *"There is also the fact that I can't read Zander at all. My ability does not work on him. That makes me feel anxious around him, I guess."*

"I can't hear anything either." Grayson confesses. *"I have met a couple people over the years that I don't have access to their thoughts."*

"So, are you willing to give scuba diving a chance darlin'?" Lucien asks me, putting no pressure in his statement at all.

I nod that I will give it a try while inside I want to stamp my foot and scream no. What if I have a panic attack while I am diving?

"We don't have to do this if you don't think it is an activity you want to pursue." Lucien insists. "We can take up rock climbing, for instance, if you rather."

"I will try." I state softly, keeping my attention focused on Lucien. Zander is the last person I want seeing me in a bikini.

Rising from the table I step over to Lucien and kiss him softly.

"I'm going to turn in." I say with a huge yawn. "I have a busy day tomorrow getting settled at the house."

"Alright. I will stop by after work." Lucien says, his expression darkening seductively.

"It was nice seeing you again, detective Cody." I tell Zander politely before disappearing into the house with Rune.

Chapter Twenty-Three

I am so excited to move into my new house that I am awake before the sun comes up. Rune, feeling my happiness, dances around me eagerly as I feed him and let him out into the back yard.

I make a big pot of coffee and start breakfast for everyone while I wait for them all to get out of bed. I take out muffin tins and get started making my mini quiche's that were always a favorite of my adopted parents.

I sauté onions and mushrooms in a little olive oil, adding season salt, garlic powder, and pepper while I brown sausage in another pan. I find some diced stewed tomatoes that will work in the pantry and some shredded cheese from the fridge. I crack open a dozen eggs into the blender with a little bit of milk to scramble them up nice and fluffy.

Once I have all of my ingredients prepared, I pour my egg into the muffin pans, about two-thirds full and then add a little bit of everything else. I place my muffin pans in the preheated oven and then plug in the crockpot to place my mini quiches in to keep warm.

Lucien and Victor stumble sleepily into the kitchen and perk up slightly when they smell my breakfast cooking.

"What's that Jac?" Victor asks eagerly. "That smells divine!"

"Mini quiches." I smile at him affectionately.

"Sausage, onions, mushrooms, stewed tomatoes, cheese and, of course, scrambled eggs. I have them cooking in muffin pans in the oven. My adopted parents loved them."

"You're up early this morning, darlin'." Lucien pulls me into his arms and kisses me tenderly right in front of his dad, making me blush bashfully.

I hear Victor chuckle as he takes a seat at the table here in the kitchen with a sigh. I take a moment to cuddle up to Lucien with a happy sigh and enjoy his closeness before my busy day begins. Lucien happily obliges me and wraps me in his arms while he lies his cheek on the top of my head.

"So, what exactly are you planning on getting done over there today?" Lucien asks as he sits at the table next to his dad.

"Unpack my clothes, make my bed. Put away all of my bathroom stuff." I sigh happily. "Wash all my dishes, organize my kitchen, organize the pantry. Unpack all of my boxes from my adopted parents' cabin. Perhaps take a few minutes and swim in my pool or relax in the hot tub."

"Sounds like you aren't going to get all of that done in one day." Victor laughs. "I would force Grayson to help you with all of that. He loves washing dishes by hand."

"I'm sure he does." I laugh at the teasing in Victor's voice. "I want to have everyone over for dinner tomorrow night. You guys, my grandparents, and aunt Kyna."

"That sounds great Jac." Victor nods his head approvingly. "Now, make sure you introduce yourself to the security guards in the booth outside the gate. You want to get to know them, offer to feed them, bring them coffee or whatever. The more you allow them to get to know you the harder they will work at keeping you safe. They work in eight hour shifts around the clock so make sure you meet all three of them."

"It probably wouldn't hurt to introduce Rune to them so they can come onto the property without problems." Lucien suggests. "Only the three normal security guards because there will be temporary guards once in a while to cover for vacations."

Nicole and Grayson wander into the kitchen as I am taking the quiches out of the oven and placing them in the crock pot. I set the crock pot right on the kitchen table and hand everyone plates so they can dig in.

After eating I hurry upstairs and grab my suitcases that are already packed to carry them downstairs. Grayson, seeing my eagerness to get started mumbles his way up to his bedroom to get dressed.

I am surprised to see that Nicole is already to join Grayson and I today to help us get settled in.

"You don't have to come and help if you have something else to do." I tell Nicole, feeling guilty after all the hard work she already did.

"I would love to come and help the two of you get settled." She smiles at me happily.

"I would love to have you." I smile back at her sincerely.

I drive my sport's car, Lucien drives my SUV, Grayson drives his car, Nicole drives her own vehicle, and Victor follows us over so Lucien can catch a ride to work with his dad. Since my garage is still full of boxes both of my cars will have to sit on the driveway for now. I plan on storing most of the boxes from the cabin in the small second floor space of the garage to keep them out of the way.

First thing, after Lucien and Victor leave for work, I take Rune over to the security booth so we can introduce ourselves. An older man who must be in his fifties comes out to greet me with a welcoming smile. He is nearly as tall as Grayson, nearly six and a half feet, with short snowy white hair, full beard, and as many muscles as my brother.

"You must be Jacqueline." He shakes my hand. "I'm Alex Myers. Victor told me you were moving in today."

"It's nice to meet you Alex, please call me Jac." I return his hand shake firmly. "I wanted to introduce you to Rune. I want you to be able to walk the property without the wolf giving you a problem."

I encourage Alex to squat down with me in front of Rune and I mentally share with my wolf what the security guards' purpose is here. Rune seems to think he is an equal with Alex and accepts him as belonging here.

Rune nudges Alex's hand before sitting down next to me.

"Victor told all three of us about your abilities and I have to say seeing this first hand is really impressive." Alex tells me sincerely.

"I hadn't thought about you guys knowing that but I suppose that is an important piece of information." I reply thoughtfully. "I'm still getting used to people knowing about it and accepting it."

"I work six in the morning until two every afternoon. My replacement is Henry Bennett and he will work until ten every evening. Chris Murphy will work until I come in the following morning at six." Alex explains to me. "Our cell phone numbers are in the house by the coffee pot and you can also talk to us through the speaker by the front door."

"I made quiches this morning and brought you some." I hand him a covered bowl with a smile.

"Thanks, Jac." Alex smiles appreciatively as he opens the lid to the bowl and makes a growling sound deep in his throat. "Smell delicious. Feel free to share your cooking. It has been a long time since I was able to enjoy home cooking on a regular basis."

"Deal." I laugh at his good-natured reply.

I make my way back to the house and smile as I see Nicole has already begun on the kitchen busily washing my brand-new dishes by hand. Grayson has carried my suitcases upstairs to my bedroom so I get started unpacking. It takes me about an hour to put all of my clothes away and put all of my toiletries into my bathroom. My empty suitcases go into the small attic space I have down the hallway.

Someone from Nicole's crew must have taken the time to wash my new sheets for me as they are sitting in a clothes basket on my bed smelling like they were dried outside. After making my bed I stand back and look at my new bedroom with satisfaction. I run my hand over the quilt my adopted mother, Zacari, made for me lovingly.

The stone floors are cold against my bare feet so I guess I will have to invest in some throw rugs. I will have to note what colors I want for each room so I can go online and order matching rugs.

I make my way downstairs and when I look outside, I see Rune is busy making a circuit of the yard, taking in all of the scents. Peeking into Grayson's room, I find him putting all of his clothes away. He hasn't even slept here for one night and already his bedroom is a disaster. I shake my head as I join Nicole in the kitchen.

She looks young for her age, especially when she stands next to Victor who is almost completely gray. Her mahogany hair falls in waves to just below her shoulders, her face a youthful oval with perfectly shaped eyebrows, full lips, and exotically slanted hazel eyes. She keeps herself athletically slim by doing aerobics and light weight lifting several days a week.

I dry and put away all of the dishes she has washed, making room for the others she is still working on. Soon we have all of the dishes, pots and pans, silverware and other odds and ends put away where they belong.

With the kitchen completed, Nicole and I move out into the garage to get started on the rest of my purchases and to sort through boxes from the cabin. After a couple hours, Grayson comes out to the garage to help us sort stuff. We are making a lot of trips back and forth to the house as we open up stuff, I bought for the house that has been waiting for the remodel to be done.

Stretching my aching back, I sit down on the concrete with an exhausted sigh. I look around the garage and see that we have made room for one car to fit in the two-stall garage at least.

"Let's put a couple of those freezer pizzas in the oven and then sit in the hot tub for a while." Grayson suggests as he plops down next to me.

"That sounds like heaven." I agree and get to my feet slowly. I head inside to put the pizza in the oven while Grayson uncovers the hot tub and brings it up to temperature.

I change into my new blue bikini and grab three large beach towels out of the linen closet to bring outside. After the pizza is done, I slice it and bring it out to the patio table so we can eat outside. Nicole remembered to bring her bikini and I think she looks fantastic for a woman in her fifties.

I have Grayson bring the extra pizza I cooked out to Alex in the security booth while Nicole and I slip into the hot tub. Rune lies down next to us on the patio with a happy groan. The hot water feels heavenly on my sore muscles and I relax back with a groan of my own. Grayson joins us after several minutes and sighs happily at the feel of the hot water.

After the rejuvenating soak, it is time to get back to work. The three of us head back to the garage and start on the rest of the boxes. We work tirelessly for the next few hours until it is just time to call it a day.

I take Rune to the security booth to meet Henry, who works second shift. Henry is in his mid-thirties or so and has a lot of tattoos showing on his arms and I can even see one peeking above the collar of his shirt. He has brown hair, blue eyes, a slim athletic build and charming smile.

"You must be Henry." I shake his hand.

"You must be Jacqueline." He chuckles.

"Please, call me Jac." I smile warmly. "This is Rune."

I spend a few seconds doing the same introduction with Henry and Rune as I did with Alex. Henry is just as impressed as Alex was. Henry seems a little harder around the edges than Alex. I learn that Henry was an undercover cop in Boston where he spent years getting cozy with a big-time mafia family. I let him know that I am making a big pot of spaghetti for dinner and will bring him out some if he is interested, he readily agrees.

Before starting dinner, I take a long hot shower and change into a pair of leggings and a t-shirt with a pair of thick socks against the cold stone floors.

While I am chopping vegetables to go into my spaghetti sauce Nicole takes a shower as well and changes clothes before helping me with dinner.

Looking around at my new home I cannot help but smile happily. It is all mine. The remodel made it feel homey to me and I really think I will be content here.

Chapter Twenty-Four

I am surprised to see Victor and Lucien stroll in before dinner is ready. I wasn't expecting anyone this evening, so I am glad that I made a big pot of spaghetti just in case. When I see that Lucien is carrying a duffel bag, I raise my eyebrow at him questioningly.

"I think it is wise to have Lucien here until we are certain that you are safe from Seth." Victor steps up to me and kisses me on the forehead. "Make him sleep on the sofa."

"Thanks Dad." Lucien exclaims.

"We don't need to impose for dinner, Jac." Nicole says as she slips on her jacket and grabs her purse.

"I made enough for a small army and I am sure that Grayson, Lucien and Henry aren't going to eat it all."

Nicole helps me add two leaves to my dining room table to make it comfortable for everyone. While Grayson is setting the table, I make a large portion of spaghetti in a bowl with a lid and wrap a couple pieces of garlic bread in paper towel.

Lucien runs Henry his dinner while I place the food on the table and make sure there is cheese, salt, and pepper, as well as any other condiments needed.

Victor insists that I sit at the head of my own table, which I must admit feels a little strange. Lucien sits on my left and Grayson on my right with their parents next to them.

My first dinner goes smoothly, and I feel proud of myself for that and all the work I got done today. Victor and Nicole leave shortly after dinner and I don't blame them because she must be exhausted after helping me all day long.

I happily clean up after dinner by myself just because I am eager to putter around in my own kitchen. After the dishwasher is running and everything is wiped down, I join Lucien on the sofa.

"Are you uncomfortable with me staying here?" He asks me seriously.

"No, I was just surprised." I confess. "I guess I expected a heads up, but I don't blame you guys for thinking it is a good idea."

"Good, because I don't want you uncomfortable." Lucien breathes a sigh of relief.

"I'm not, but I don't want you sleeping on the sofa." I whisper nervously as I look down at my fingers twisting in my lap.

"Why not?" He tips up my chin, forcing me to look at the turbulent expression in his eyes.

"We are both adults and I think you will be much more comfortable in my room." I manage to state in a tiny voice.

"That isn't what my dad had in mind." Lucien tells me, his voice going husky.

"Not his decision." I shrug. "Besides, there really is no rush for us to be going on to the next level in our relationship so soon."

"Agreed." He nods his head, looking a bit relieved.

"Did you think I was seducing you?" I laugh.

"I wasn't sure." He confesses. "I wanted us to be on the same page."

"Good, now we are." I state as I rise from the sofa. "I'm going to change into my bikini and sit in the hot tub if you care to join me."

"What's Gray doing?" He asks as he stands up with an eager grin.

"Lifting weights upstairs." I smile at him mischievously. "I will grab us a couple towels."

Suddenly nervous, I am trembling as I slip into the steaming water of the hot tub to wait for Lucien. He doesn't make me wait long. It looks like he took a quick shower as his hair is already wet.

He slides over to me right away kisses me until I am desperately trying to feel the same desire as him. He sits back and pulls me over his lap, so I am straddling him and gazes up at me heatedly. Nibbling my lower lip nervously I decide to try and be bold, so I lean into him and kiss him first. He stays still while I make the first move and softly kisses me back.

I run my fingers over his well-defined muscles and smile when he groans softly. He has tattoos that I never knew were there on his chest and arms. I trace the dark colors and love the feeling of his skin under my fingers. Lucien is gorgeous with just the right amount of muscle and the tattoos just add even more.

I can't help but wonder if he will be the one I give my virginity to. Will he want it? I wonder anxiously. Will it hurt as much as my adopted mom said it would?

I turn around and sit between his legs with my back

against his chest. He wraps his arms around me and softly strokes my stomach, giving me goose bumps.

"I have something I need to tell you." I tell him, my voice trembling.

"What?"

"I should have told you already, but I was afraid of how you would react and now it is important that you know." I hedge.

"You can tell me anything Jac." Lucien squeezes me reassuringly.

"Last week, the day after Annie went missing, I drove over to the park across from her house where she was abducted. I wanted to see if I could get a vision and maybe help bring her home. Detective Cody was there and he came over to see what I was doing and realized that I was Seth Pickett's daughter." I share with him, feeling guilty. "I didn't tell anyone that I had already met detective Cody because I knew all of you would treat me like a naughty teenager and ground me to the house. Well, the day after Bobbi went missing, I drove over to the opera house to do the same thing. Detective Cody was there waiting for me because he knew about my gift at the park and had a feeling that I would come to do the same thing."

"I understand why you didn't say anything Jac, but you are leaving something out." Lucien says perceptively. I squirm uncomfortably because I am terrified Lucien will somehow see this as my fault. "Come on darlin'." He whispers into my ear.

"Both times when I saw Zander at the crime scenes, he hit on me leaving no doubt that he was attracted to me." I manage to whisper. "At the opera he kissed me. He had me blocked against the wall and was holding my chin still so I couldn't get away."

Lucien tenses and is quiet for so long it scares me before he finally speaks.

"Did he hurt you?" He asks, his voice deceptively soft. I shake my head.

"No." I answer as tears of shame course down my cheeks. "But he is going to tell you that I am attracted to him."

"Did you want him to kiss you?" Lucien continues.

"No, I did not." I tell him honestly. "I told him that I was with you and he told me that he knew I was fighting it but that I wanted him as much as he wanted me. He said he would keep our secret for now. I didn't say anything because I just figured I wouldn't see him anymore, but now you want him to take us scuba diving."

Lucien turns me around, so I am straddling his lap once more and he looks at me seriously.

"Why did you wait to tell me this?" He asks me tenderly.

"Because! He is right! I am attracted to him for some reason." I exclaim in anguish. "I can't stand being around him, but he is right."

Lucien reaches up and strokes my cheek affectionately as he smiles at me heatedly.

"Who do you choose to be with Jac?" He asks seriously.

"You! Only you." I reply, just as serious, as I wipe the tears from my cheeks. "You aren't angry at me?"

"I am a little disappointed, but I understand that your independence is important to you." He explains. "You spent your whole life being kept from living life because it was safe and for your own good. I too want you to be safe, but I promise not to ground you. I am your boyfriend after all, not your guardian."

"You aren't going to kill Zander, are you?" I ask timidly.

"Nope, but I am definitely telling him that I know what happened." Lucien states firmly. "If we are so set on scuba diving, we can hire a professional instructor and take classes together."

A huge sigh of relief escapes my lips as I lay my head on Lucien's chest. He wraps his arms around me and holds me tightly as he kisses the top of my head.

Grayson slips into the hot tub with a groan.

"Am I interrupting anything serious?" My twin asks. "I can leave if you guys are discussing something."

"No, you're not." I tell him honestly.

"Looked pretty serious from the window." Grayson says.

"Zander has been hitting on Jack." Lucien shares with his brother.

"Ah. Yep, that's serious." Grayson nods his head. "Guy talk with detective Cody tomorrow?"

"Definitely." Lucien replies.

"Are you going to like living here?" I ask Grayson curiously.

"Oh yeah." He laughs. "I was afraid I was going to have to live with Mom and Dad forever. Why wouldn't I like living with you?"

"I don't know." I hedge. "We are just getting to know one another and sometimes people find out that they hate each other after moving in together."

"I could never hate you, sis." Grayson whispers tenderly. "It's a good thing that you bought a new sofa. Poor Lucien is going to have a rough time of it for a while."

"Lucien won't be sleeping on the sofa." I state nervously.

Grayson stops laughing and looks at the two of us questioningly.

"It's a king-size bed Gray." Lucien says nonchalantly. "It's not like I am going to be corrupting her already. Her virtue is safe."

"Good. I would hate to have to put you in your place big brother." Grayson laughs.

Chapter Twenty-Five

I change into my nightgown in my bathroom and then stand there nervously, too afraid to come out. The nightgown is one of my new ones. It is dark blue with a tight bodice, spaghetti straps, and swirly skirt that stops mid-thigh with matching bikini panties.

Finally, I take a deep breath and step into my room to find Lucien looking out the window wearing a pair of boxers. I nibble my lower lip anxiously and note that he looks completely relaxed compared to me.

"I can sleep on the sofa." Lucien suggests after turning and seeing me. I shake my head before blushing bashfully.

"I don't want you to sleep on the sofa." I tell him sincerely. "If I happen to snore terribly maybe you will want to tomorrow." I joke half-heartedly.

Lucien steps up to me and kisses me until I am trembling nervously. Scooping me up in his arms he carries me to the bed and lies me down before reclining over me. He captures my lips with his becoming more demanding. I arch up into him with a moan as his desire pulses through me and kiss him back. Eventually, he lifts his head and the expression on his face is intensely seductive.

Tucking us both under the covers, he pulls me alongside him, and I lay my head on his chest with a contented sigh.

"I truly never thought kissing could be so enjoyable."

I whisper bashfully.

"Oh, that's because you are kissing me, of course." He teases before kissing me on the head.

"I'm really glad that you didn't get mad at me about Zander." I tell him honestly.

"You aren't the one I am angry at darlin'." Lucien replies. "He knew about us before you even met him that day at the park. You were officially off limits to him."

"I don't suppose you have any leads about Bobbi?" I ask softly.

"No. The water destroyed any evidence we may have had." Lucien tells me.

"I can try touching her clothes or the duffel bag she was found in." I suggest. "Zander knows about my gift and no one else needs to know."

"I will bring it up with Dad and see what he thinks." He says thoughtfully. "Is helping these girls worth feeling the hell they went through?"

"Yes." I reply automatically.

"Alright." He squeezes me tightly.

Unaccustomed to sleeping with anyone, I am wide awake as soon as Lucien tries to slip quietly from the bed.

"Go back to sleep." He kisses me on the cheek. "You worked hard yesterday."

"It is still early enough for me to meet Chris and introduce him to Rune." I yawn as I slip into the bathroom quickly.

I throw on a pair of leggings, t-shirt, and thick socks before heading downstairs to make a pot of coffee. Lucien comes out of the downstairs bathroom freshly showered, dressed, and ready for work.

"How did you sleep?" I ask bashfully as I step up to him to get a kiss.

"Your bed is fantastic." He replies after kissing me tenderly. "I think it was made for me. How about you?"

"I agree, it's perfect." I smile. "I will make breakfast after meeting Chris."

I slip on a pair of tennis shoes and take Rune outside with me.

Chris Murphy is in his early forties and is big like Grayson, muscled everywhere. He keeps his dark hair shaved nearly bald and he has tattoos peeking our everywhere there is skin. He is quiet, is as impressed as Alex and Henry were with my introduction of Rune and refuses my offer of breakfast stating he has somewhere he has to be right away this morning.

Grayson is up early and by the looks of it is all set for his morning workout. I had Grayson order the equipment for the third bedroom upstairs and he has a huge weight lifting machine that can work all of the muscle groups and a treadmill.

Lucien feeds Rune while I get started on making breakfast. I whip up a batch of homemade buttermilk pancakes with bacon and over easy eggs. Grayson gets in a quick cardio workout on an empty stomach while I am cooking.

"I thought about making burgers and brats on the grill for dinner tonight." I mention. "Corn on the cob, cut potatoes in quarters and bake them with a little butter and spices. What do you think?"

"Want me to man the grill?" Lucien asks.

"That would be fantastic." I smile.

"What are you thinking of making for dessert?" He wants to know.

"A blonde brownie with a maple butter sauce and ice cream." I share. "It is absolutely heavenly."

"I can't wait to try that." He smiles eagerly.

Lucien heads over to his parent's house early so he can talk to his dad about my idea to get a vision from Bobbi's clothes. He rinses and loads his breakfast dishes into the dishwasher before kissing me goodbye.

I run some breakfast out to Alex while it is still hot and then clean up my kitchen before heading out to the garage to unpack some more boxes. My area rugs arrive while I am working in the garage, so I take some time to take them inside to lay them around the house where they belong.

I step back and take a look around at the difference that the area rugs bring to the house and I nod with a happy smile. Not only will they be warmer on people's feet but they add color to each room.

Stunned, I stare down into the box I have just opened I find myself staring at a bunch of girl things that don't belong to me. They must belong to my adopted parent's real daughter that went missing, Wilhelmina.

She must have really loved dolphins, which isn't a surprise considering how close to Puget Sound the cabin is. There is a small stack of books that look like they could be journals and when I open the top one, I see that is indeed what they are.

I have gotten many small visions from touching her

things, all of them joyous memories of her life in the cabin. She was very close to her mother, Zacari, and lit up whatever room she was in. She had many friends in school who were constantly at the cabin for sleepovers or studying.

I set the box aside and wonder where in the world this box was at the cabin because I don't remember any boxes that I hadn't sorted after my adopted parents died.

Shortly after lunch, I have the rest of the boxes in the garage sorted. The ones from the cabin that I am storing are placed in the small attic space of the garage. All of the items I purchased for the house have all been opened and placed inside where they belong. I take a couple minutes to park both of my vehicles inside the garage and put the remotes on the car's visors.

Grayson has been in his room unpacking all day so far. Poking my head in his room, I am impressed to see just how organized it is and I pray fervently that he is able to keep it this way.

I head upstairs and take a long hot shower and change into an adorable Stetson blue chambray spaghetti strap ruffled western sun dress. I wear a pair of brown leather cowboy boots and some turquoise jewelry as accents. I French braid my hair and apply light natural looking makeup and some black eyeliner with plum colored lip gloss.

Down in the kitchen, I scrub a ten-pound bag of russet potatoes, quarter them and spread them through three glass baking dishes with butter, sliced onions, and spices. After placing the potatoes in my extra fridge in the pantry, I get started forming hamburger patties out of the ground beef before placing them in the freezer to harden slightly before cooking.

Deciding to do my corn on the cob in a cooler I shuck about twenty ears of corn and leave them ready for the hot water.

The last thing I have to prepare is my brownie dessert. I mix up the batter for the brownies before I mix up the maple butter glaze that goes on top. The maple butter glaze goes into the fridge for now as well as the pan of brownie batter so I can just throw it into the oven later.

The weather for the beginning of May is perfect. There isn't a cloud in the sky and the temperatures are supposed to be in the low seventies until sunset. I clean up the patio area and decide that we can eat outside. There are eight of us eating and the patio table is just big enough for all of us.

I glance down at my Fitbit and see that I should probably put the potatoes in the oven to cook since they will take the longest. Fortunately, my new kitchen has a double oven so I have plenty of space to bake all three pans.

I am heading back outside when I see the gate open and Henry has let in my grandparents with Aunt Kyna. I let all of my security guards know about my dinner party ahead of time so they would be prepared for my guests.

This is the first time my grandparents and Aunt Kyna have seen my new house and they look quite impressed. I give them a tour and introduce them to Rune so my wolf will be comfortable with them.

I cannot describe the joy I feel when my grandmother hugs me tightly and kisses me on the cheek lovingly. I missed her so much in these last few days since I saw her last. I look forward to spending more time with her and getting to know her better.

It pleases me immensely to see Grandpa walk right

up to Grayson and give him a hug. Grayson smiles at him and seems happy with the effort our grandfather is putting in to make it right.

Lucien, Victor, and Nicole show up right on time. Grayson introduces our birth mother's parents to his adopted family as they have never met each other yet.

After everyone chats for a few moments, Lucien gets the charcoal grill ready for the meat while I check on the potatoes. I pour the hot water over the corn and close the lid to the cooler. Nicole, Aunt Kyna, and grandma all help me finish with the dinner prep. The patio table is set, condiments set out, and drinks handed out to everyone.

I take time to mingle with everyone while the food is still cooking and am pleased with how well my dinner party is going. My mother's family is getting along great with Grayson's adopted family and I seem to fit right in between everyone.

Dinner goes smoothly with no uncomfortable moments or lapses in conversation. Nicole, Aunt Kyna, and grandma all help me clean up afterwards.

Once the kitchen is clean again, I pull my brownies from the oven and serve them warm with the maple butter glaze and ice cream. Everyone raves over how good they are and all of the guys have seconds.

Grayson takes dinner and dessert out to Henry while we all sit on the patio chatting. Grandma and I make plans to do lunch tomorrow while Grayson agrees to start working out with grandpa.

I am surprised when grandma hands me and Grayson gift bags. Inside mine I see a coffee mug that has the Burt family crest on it. When I take it out of the bag is get a vision of Phemie and her excitement at the mug as a

Christmas gift. Feeling her happiness when I use it every morning for my coffee with be a joy.

Grayson's gift is a framed photograph of our mother that must have been taken shortly before her abduction. She was wearing one of those karate things that people wear with the different colored belts. She is holding a colored belt in her hand and smiling proudly for the camera.

I can feel that he is deeply touched by the gift.

It is starting to get dark by this point and everyone takes their leave, excitedly praising me for my first patio party.

Chapter Twenty-Six

Grayson changes into a pair of shorts and a tank top before heading through the gate to go for a jog. He was feeling bad about all of the calories he had just for dinner alone. Lucien and I change into our swim suits to sit in the hot tub.

"Dad said we will bring over Bobbi's things tomorrow morning." Lucien tells me as he sits back in the steaming water with a sigh. "Detective Cody said he wanted to be here but I told him after what he pulled; he wasn't welcome here."

"How did that conversation go with him today?" I question anxiously.

"He was very professional about it." He shares with me. "He apologized and said he knew we had just met each other and wasn't for sure if we were committed to each other. I guess I can buy it. It is sort of a guy thing that a girl is considered available if she just met someone and they haven't gotten to that point in the relationship where they are committed."

"Well good." I nod my head with relief. "Hopefully, I won't have any further problems with him."

"If you decide to go check out the next crime scene let me or Dad know?" Lucien asks softly. "The last thing we want to do is put you in a position where you are alone with Zander. I don't trust him."

"Agreed." I smile at him, feeling mischievous. His

eyes darken seductively at the change that comes over my face and he pushes through the water to recline over me. He kisses me deeply and I am instantly lost in the desire surging through Lucien.

I am feeling so much that it is all I can do to cling to him and kiss him back fervently. His thumb brushes over my pebbled peak underneath my bikini top and I feel an instant warmth between my legs.

I whimper into his mouth as he lightly pinches and strokes and I pray that he doesn't stop. He growls and I feel it reverberate through his chest as he parts my legs and lies against me, his hardness pressing into me.

I ache between my thighs and I grab his hips to pull him more snugly against me as I moan for more.

Lucien's feelings coursing through my veins are heating my blood. He has a lot of the same sensations that I am having but instead of the ache that I have between my legs he has more of a throbbing that feels like it is going to stretch beyond what it is capable of. It feels painful and I make sounds of distress in my throat as all of these sensations are swamping me all at the same time.

What he is doing to my breasts seems to be directly linked to the area between my thighs and the more he plays with me there the more I ache down below.

Suddenly, I feel his fingers slip beneath my bikini bottom to softly stroke where I have never been touched before. His thumb fondles a small spot that without warning shoots me into space where I explode, crying out into the curve of his shoulder softly.

When I finally come back down, I can still feel Lucien's pain as his hardness still presses into me. His heart beat has slowed, just like mine but for some reason he still feels discomfort.

"Did I just orgasm?" I whisper into his chest bashfully. I can both hear and feel Lucien chuckle softly.

"Yes, darlin'." He murmurs.

"Why do you still hurt?" I ask him uncertainly.

"You can feel that?" He returns in surprise.

"I think I can feel everything you are feeling physically." I confess. "I admit it got really intense for me."

"Wow!" He exclaims as he sits back and pulls me onto his lap. "I hadn't thought that your ability would work that way."

"Me either." I murmur as what strangely sounds like a purr emerges from my throat.

I curl up into his chest as he wraps his arms around me and I cannot ever remember feeling this content or at peace. Several minutes pass and Grayson slips into the hot tub with us groaning at the sensation of the water.

"How was your run?" I ask, keeping my head on Lucien's chest.

"Wonderful." Grayson replies with a blissful sigh. "I think I worked off maybe half of dinner and that awesome dessert you made."

"I had no idea our mom was into karate." I state, thinking of the gift Grayson got.

"I didn't either. She sure looked proud in that picture though." Grayson replies.

"I think it is a good idea for me to find a partner to spar with." I bring up hesitantly. "My adopted dad and I would spar together all the time. He was insistent that

I knew how to protect myself. They had me in different kinds of martial arts my whole childhood. Apparently, it was an important reason for me to be allowed to socialize with other people."

"You know how to spar?" Grayson exclaims in disbelief. "You seem so helpless!"

"Hey!" I exclaim. "My dad had me learn mixed martial arts, Krav Maga, and Taekwondo. I can hold my own on the mat."

"Let me order a mat that we can use outside on the patio." Grayson suggests. "We don't have enough room inside to spar. This way we can practice outside when the weather isn't bad."

"Sounds like a wonderful idea." I reply. "I am getting soft. I haven't even lifted weights since my parents died. It couldn't be a better time for me to get back into a regimen."

"Agreed." Lucien says. "Grayson and I can both spar with you. Our parents had us both take martial arts growing up and we both kept up with it for different reasons."

"I found my adopted parents real daughter's journals in the garage today." I state softly. "I didn't even know that box was in the cabin. She was such a happy girl. I can't wait to read them."

I yawn and suddenly I am completely exhausted. Lucien stands up and swings me up in his arms before heading for the house.

"Good night Gray." Lucien says.

"Night guys." Grayson replies.

I check my email as I sip my morning coffee and smile as I contemplate my life going back to some semblance of normalcy.

There is an email from a Charlotte Neumann and she tells me that she found me on the DNA site where my family tree is. Apparently, the site lists us as first cousins once removed. I am not exactly sure what this translates to on a family tree so I log into the web site that has my DNA.

I look at Charlotte's family tree to see how we are related and I can see Seth's mother and Charlotte's mother were sisters. It says that Charlotte lives in Baton Rouge which is just north of here a little bit. I wonder if Charlotte is aware of the horrible things that her cousin, Seth, has committed.

I send her an email back explaining that Seth is my birth father and that I would love to meet for coffee somewhere. To be able to get to know both sides of my family tree would be a real treat for me, Grayson as well, considering they are worth knowing.

Lucien and Grayson both come downstairs at the same time and I excitedly tell them about finding Charlotte.

"Do you think it is a good idea to meet anyone on Seth's side of the family?" Grayson asks suspiciously.

"How are we going to know if we don't at least meet her?" I point out reasonably. "Seth could be the black sheep of a wonderful family. What if this Charlotte has no other family but us?"

"Give this girl a chance Gray." Lucien agrees with me. "You guys can meet her in public just like you and aunt Kyna did with Jac. Make your decision after you meet her and not before."

"Alright." Grayson nods his reluctant agreement.

"Maybe we will discover that you look just like our great grandfather who was a great guy." I suggest hopefully.

"Yeah, maybe." My twin states cynically.

"So, what is the deal with you and grandpa working out together?" I ask curiously.

"His doctor wants him to exercise more and eat better." Grayson explains. "I guess his last blood test result wasn't good and the doctor told him he was in danger of either a heart attack or stroke."

"What time was your dad supposed to be here this morning?" I ask Lucien, anxious about touching Bobbi's clothes.

"Any time." He tells me after looking at his watch.

I rise from the table and put my laptop away before starting a big pot of oatmeal for breakfast. Victor shows up just as the oatmeal is finished so we all sit down together to eat breakfast. I also toasted several pieces of whole wheat bread to go along with the oatmeal and set out orange juice as well.

The oatmeal is completely gone by the time all of the guys have had seconds. I clean up the dishes while Lucien and his dad talk about the case softly between the two of them. Finally, I join them at the table when I can't logically put it off any longer.

Victor places several crime scenes bags on the table in front of me and looks at me anxiously.

"You don't have to do this." He says seriously.

"Yes, I do." I state firmly. "This is the exact reason I am getting a master's degree in forensic psychology with a minor in criminology. I wanted to use my gift to help others."

"It could give you nightmares." Victor persists, ever the father figure.

"I know, but Bobbi is counting on me." I whisper as I open the bag that her purple sweatshirt is in. I simply lie my hand on the blood-stained fabric near the neckline and close my eyes.

I feel her terror as Seth grabs her as he hides behind the curtain at the opera house. She quickly falls asleep from the choke hold only to wake up some time later inside the darkness of the car trunk. She cannot see anything but she hears two men outside arguing over her. One of them is saying she needs to die so they don't get caught. The other voice is saying that he didn't get a chance to play with her first and he is angry, very angry.

She can tell that the trunk opens from the bright sunlight shining slightly into the duffel bag she is zipped inside of. Suddenly, she feels a sharp pain in her thigh as someone jabs her with a needle.

Bobbi is awake but feels groggy and someone is holding her in a standing position. She feels a cold wind on her face and it smells like salt. She can't see because there is a bag or something over her head.

Before she can figure out what is going on, she feels a hot, painful slice across her throat and she suddenly is struggling to draw in air. She can't raise her hands to her throat to find out what is wrong as they are tied somehow. She tries to scream and all she hears is a gurgle before darkness.

I pull my hand out of the bag and take a deep cleansing breath before I relate to Lucien and Victor exactly what I saw and heard. I knew she was dead, but to actually feel the knife slicing her throat and then her death was nearly too much for me.

"Seth didn't want to kill her." I state firmly. "Whoever he was arguing with is the one responsible for killing the girls."

"Are you alright?" Lucien asks as he pulls me into his arms tightly.

"I will be." I whisper. "I felt her die Lucien."

He holds me until I finally stop trembling and then I retreat to my bedroom where I curl up on the bed with Rune next to me.

Chapter Twenty-Seven

Grandma is meeting me at noon at a restaurant in the quarter called Port of Call. I pull out of the gate a few minutes before since the restaurant is only a few blocks away.

Grandma is already at a table waiting for me when I step inside and she stands to hug me affectionately.

"So, tell me about your childhood in Washington." Grandma suggests after we order our lunch from the waitress.

"Well, I never knew I was adopted until my family attorney read the will to me several weeks ago. My parents had disappeared while they were on their yacht last October." I begin with a little history. "I grew up on Bainbridge Island just outside of Seattle in a very modest cabin just a short walk to Puget Sound. I guess my parents had a daughter before me that went missing and was never seen again. Because of this, I was homeschooled and my parents were very overprotective.

"My dad, William, was part owner of Delta Logistics, so he worked in Seattle while my mom, Zacari, was a stay at home mom. They were both great parents and doted on me in their own way. They both played games with me, read to me, and really tried to make up for my lack of friends. I spent a lot of time on the beach or swimming with my dad.

"I finished high school right before my sixteenth birthday and started online classes for college. It was at that time that I insisted on getting a job in town because I wanted my own money that my very frugal father insisted I didn't need. Finally, my mother argued on my behalf I was allowed to get a full-time job at a McDonald's so I could save money to buy my own car.

"For the first time in my life, I was finally around other people on a regular basis so that I could make friends. My mother once again came to my defense and pushed for me to be allowed to actually attend some classes at the university in Seattle. There I made more friends and I felt like I was finally becoming a normal girl. I finished my associate's degree and nearly completed my bachelor's degree before my parents went missing on their yacht.

"I don't mean to make my childhood sound negative. I guess I tend to remember all of the things I was missing, especially after finding out their birth daughter went to public school, had tons of friends over to the cabin for sleepovers, was spoiled because Dad bought her everything she desired." I look down at the table anxiously, wondering what Grandma must be thinking.

"They were just trying to learn from their mistakes, Jac." Grandma says supportively. "Sometimes when something traumatic happens like that you want to make sure you don't make the same mistakes twice and sometimes that means making different mistakes. It sounds like they loved you very much."

"I know they were." I confess with a sigh. "While I was growing up, I didn't realize what I was missing so much. I wanted friends, but didn't know what it was like to have any."

"Which explains why you moved down here so quickly after finding your birth family." She smiles at me lovingly. "Tell me. Your new house has a lot of security. Why?"

"Seth has attempted to contact me twice since I arrived here." I explain with a sigh. "My business partner, in Delta Logistics, and I have had a falling out. I don't trust him now that I have caught him lying to me about something really important. My attorney thought it a prudent investment when I bought it."

"What did he lie to you about?" Grandma asks after finishing a bite of her burger.

"My adopted parents didn't just disappear in a storm like he had originally told me. Lucien read the police report and it stated that they had been murdered before the yacht went down. Someone had slit their throats." I explain to her.

"Do you think he would have had anything to do with that?" She questions in shock. "Didn't you know this man your whole life? He was close friends with both of your parents?"

"Yes. I have called him uncle John as a term of endearment for forever." I nod sadly. "I don't want to believe he is capable of something so terrible, really I don't. My attorney is having the company audited for my protection. Mr. Sorenson said that my father has been suspicious of John for some time but could never accomplish the audit himself."

"You seem happy with Lucien." Grandma says with a grin. "He seems like such a nice young man."

"I am." I blush. "I never dated up in Washington so he is my first real boyfriend. Do you find it inappropriate that he is Grayson's adopted brother? Do you think that means I shouldn't see him?" I ask her honestly, remembering what Zander said.

"No." She waves her hand dismissively. "You and

Grayson were separated at birth and were raised by two different families. Lucien may be a brother to Grayson, but he is not a brother to you. I would be careful that you don't stay with him if you discover later that the two of you weren't meant to be together."

"I know. That could make things uncomfortable between me and Grayson's family, but you are correct, of course." I agree with her.

"Have you and Lucien had sex yet?" Grandma gazes at me directly after asking the question.

"No." I shake my head. "Honestly? I am really attracted to him and I like it when he kisses me, but I am really hesitant to go too far too soon since I have no experience dating."

"He doesn't pressure you?" She presses.

"No. Lucien would probably tell me no if I begged him to have sex." I explain with a laugh. "He is an old-fashioned guy that way, which just makes me more comfortable with him."

"I was very happy to hear Grayson agree to train your grandfather after how cruel Francis was." Grandma sighs. "I admit to being terrified when the doctor told us about Francis' latest lab results."

"I think Grayson is just relieved that this has all worked out the way it has." I explain to her. "Grayson is very family oriented. He is more than willing to forget the past now that Grandpa is working on accepting him."

"Kyna told me you got in Francis' face at her house that morning defending Grayson." She chuckles. "Poor Francis. He really suffered these many years after we lost your mother. I was able to accept what happened and move on, but not your grandfather. Phemie was his princess and her death nearly destroyed him. It took you lecturing him for him to finally see that Grayson is nothing like Seth Pickett."

"I could see the pain Grandpa was in." I confess. "I have to tell you; I have never felt for another woman in my life the way I felt for you that first time we met. I confess that I wanted to feel that way for my birth mother if I got the chance to meet her."

"Your mother wanted to keep both of you." Grandma tells me, her expression faraway and sad as she relives the memory. "She argued with Francis that it wasn't the babies' fault who their father was. For the first time, I was on Phemie's side and not her father."

"I didn't know that." I reply in shock. "She was just a child herself!"

"She really grew up after what happened to her." Grandma says. "I have a confession of my own. I feel for you how I always wanted to feel for Euphemia. Her and her dad were always so close, but her and I never really saw eye to eye. I couldn't have loved a daughter more, but I feel that with you. I am blessed that you and your brother have come back into our lives."

A tear trickles down my cheek at her declaration and I nod at her without speaking because my throat feels all choked up.

"I love you Grandma." I manage to whisper several minutes later.

"I love you too Jacqueline." She strokes my cheek tenderly.

We finish up our lunch chatting about this and that before making plans to meet again in just a couple days.

Lucien is mowing the lawn when I get home and Grayson is still gone with our grandfather. Rune follows me inside the house and lies on the floor next to my desk while I turn on my computer.

Charlotte has emailed me back and is excited for us to meet. She hopes it won't be too much trouble for me to drive up to Baton Rouge to meet as her car isn't the greatest for the drive to New Orleans. I reassure her that I can drive up there without a problem and ask if tomorrow morning would work for her. I ask that she pick the place as I am not familiar with the area.

I intend to use the time with Charlotte to find out as much as I can about her aunt, Seth's mother. Maybe, if I can find out who Seth's real father is it will help us discover where he is taking the girls.

It bothers me that someone at my own company, Delta Logistics, knows Seth enough to mail him stuff while he was in prison. I desperately want to solve this mystery surrounding my birth father so we can send him back to prison, for the rest of his life.

"Your attorney called the house while you were gone with your grandmother." Lucien says as he steps into my office, all sweaty from mowing the grass. "He said you forgot to buy lawn equipment and sent over what you would need. It arrived shortly after you left."

"You didn't need to do my lawn, you know." I scold him with a smile. "But thank you. I can't believe I forgot to buy a lawnmower!"

"You're welcome." He smiles down at me. "Ted called. The guy we got Rune from? He has a female Mackenzie wolf that he was hoping he could place here with you. They are an endangered species and Ted is hoping you will allow Rune to mate with her."

"We could go and take a look at her." I nod immediately. "We should probably bring Rune along to see if they are compatible?"

"Ted suggested we bring Rune along." Lucien nods. "He wants you to meet Freya first to see if she can bond with you. If she is a good fit for both you and Rune, he will take care of the necessary permits to make this legal."

"I am guessing he has a plan for the pups?" I ask curiously.

"He does." Lucien replies. "He knows a couple guys who work with a few packs of wolves up north in Canada and Alaska. It is the hope that the pups will become an accepted part of the packs up there and increase numbers."

"When does he want me to meet Freya?"

"Today if you have time." He raises his eyebrow questioningly.

"Sounds good. Did you want to go now then?" I turn off my computer and get to my feet.

"Let me shower and change clothes first, then we will head over." Lucien says before heading upstairs.

I take a few minutes to pull out some chicken breast from the freezer so it will thaw while we are gone. I can bake it later along with some pasta and homemade alfredo sauce.

Lucien comes back downstairs just ten minutes later, freshly showered and changed. We put Rune in the back of my SUV and head out to Ted's plantation on River Road.

Lucien texts him that we are on the way as we are heading out of the driveway. We are pulling into Ted's place within a half hour and Rune is pacing in the back anxiously.

Rune stays in the car for now while Lucien and I meet Ted outside his barn. He leads us inside to a stall where a pale silvery white wolf is lying down. I reach out mentally to the beautiful wolf and she raises her head curiously. Our eyes meet and she cocks her head to the side as we gaze at each other. When I feel no danger from her, I open up her stall and step inside where I squat down to her level. Holding out my hand to her I communicate to her telepathically that I mean her no harm and send her images of Rune knowing she can smell him on me.

It takes her nearly a full minute before she finally approaches me and sniffs my hand hesitantly. I can feel her interest in Rune and her eagerness to meet the male wolf.

"Go get Rune." I state softly as Freya looks at me.

As soon as Rune enters the stall Freya turns to him excitedly and I can feel their eagerness. Rune steps up to her slowly making quiet whining noises and I see Freya do the same thing. They lick and nuzzle each other's muzzles before bumping their bodies together. I feel their acceptance of each other.

They make a beautiful pair. Rune is nearly all black except for the white tips to his guard hairs and Freya is a brilliant silvery white.

Rune steps up to me and bumps my chin, showing his submission to me before he looks back at Freya. She cocks her head to the side and I can feel her consider his action curiously. Rune does it again and then steps up to Freya to growl at her softly. His body language to her shows he is the alpha. He is trying to tell her to accept me as her alpha too.

Freya slowly steps up to me and gently taps her nose

under my chin, whining softly. I stroke her face and ears to show my acceptance of her and am surprised when she rolls onto her back as well. Rune steps over and nuzzles her face affectionately while whining softly once more.

I have Lucien step into the stall so I can introduce Freya to him. The female accepts Lucien quickly before bouncing around the stall with Rune happily. Freya has herself a new family.

Chapter Twenty-Eight

Ted suggests that I allow one of his friends to put in a wolf den on my property for Freya to have her pups in. They can construct it out of natural boulders and stones to make it weather proof. He explains that it should only take a day or two to put it up and it would be best for the pups to be born in this type of environment since they will be introduced into the wild.

I agree and he gives me his friends business card so I can give the contact information to my security guards.

Freya jumps into the back of the SUV with Rune without hesitation and we soon have the wolves back home without incident. Rune and Freya run through the yard together getting to know one another. I see several instances where they show one another affection which just makes my heart melt.

Charlotte texts me and suggests a diner Monday morning at ten if that is not too early for me. Lucien tells me that it is about an hour and a half drive so I will want to leave about eight-thirty in the morning. Lucien begs me to take Grayson with me as he is not comfortable with me driving all that way by myself. I readily agree since Charlotte is his cousin too.

Sunday passes quickly with Lucien spending some time with me out on the grass sparring. We are unfamiliar with how each other fights so it is a fun learning experience. Lucien helps me with some of my moves and teaches some that I do not know while I show him some from Krav Maga, the Israeli form of martial arts.

I also get started on my weight lifting routine upstairs in the third bedroom. The machine that Grayson picked out is perfect. I can work every muscle group without problem or being too complicated. I run a few miles on the treadmill before heading downstairs to make dinner.

Lucien has already left for work when I step into Grayson's room the next morning to wake him up and find him in bed moaning.

"Are you alright?" I ask him as I check his forehead for fever.

"I have been throwing up." He groans as he clutches my stomach. "You should go meet Charlotte without me. I will be fine. I am sure it is just the flu and it will pass."

I get Grayson a pitcher of water with a glass to keep him hydrated while I am gone. I will most likely be back around lunch time anyways.

The thought of driving my sports car on the highway actually excites me as I pull out of the gate, waving to Alex as I go by. Knowing that Lucien will just try to get me to reschedule my coffee date with Charlotte I do not text him that I am going alone. I will be home by lunch time.

The drive to Baton Rouge is great. I listen to the radio with the top down and sing along as loud as I can. My Audi Spyder is such a fun car to drive.

Coffee Call, the restaurant, is easy to find and I find parking right near the door. Charlotte and I exchanged pictures by text so we would recognize each other. She is already standing just inside the door to the diner.

I am surprised that she is a dainty girl just like me. She is only a year older than me with golden blonde hair and baby blue eyes. Her face is heart shaped, her nose is slightly upturned at the end, and her lips are beautifully curved. She is a very pretty girl.

She is wearing a worn pair of blue jeans and a well-washed Louisiana State University t-shirt. Her shoes, although clean, look they are close to having holes from wear.

I feel guilty for wearing an expensive new summer dress and driving my sports car when it is obvious, she is poor. My adopted parents never let me wear such worn out clothes but I was never allowed to buy anything name brand either.

"Charlotte?" I step up to her with a welcoming smile. She returns the smile and I can feel her eagerness at meeting me and her hopefulness, probably that we get along.

"You must be Jacqueline." She shakes my hand firmly.

"Please call me Jac." I shake her hand and instantly see a vision of Charlotte sitting at the bedside of a woman. The woman is whispering to Charlotte while Charlotte cries. It is her mother's death bed. Charlotte looked similar in the vision but I am guessing it was a year or two ago. "Where do you want to sit?"

"That back corner table will give us some privacy." She says softly. "My friends call me Charlie."

I follow her to the table she suggested and we both have a seat with nervous smiles. The waitress takes our order for coffee and beignet fingers which I am completely excited to try out.

"I have to confess I am surprised you wanted to meet me and my brother after finding out who our birth father is." I tell Charlotte. "Surely, you know what he was in prison for and who our birth mother was."

"I do." Charlie sighs sadly. "It goes both ways though. I am Seth's family too. You must be wondering if I am as messed up as he is. I am aware of Seth. I confess I have never met him. My mother didn't have me until late in life and by the time I was born Seth's mother had disappeared years before. I only know what my mother told me before she passed."

"I was raised by a family in the Seattle area. I did my DNA test just a couple months ago and that is how I found my twin brother Grayson and a great aunt on my birth mother's side of the family." I share with her. "My adopted parents passed last fall. I flew down here to meet Grayson and my aunt Kyna and just decided to live here where I could be close to family. I was more excited to meet you than nervous that you would be like Seth. Do you know anything about Seth's mother?"

"My mom, Hope, was seven years younger than Seth's mother, Ava. They used to be quite close until Seth got older and started causing problems. Ava worked at Old Absinthe House when she got pregnant with Seth. She told my mom about the guy she met there but I guess he was married and had a family. Mom said that Ava was pretty close with a couple of the other waitresses there."

"Do you have family on your dad's side?" I ask curiously as it sounds like Charlie is all alone.

"No." She shakes her head. "He died when I was little and he made my mom promise him to stay away from his family because they were bad news. You, Grayson, and Seth are the only family I have. What happened? I thought Grayson was coming today?"

"He woke up sick this morning." I chuckle.

"I have been following the news down there in New Orleans." Charlie says. "The missing girls. That's Seth isn't it?"

"Yes." I sigh. "He has tried getting a hold of me a couple times now. I admit the man freaks me out totally. The first girl he took I helped find because he left clues just for me."

"My mom told me that Seth always claimed to be telepathic." Charlie states nonchalantly even though her emotions are screaming fear, fear that I won't believe what she is saying.

"Yes." I whisper softly as I stare into her blue eyes intensely. "They say that sort of thing passes through the family."

"Yes." Charlie whispers back as she searches my gaze just as intently.

"Grayson and I can communicate telepathically." I attempt to send her mentally and see her eyes widen when she hears my voice in her head.

I laugh when I feel her relief that I am gifted. My guess is that she is as well somehow.

"I am an empath. I can feel what others feel, can tell when they are telling the truth, as well as having visions when I touch people or objects. Grayson is telepathic." I share with her telepathically.

I watch as Charlie focuses on my coffee cup and I actually see it levitate just a little off of the table.

"That is awesome!" I exclaim softly and Charlie blushes. "That must really come in handy and be so much fun to play with! I think I am jealous."

"It would be so handy to be able see when people

are lying or being deceitful." Charlie sighs sadly. "I have a hard time making friends because I am going to be rejected when they find out what I can do. I don't date for the same reason."

"Me too." I nod. "I really didn't have any friends in Seattle for that same reason. It helps that Grayson's family knows about his gift and they accept mine as well. It is a huge relief to have people around you that accept you no matter how strange you are."

"Are you dating anyone?" She asks curiously.

"I am." I blush anxiously. "Grayson has an older brother. His adopted brother that is his adopted parent's birth son."

"Oh." Charlie nods as she thinks about it for several seconds. "So, you just met this guy just a couple weeks ago?"

"Yes. We just instantly connected." I confess. "I wasn't sure about him being my twin's brother at first and I know it sounds strange, but we aren't related and didn't grow up together so."

"If you found a guy who knows about your abilities and accepts you for it, I can't see why not." Charlie exclaims firmly. "That is a blessing many of us will never have."

"Are you in college or work somewhere?" I ask her.

"I have a scholarship to Louisiana State." Charlie explains. "I will be done with my bachelor's in accounting after this summer semester. I want to go on and get my master's degree but that will be a lot of loans to pay back."

"Well, if you would be interested in working for a shipping company down in New Orleans let me know." I tell her casually.

"Why?" She laughs.

"Because I am one of the CEO's." I whisper uncomfortably. Her eyes practically bug out of her head.

"You own a shipping company?" She asks incredulously.

"I do now that my adopted father is dead." I share with her honestly. "I am in college working on my master's in forensic psychology with a minor in criminology. I want to work for the FBI or law enforcement. I really have no interest in running Delta Logistics but I am almost half owner so."

"Wow." Charlie shakes her head in disbelief. "I will definitely keep that in mind."

I pick up one of the beignet fingers and take a big bite before moaning at the crispy sweetness. They have a slightly different consistency than a regular beignet but they are fantastic.

"I hope my new lifestyle doesn't make you uncomfortable." I tell her honestly. "My parents were extremely frugal when I was growing up. I wore second hand clothes, wasn't allowed to have my own cell phone or computer, couldn't have friends, had to beg to get a job at McDonalds so I could buy my own junker car."

"It's alright." Charlie replies with a smile. "My mom worked hard when she was alive and we did alright. When she got sick, her doctor bills used up the savings from my dad's life insurance. When she died, her life insurance didn't go near as far as I would have liked it. I work for a small company here in Baton Rouge to help me get through school."

"How long ago did you lose your mom?" I ask.

"It will be a year soon." She replies sadly.

"I would love for us to stay in contact." I tell her. "I think considering all we have in common and the fact that neither of us have much family left…."

"I agree." Charlie smiles at me brightly.

I text her my address and make her promise to come to my house for dinner next Saturday night. I even let her know that I have a sleeper sofa in my office if she doesn't want to make the drive back to Baton Rouge until the next day.

We hug each other tightly before leaving the restaurant, both of us pleased to have found the other.

Chapter Twenty-Nine

Before driving away from the restaurant, I make sure to put home into the GPS just to make sure I don't get lost on the way back to New Orleans. It looks like it might rain so I put up the convertible top and sigh regretting that I won't feel the wind in my hair on the way home.

I am surprised when my GPS has me take an exit off of the highway that I did not take on the way up here but I turn off anyway. It looks like this could be a scenic route back to New Orleans so I shrug and continue down the small country road the GPS is leading me through.

Soon, civilization drops away down the route I am taking as gas stations and houses disappear. The pavement is beginning to crumble and I find myself swerving to avoid potholes the size of a small canyon.

I groan in frustration and pull over to the side of the road so I can reset my GPS to take me back to the highway. Unfortunately, I cannot seem to get it to respond to me at all as it seems to be frozen. I have made way too many turns on this road to be able to find myself back by memory so I suppose I just have to trust the car will see me safely home eventually.

With a sudden thought, I take out my cell phone with the intention of using the map on it to find my way home but I have absolutely no service. Shaking my head in disgust I throw my cell phone on the passenger seat and pull out following the GPS on my car just as it starts to pour down rain.

Every once in a while, I pass a shack that looks like it may have been lived in like fifty years ago, but actually shows signs that a person really lives there. The rain seems to be intermittent where it will pour for several minutes before slowing to a sprinkle.

After not seeing another building of any sort for at least a half hour I am following the curving country road and apparently going way too fast when a sudden downpour slams down around me making visibility impossible. I tap on the brakes to slow down but suddenly discover I have none. The brake pedal goes all the way to the floor and the car does not respond at all.

I fail to see the sharp corner in the road until it is too late and my car careens off of the broken pavement and into the woods, slamming into a tree out of sight of the road. The last thing I remember is screaming as the car crunches into the tree and my air bag explodes into my face.

"You're ok Jacqueline." A deep southern drawl whispers into my ear as I feel myself being lifted out of the wreckage of my car.

I try to open my eyes, but everything is blurry and my head hurts so badly I whimper pitifully as I close them once more. Nausea and dizziness washes over me and so does the need to throw up.

"Need to be sick." I manage to gasp as I swallow down the urge to vomit. He squats down with me cradled in his arms and supports me while I throw up until I dry heave painfully.

It is pouring cats and dogs and I am completely drenched as is the good Samaritan who pulled me from my car. I can't even open my eyes to see who it is that is helping me. I remember he used my name but his voice didn't sound familiar to me.

Where am I? Why was I driving in such bad weather?

I struggle to remember, but I can remember nothing.

He places me on a long vehicle seat so that I am lying across it before closing the door. The car begins to move and I pray he is taking me to a hospital because I must have a concussion from the car accident.

We drive for a short distance before the car slows down to navigate over a rutted road or driveway. It seems to take forever for the car to stop slamming over the bumps and pot holes which just makes me feel worse.

He pulls me out of the back seat and into his arms.

"You are safe now baby." The deep southern drawl encourages me.

"Who?" I manage to croak.

"You're with Daddy now." He murmurs soothingly.

Daddy? Dad died months ago; my fuzzy brain tries to make sense of what I am hearing.

There is something my head is trying to warn me about but I just cannot grasp it.

He carries me inside of a building that smells musty and lies me down on an equally smelly bed. I attempt to open my eyes again but the dizziness that instantly overwhelms me makes me close them again with a moan of distress. He starts to strip off my wet clothes and even though I weakly protest he has no problem undressing me completely.

I am wrapped in a stinky blanket that is rough like wool. Judging from the sounds I am hearing he is messing around with a wood stove. I hear and smell it light before I hear water pouring nearby.

Exhaustion sets in and all I want to do is go to sleep so I relax inside my itchy blanket and let myself drift off.

"Stay awake baby." The deep voice is insistent right next to me. "You probably have a mild concussion and can't go to sleep."

"Tired." I protest.

"I know you're tired." He runs a wet cloth over my forehead and I cringe against the stinging pain as he cleans an open wound there.

"Who are you?" I whisper softly as it seems to just make my head pound furiously.

"I told you who I am Jacqueline." He insists, his voice irritated.

"Dad's dead." I persist, my brain still not functioning correctly.

He continues to clean my head wound without speaking further but I can feel his fury washing over me making me afraid. His emotions do not feel familiar to me. Why is he so angry?

Seemingly satisfied that my wound is clean, I feel his weight leave the mattress I am lying on. I hear rustling sounds nearby and I can tell after a few seconds that he is taking off his wet clothes as well. I also hear him getting dressed so there must be clothes here, wherever we are.

After a short while, the fire he started has warmed up the room we are in enough that I have stopped shivering. I open my eyes again and this time manage to fight the dizziness long enough that it eases and I can look around curiously.

I am in a shack of some sort where I can see outside between the boards making up the walls. I am lying on a double bed, the only one in the one room building, there is a small handmade table with two chairs, and a cast iron wood stove.

A giant of a man is tending the wood stove with his back to me. He is wearing a red and black flannel shirt, no doubt found here in the shack. I frown as I stare at him and wonder how he knows my name but he doesn't look familiar to me; until he turns around.

Seth Pickett!

I shake my head, as I feel panic welling up inside me, but the slight motion causes my head to hurt too much. My whimper of distress causes Seth to turn and look at me. He watches me curiously as I stare at him in terror.

"What have you done?" I moan as I try to sit up and fail, the movement making me want to be sick again.

"What was necessary for us to spend some time together." He replies, his voice soft. "You are my daughter."

"Unfortunately, you supplied the sperm necessary to create my existence, but I am not your daughter." I state furiously.

He shrugs but does not argue the point and turns his attention back to the stove. I can smell that he is cooking something but the smell just turns my stomach.

I wonder if I can somehow reach out to Grayson for help. Will he be able to hear me from wherever I am?

Seth steps over to me quickly and leans down over me with a knife to my throat.

"No calling for help Jacqueline." He threatens seriously. "I don't want to hurt you, but if you disobey me, I will have no choice."

"I won't call for help." I tell Seth mentally as I am too afraid to nod my head with the knife there. He searches my expression and I can feel him inside my head before he stands up, placing the knife inside his belt.

"Who killed Bobbi?" I ask him bluntly. He looks down at me in surprise, he didn't think I would know about that.

"You wouldn't believe me if I told you." He states simply.

"How did you get my childhood book?" I persist.

"Again, you wouldn't believe me if I told you." He repeats. "I will tell you that you have made some very intelligent decisions lately."

"What does that even mean?" I ask as I manage to sit up, keeping the blanket wrapped around my nakedness.

"I am glad that you met Charlotte today." Seth continues as if I didn't speak. "She needs family in her life. Especially family that is gifted like we are."

"You know about her?" I ask in surprise.

"Of course, I do." He nods as he sits back down on the end of the bed. I curl up in a fetal position as far from him as I can get which makes him smile sadly. "Her mother was my mother's younger sister. I spent a lot of time with aunt Hope growing up. Aunt Hope had the same ability that Charlie has."

"If you were in prison this whole time and have never met Charlie how do you know what ability, if any, that she has?" I can't stop myself from asking.

"I can find out anything about anyone." He shrugs. "I

found out where you were going this morning. I found out that, last minute, you would be going alone. You think you are safe inside your highly secured home, but you aren't baby."

"Don't call me that!" I yell at him angrily and cringe away as he crawls across the bed towards me. He places his hands on either side of my shoulders blocking me in before leaning close to me.

"Go ahead and ask me the question that has been burning inside that mind of yours Jac." Seth whispers into my ear as he strokes my cheek softly. I push feebly against his massive chest but I am too weak to do anything.

"Please." I whimper, terrified that he will want to hurt me like he hurt all of the other girls.

"I don't want that from you." He confesses as he nuzzles his cheek against mine. "I simply want to get to know my daughter. Ask me, Jac."

"Why?" I breath softly.

"Be more specific." He continues to murmur into my ear, touching me gently.

"Why do you hurt those girls?" I continue to weakly push against him, desperate to put some distance between us. Seth chuckles and sits back at the end of the bed with a smile.

"My mother worked nights at a bar so when I was too little to stay by myself, she had the neighbor girl come watch me." Seth begins, his facial expression far away. "She was a tiny little thing, even though she was older than me. After I fell asleep, she would come into my room and touch me under my pajamas. This just kept progressing until she would use her mouth on me and then show me how to do the same to her. When she stopped babysitting me her little sister took over where she left off. She would do the same things to me that her older sister did. Eventually, I was old enough and I didn't need a babysitter anymore but I had developed a taste for tiny little pubescent girls. I admit, when I was still a little boy, I would beg her not to touch me, beg her to stop. It felt dirty, naughty. I didn't find out until years later that their father had been sexually abusing them from the time they were toddlers."

"Just because that happened to you doesn't mean you had to abuse others." I point out furiously. "I felt what you did to my mother!" I scream at him, tears streaming down my face.

Seth shrugs.

"It is what I desire." He states simply.

"You are a monster." I sob. "I am ashamed that we share the same DNA."

Chapter Thirty

Seth checks on the food that he is cooking on top of the wood stove before moving it off of the direct heat. He rummages around in a duffel bag that is on the table and pulls out some more clothes.

He steps up to the bed and scoops me up in his arms no matter how much I push against him. Setting me on my feet he sits down in one of the chairs next to the small table and supports me so I won't fall. Standing upright is really making me dizzy and I have no choice but to lean against Seth or I will be sick. He pulls the blanket from around me, letting it fall to the floor even though I attempt to clutch it.

"Stop!" I whimper, terrified that he is going to hurt me now.

"You look just like your mother." He says, his voice sounding mesmerized as he runs a finger across my chest lightly. I am sobbing at this point and trembling so badly that there is no way I could stand on my own let alone fight this massive man. He pulls me up on his lap and slides a thick pair of leggings over my feet. Eager to have clothing on I try to help him pull them up over my hips, although I cannot stop myself from weeping uncontrollably.

Once the leggings are on, he slips a sweatshirt over my head and down over my arms before putting a pair of socks onto my feet. Instead of returning me to the bed he leaves me on his lap where I have no choice but to lie my head on his chest. I am so weak and dizzy I can't hold my head up any longer.

"Your sweet innocence makes men want to protect you." Seth states suddenly. "All the men in your life want to command your obedience to force your protection and you see it as a theft of your independence."

"Protection from you." I tell him honestly.

"Touché." He laughs. "How angry do you think Lucien will be when he finally gets to talk to you?"

"He should be angry at me." I point out logically. "Look at what my foolish decision cost me?"

"I haven't harmed you." He says tightly.

"I am pretty sure my car accident was somehow your fault." I tell him suspiciously. "I would consider a concussion to be harm."

"Your mother stood up to me as well." Seth remembers, his voice happy. "She was so different than all of the others. I had to move her to protect her from ending up like all the others. Her and I needed to get to know each other better before he took her away from me. The others cried and whimpered but not Euphemia. She fought me like a little warrior using her karate skills on me every chance I gave her. She cried for me when I told her what my babysitters did to me. She told me that she was sorry that my mommy didn't protect me like she should."

"You confused a poor innocent girl!" I yell at him. "She didn't need to feel sorry for you! She should have killed you if she had the chance."

"Like you, baby?" Seth taunts me angrily.

"I told you not to call me that!" I slap him across the face as I slide off of his lap where I fall to my hands and knees. I struggle to get to my feet but I am too weak.

He picks me up and pins me down on the bed with

my wrists held in one of his huge hands above my head while he reclines over me closely.

"You are my baby, Jac." He nuzzles my cheek again. "Daddy's little girl. Just like Phemie was her daddy's little girl."

"No!" I hiss up at him furiously.

"Oh yes, baby." He continues to taunt me. "I know your tired, but I wouldn't trust a deviant like me. You look so much like your mother and I know you are a virgin, just like her. Oh, I could relive those fond memories since I have you here with me."

"Please." I struggle to free my wrists to no avail.

"Stay awake." He instructs me seriously. "It would be so easy for me to pretend you are your mother while you sleep. Such innocence."

He parts my legs and presses his hardness into me as he nuzzles my neck before nibbling on my ear.

Before I can react to the horror, he is off the bed and tending to the stove. I scoot up into a sitting position and curl up into a ball with my arms wrapped around my drawn-up knees in the far corner of the bed.

I am no longer tired with his threat still ringing in my ears so I watch his every move instead.

The hours pass slowly and soon it grows dark outside, the temperatures outside falling near freezing. I can feel multiple drafts slipping between the boards at my back.

"What happened to your mother?" I ask, finally unable to take the silence.

"She was responsible for what those babysitters did

to me." He shrugs.

"It sounds like you grew to enjoy what they did to you." I state reasonably. "You prefer pubescent girls just like they were at the time."

"Oh, did I leave out a key part of the story?" He replies, rage rolling off of him in waves as he turns to me. "Their father, the babysitters, he not only sexually abused his daughters but he was also raping my mother and forcing her to keep it a secret. He threatened to use me instead of her, so for a while she kept his secret and allowed him to hurt her. One night when I was only fourteen, I heard them arguing in her bedroom before he came into my room. My mom listened while he forced himself on me and she never said a word to anyone. She allowed this to continue and no matter who I told no one would listen because I was just a troublemaker who had been expelled from every school he attended. I was drinking and using drugs by the time I was eleven years old and hanging out with adults. I was just trying to get attention, right? I ran away only for the police to bring me back home where he would punish me for my disobedience. This happened over and over again until it finally came to an end on my eighteenth birthday."

I stare at him stunned as the truth of his words washes over me. He is not lying to me and my guess is that he killed both his mother and the man who was assaulting him.

Dropping my gaze, I look away from him as I have no idea what to say to him. When I look up again, I see that Seth has managed to cross the room without making a sound and he is standing right in front of the bed. He gazes down at me before reaching out to grab my chin in between two fingers tightly. He sits down next to me on the bed and stares into my eyes for several long seconds before he releases my chin.

"You need your rest." He tells me as he yanks on my ankle and pulls me down beside him on the bed. I fight and struggle to get away from him but he seems to know what I am going to do before I do it.

He pins me down just the same as he did before and stares down at me curiously.

"Your eyes are no longer dilated." He whispers softly. "It is safe for you to get some sleep."

"What about you?" I question him as I shake my head, forcing down the panic.

"I intend on getting some sleep as well." He chuckles without releasing me.

"That isn't what I meant." I squirm under him to free myself.

"Your virtue is safe, daughter." He informs me as he finally lets me go and pulls the thin wool blanket over the two of us. He rolls me onto my side with my back against his chest and pulls me back against him snugly with his arm wrapped around my waist tightly.

He is telling me the truth but it still takes me a long time to relax with him practically wrapped around me. I finally slip to sleep but it is filled with images of Seth's childhood trauma.

"Jac!" I hear my name being called and someone is tapping my cheek gently. When I open my eyes, it isn't Seth staring down at me it is detective Zander Cody.

"Zander?" I push him away and sit up in confusion as I look around the shack for Seth. "Did you catch him?"

"Catch who Jac?" Zander asks.

"Seth!" I exclaim as I see no proof that he was here at all. The duffel bag is gone as are all of the wet clothes.

"No, I only found you in here." He tells me. "There are tire tracks outside and I found your car smashed into a tree a distance from the road. What the hell were you doing all the way out here Jac? You were supposed to be driving back to New Orleans on the highway!"

"The GPS on my car told me to come this way." I answer softly. "I didn't realize that it was a mistake until I pulled over and it wouldn't let me reprogram it. My phone had no service so I couldn't use the GPS on that to find my way back to the highway. It started to downpour when I was driving a little too fast and I didn't see the curve in the road until it was too late."

"Seth pulled you from the wreckage and brought you here?" Zander asks as he runs a finger gently over the large bump on my forehead.

"Yes. I was so dizzy, nauseous, and my head hurt so bad I couldn't even open my eyes for a long time. When I finally realized it was him, we were already in the shack. I wanted to reach out to Grayson telepathically, but Seth threatened to kill me if I tried."

"How do you feel?" He looks into my eyes closely. "Did Seth hurt you at all?"

I remember how he pinned me underneath him and pressed his hardness in between my legs and shudder.

"No." I shake my head, not wanting to talk about it.

"Jac." He pushes, knowing I am hiding something from him.

"My virtue is intact." I reply sarcastically. "I want to go home, please."

Zander picks me up and cradles me in his arms to carry me out to his cruiser which is parked outside the shack. He buckles me into the passenger seat and hands me his cell phone.

"Call Lucien." He says. "He is worried."

"Lucien Devereaux." Lucien answers his phone crisply.

"It's me Lucien." I whisper, trying not to weep with happiness at hearing his voice.

"Jac!" Lucien exclaims. "Darlin' are you alright? Where are you? Why are you using Zander's phone?"

"Seth followed me to Baton Rouge and I think he somehow caused the brakes on my car to fail. I got into an accident on some backwoods country road and Seth was there to pull me from the wreckage. Zander found me this morning. He is bringing me home. I am fine, I promise." I explain quietly.

"Let me talk to Zander darlin'." Lucien instructs me, his voice angry.

I hand the phone back to Zander and they discuss what they know so far and where to go from here. Zander tells Lucien that he is bringing me to the University Medical Center Emergency Department to have my concussion looked at before he hangs up.

"You are lucky you didn't pull this stunt if you were my girlfriend." Zander states furiously.

"Why?" I seethe at him, just as angry. "Would you punish me Detective Cody?"

"You're damn right I would!" Zander explodes as he turns to me and pins me back against the seat, grabbing my chin in his hand. "I would put you over my knee like the naughty girl you are and blister your ass until you sobbed for me to stop."

Stunned, I can only stare at him in shock at the boldness of his words. I flush and try to free my chin from his grip but he just tightens his hold as he gazes into my eyes deeply. I am not comfortable with my reaction to his words and I squirm as shame rushes through me. Zander smiles as he sees the truth on my face and reluctantly releases me.

He starts the car and chuckles throatily before heading down the rutted two-track.

"Oh, baby." Zander croons. "I don't think Lucien realizes you aren't as innocent as you portray yourself to be. You need a man in your life who can bring out that naughty girl that lurks there beneath the surface."

"I don't know what you're talking about." I look away from him, my voice prim and proper.

"Lie to yourself all you want Jac." He purrs in his husky voice. "I saw the truth in those beautiful blue eyes of yours."

Chapter Thirty-One

Zander is quiet during the ride into New Orleans which takes us nearly an hour thanks to how far away from the highway I truly was. I nearly fall trying to get out of the car as a wave of dizziness sweeps over me suddenly so Zander picks me up to carry me inside. Lucien is right inside the door to the emergency department; as are his parent's, Grayson, Aunt Kyna, and my grandparents. Lucien takes me from Zander and I instantly hide my face in the curve of his neck because I can still feel how angry he is at me.

Victor has spoken to one of the doctors already so I am taken right into an exam room with Zander and Grayson following behind. Everyone else must be in the waiting room for news.

Lucien sets me down on the bed but barely moves enough for the doctor to examine me. Once the doctor has looked me over and asked me a long battery of questions, he says he will give me a shot for the pain, explaining that I do indeed have a mild concussion. I will need seven to ten days of rest with minimal television or computer use. Nothing physical or strenuous at all. He will give me a prescription to take at home for the pain and nausea.

He leaves the room and I am suddenly afraid because I can feel Lucien's anger is at an exploding point. I curl into a ball on the bed and just wish I could disappear.

"Darlin', why didn't you tell me that Grayson woke up too sick to go with you?" Lucien asks tightly. "I am sure Charlotte would have been understanding that you needed to put off meeting her for just a day or two."

"Don't Lucien." I whisper, embarrassed to be doing this in front of too many people.

"Don't what?" He continues, getting angrier. "Don't protect you from the monster that is determined to get you all to himself? Don't keep you safe?"

"Not here Lucien." I beg one last time.

"Lucien." Grayson puts his hand on Lucien's arm. Lucien shakes it off, too furious to see reason.

"Get off Gray." Lucien yells, giving free reign to his rage.

"Now, son." Victor steps up to Lucien as well, his voice soothing. "After being in Seth's control for that long I am sure Jac has seen the error of her ways."

"No, Dad." Lucien's face is turning nearly purple he is so upset. "This is between me and Jac."

"No, this concerns all of us." Grayson insists calmly.

"She belongs to me!" Lucien roars as he turns towards his brother with a crazed look in his eyes.

Grayson shakes his head sadly before he lifts his arm and very calmly punches his brother in the face.

"Get him out of here Dad." Grayson states as he sits on the bed with me and pulls my trembling form into his arms.

Victor helps Lucien off of the floor and leads his reluctant son from the room.

"Are you alright?" Grayson asks me once my tears have dried up and I am no longer trembling. I nod before looking up at Zander uncomfortably.

Zander is watching me with concern mirrored in those blue eyes of his.

"I know you told me some of what happened yesterday, but I need you to start with leaving the house to meet your cousin Charlotte." Zander asks gently as he sits down on a chair next to the bed.

I start with putting in the name of the restaurant into my GPS into my car before driving through the gate and don't stop until I woke to find Zander in the shack with me. I tell them everything that Seth said and did, even the parts that fill me with horror and shame. The only thing I don't bring up is what punishment Zander brought up if I were his girlfriend and my reaction.

Zander asks me many questions; did I see what the car looked like Seth was driving, did my brakes feel funny before they suddenly went out, did I notice anything strange while I was at the restaurant with Charlotte and many other things that weren't included in my statement.

A nurse comes in and gives me a shot after confirming that I am riding home with someone. She goes over my discharge papers with Grayson and explains to him in detail what I am allowed and not allowed for the next seven to ten days. She also gives him a list of primary care physician's that are accepting patients in the area, encouraging him to find me a doctor to see soon.

She puts me in a wheelchair after telling Grayson to go get his car and drive it up to the hospital. As soon as she wheels me towards the doors everyone comes out of the waiting room and wants to know if I am alright. The shot is already taking effect so Zander explains to all of them what the doctor and nurse told me, leaving out everything about my time with Seth.

Zander walks alongside my wheelchair out to where

Grayson is waiting with the car. Zander picks me up gently and places me in the passenger seat of Grayson's Camaro before buckling my seat belt.

"Thank you for saving me." I whisper to Zander softly. "You followed me to Baton Rouge, didn't you?"

"I did." He chuckles. "Someone has to keep you an eye on you. Apparently, your new family doesn't know you like I do yet."

Zander hands Grayson something across the car.

"That is her cell phone from the wreckage." Zander explains to him. "Buy her a new cell phone, this one is broken. I am having her car towed back to the crime lab where they are going to go through the computer for tampering. I will be in touch to let you both know what we find."

"Thank you, Zander, for bringing my sister home to me." Grayson states sincerely.

"Any time, man." He replies and shakes hands with Grayson. "I will be over to the house in a couple hours if that is alright. I need to have my IT techs take a look at the internet at your house to see if Seth has been hacking in."

"Of course." Grayson nods. "I will let the security guards know you are coming."

The shot for pain that the nurse gave me is really making me tired but I struggle to stay awake as Grayson drives us home. I am feeling higher than a kite but I am afraid of what I will see if I go to sleep. The stories that Seth told me are haunting me.

I am surprised to see that two of my security guards are on duty when we drive through the gate. One of them stays in the booth while the other one patrols the grounds and house. There will now be two of them working together at all times which means they have hired a couple more guys.

Grayson carries me into the house and when he heads for the stairs to my bedroom I struggle earnestly.

"Please!" I plead as I push on his arms to be released. "I will sleep on the sofa. I don't want to be up there all alone."

"You will be more comfortable in bed, Jac." Grayson reasons with me.

"No!" I continue to struggle.

"Alright." He agrees. "I will pull the bed out of the sofa and make it up for you."

"Thank you." I sigh with relief when he sets me down in one of the recliners.

Grayson has just finished putting clean sheets on the sofa bed when his mom and dad waltz into the living room.

"What are you guys doing here?" Grayson asks with surprise.

"Helping." Nicole states firmly. "I am sure Jac would appreciate a bath after everything that has happened. I will help her wash and change clothes while Victor helps Zander with the internet thing."

Nicole disappears into the main floor bathroom while Victor goes into my office to turn on my computer. Grayson calls a local cell phone store and orders me a new phone telling the person on the phone that we will pay extra to have someone deliver it here today.

Once Nicole is ready for me in the bathroom, Grayson carries me in there and sets me down on the vanity before leaving the room. She helps me undress and into the tub where she lets me just lie in the hot water for a little bit.

"Why did Lucien react that way at the hospital?" I ask her softly, knowing that Victor explained to her what happened.

"He was inconsolable when he got to your house after work last night and you weren't home." She tells me. "Grayson told him that you had went to Baton Rouge alone to meet your cousin. Grayson told him he encouraged you to go alone because he thought you would be safe. Lucien managed to track down Charlotte and she told him that you had left the restaurant before noon. Lucien tried calling your phone but it went right to voice mail. That is when he called Victor and they called in your car with your last known location but no one in law enforcement could find it. Lucien didn't know that Zander was already tracking you. Lucien was convinced that you were dead."

"He frightened me at the hospital." I confess.

"He reacted badly." Nicole nods seriously. "I won't make excuses for him. He really cares for you Jac, but he has some issues he needs to deal with. No woman should be terrified of the man in her life."

"Thank you, Nicole." I tell her. "I can't tell you how much I need you right now."

"I am here, sweetheart." She kisses the top of my head affectionately.

She helps scrub me from head to toe before supporting me to dress in a clean pair of leggings, long sleeved t-shirt, and socks. Zander and several other guys are already in the house working on the possibility that Seth hacked into my internet.

Nicole helps me to lie down on the sofa bed, propped up slightly against several pillows. I am exhausted and want nothing more than to sleep but am terrified of the nightmares I will have if I allow myself to succumb.

Zander comes out into the living room and sits down on the edge of the sofa bed.

"How are you feeling, Jac?" He asks, his expression sincere but also concerned.

"Tired." I confess as I yawn to prove the point.

"Who has had access to the house since you bought it?" He asks.

"The Devereaux family, me, Nicole's' crew that was doing the remodel, and the guys Victor knew that were putting in the security system." I reply.

"There was also the pool company that I hired." Nicole tells him. "They were here recently as well."

"Was the gate up and functional before the construction started?" Zander wants to know.

"No." Victor answers as he comes out of my office. "Why?"

Zander holds up a small object in between two fingers for us all to see, but I am not able to make out exactly what it is.

"Someone bugged the house." Victor breathes in shock.

"It doesn't necessarily mean that someone you had hired did this, but it possibly means that Seth managed to sneak onto the property before Jac moved in to plant these himself. He is a known computer genius. The techs have also found proof that whoever installed the internet here left it exactly the way Seth needed it to monitor things here. Seth had access to all devices that log into the internet." Zander explains calmly, but I can see the anger he is controlling in his eyes.

"How do I fix this?" I ask anxiously.

"I am having all of the bugs removed." Zander tells me gently. "Your security guard, Alex, is a bit of a computer guru, and has offered to secure your issues with the internet. Alex has a military background and has successfully protected some important people. Put Alex in charge of your security detail, Jac, and he will keep you safe."

"Alright." I nod, finding it harder and harder to stay awake. Zander smiles at me knowingly before he pulls me into his embrace.

"You need to get some sleep, baby." He whispers so only I can hear him. "I know you are afraid of the nightmares, but remember that you are safe here. I am not going anywhere, I promise."

Zander pulls back and looks down into my vulnerable expression with a gentle smile.

"Grayson?" Zander says.

"Yeah?" Grayson responds.

"Come lay next to your sister." Zander suggests. "Close enough that she can smell you. It will help her to sleep and feel safe enough to keep the nightmares away."

Grayson plops down next to me on the sofa bed and covers up with an extra blanket that his mom gives him before pulling me into his arms so I can sleep with my head on his chest.

Chapter Thirty-Two

It is nearly noon by the time I finally open my eyes the next day. Grayson is standing by the windows looking out with his back to me and the house sounds quiet.

I sit up slowly, hoping to keep the dizziness away, and am happy to be able accomplish it so quickly upon waking.

"How are you feeling?" Grayson turns to me with a loving smile.

"A little better." I return his smile. "So, did they manage to secure our internet against Seth? Are all of the bugs gone?"

"Relax, sis." Grayson comes over and sits down next to me. "Alex is still working on the security issues with our electronics and the internet. He has hired three more guys for our security detail so they can work in two's around the clock."

Slowly, I make my way to my bathroom upstairs where I brush my teeth, wash my face before changing clothes. It already feels warm, so I put on a pair of jogging shorts, a t-shirt that I will be comfortable lying around in, and braid my hair.

I am careful as I descend the stairs as I can still feel the dizziness there just beneath the surface. Grayson has a cup of coffee ready for me on the kitchen counter next to my new cell phone.

"Is this ready to use?" I ask, eager to let Charlotte

know I am alright.

"Yep." Grayson nods. "It has the same phone number and everything was transferred from your cloud account to the new phone. I let Charlotte know you were alright. I didn't want her worrying."

"Thanks Gray." I kiss his cheek after he tells me what my six-digit passcode is to use my phone.

"You're awake!" Zander steps out of my office and into the great room with a relieved smile. "Feeling any better?"

I notice that he is still wearing the same clothes he rescued me in and that they are now quite rumpled. His well-trimmed beard is getting thick and he has dark circles under his eyes from not sleeping, I am going to guess.

"A little bit, yes." I smile at him, uncomfortable with my body's instant reaction to him. "You haven't slept."

"I'm working." He cocks his head to the side as he studies me with that penetrating gaze of his. My abilities don't work with Zander but I know for a fact he is aware of my response to him. I blush and move over to look out the window.

"Is there anything new you can tell me?" I ask, cursing myself for not being to stop my voice from trembling.

"Come sit with me, Jac." Zander appears behind me and leads me over to the sofa that Grayson has returned to its normal state. My blankets and pillows are gone for the moment.

Zander sets my coffee down on the table in front of the sofa with a chuckle because my hands are trembling so badly, I am in danger of burning myself.

"Seth told you about the guy who lived next door with the two daughters." Zander begins and at my nod continues. "Well, I have been doing some digging. The guy's name was Eli Garrett and he was a single father of two girls; Libby and Tia. There are numerous reports of child abuse that was never proven. Neighbors were interviewed by child services and most of them stated that Eli had a vicious temper and drank too much."

"Did you find pictures of Libby and Tia?" I ask curiously.

"Yes, why?" Zander looks at me uncertain where I am going with this.

"Seth likes tiny pubescent girls." I explain. "These two girls are the ones who introduced him to sex at a young age. He was at that impressionable age. These two girls are probably what gave Seth this preference."

"They were indeed small for their age. Pictures showed them to look underfed and even malnourished. The older girl, Libby, died of a drug overdose shortly after she turned fifteen and Tia is a prostitute." Zander explains. "Eli Garrett disappeared around the same time that Ava Pickett went missing. No one reported either one a missing person, but they both were gone."

"Seth all but confessed to killing them." I state thoughtfully.

"He wanted you to feel sorry for him." Zander points out, irritated. "He knows about your degree in forensic psychology so you are knowledgeable of what those situations were capable of doing to him."

"Yes, I know." I nod. "I also understand why he was drawn to my birth mother, Euphemia. She stood up to him. No matter how much he hurt her she didn't back down or stop trying to do what was right. His mother never stood up for him for very long. She allowed Eli to hurt Seth so he would stop hurting her. Seth couldn't forgive her for that. To him, Ava was weak. Of all of the girls that he raped before he went to prison, Euphemia was the only one who didn't dissolve into a hysterical sobbing mess. She was strong and never stopped trying to find her way home. Unknowingly, Phemie won his respect in a way. He knew that the guy who disposed of the girls he raped would come for Phemie and he couldn't allow that to happen. He wanted to keep her, so he moved her. It was that decision that led to her escape and his capture."

"If he had been able to keep you longer, he would have eventually raped you too." Zander tells me bluntly.

"Yes." I agree solemnly. "He knows in his mind that I am his daughter so it is wrong for him to treat me like that, but I look too much like Phemie. Eventually, he wouldn't be able to stop himself."

"Knowing this, will you stop going places by yourself and putting yourself at risk?" Zander asks me tightly.

"Well, I don't have much of a choice for the next ten days, do I?" I taunt him angrily. I am tired of everyone trying to lock me up like I am an errant child.

"You are acting like an errant child." Grayson states from across the room. "How do you expect the men in your life to react to that when you are constantly putting yourself in danger, Jac? Our father wants to hurt you just like he did to all of those other girls! You felt what our mother felt, Jac!"

"You told me to go by myself to meet Charlotte!" I yell furiously.

"We didn't know how closely Seth was watching

you!" Grayson yells back at me, just as angry. "I thought since you weren't going to be in New Orleans that you would be safe, but we played right into that monster's hands."

My phone pings and I see that Lucien has texted me. When I open his message, I see that there must be fifty previous messages from him. My stomach tightens anxiously as I remember his rage at the emergency department.

"Jac?" Grayson asks when he sees how much my face has paled.

"It's Lucien." I whisper as I set my phone down, too afraid to read his messages.

"Yeah, he has been messaging you since I got the new phone set up." Grayson explains to me. "I haven't seen him that messed up since his high school sweetheart, Tiffany, died. He thought Seth had killed you, Jac, after forcing himself on you. Lucien spoke to the doctor who examined Annie Wilson. Seth was so brutal with that little girl that she will never have children."

"I won't do anything like that again." I whisper as I get to my feet intending to retreat to my room.

Alex, Henry, Chris, and three other guys step into the house.

"How are you feeling, sweetheart?" Alex asks, relief mirrored on his face, as he walks up and hugs me tightly.

"Better." I hug him back.

"I wanted to introduce you to the three other guys I hired." Alex says. "This is Tony Raff, Cooper Labriola, and Daniel Sansbury. They are all marines and I can vouch for them personally. I have brought them up to speed on everything we know so far. We will be working in teams of two around the clock with one in the booth while the other patrols the house and grounds. We will be heavily armed at all times. Grayson introduced Rune to the new guys. I am sure you will not be pleased with this but until Seth Pickett is caught you will not be allowed to leave the premises without an armed escort."

"I understand." I reply meekly.

"For the time being, all six of us will not leave the property unless it is absolutely necessary. We have set up cots in the garage. None of us have wives that will miss us so until Seth is caught, we will all be here around the clock." Alex informs me. "The internet will be constantly monitored from the booth by whoever is on duty. If Seth tries to hack in again it will be seen. Only secure devices are allowed to use the Wi-Fi here. Under no circumstances, are you to open any email attachments without one of us helping you."

Tony Raff looks like he could be Italian with his dark hair that hangs down to his collar. He has a slim toned build and is only about five foot ten, short compared to the other guys. Cooper Labriola has reddish brown hair that he wears in a long spike on top. He has ice blue eyes and looks to be the youngest of the bunch. Daniel Sansbury has short black hair, big dark eyes that look nearly black, a five o'clock shadow with a cleft chin. He is nearly as tall as Grayson and although not as bulky as my brother he is certainly well-muscled. Daniel certainly looks the part of a hardened marine.

"Victor has instructed us to not allow Lucien on the property until he alone gives the go ahead." Alex informs me as he watches my expression carefully. Blushing uncomfortably, I look away as many different things rush through my mind at once.

Does Victor think Lucien is capable of hurting me? What happened after Victor left the hospital with Lucien? Do I need to do more than take a break from Lucien? Should I end it? Is Lucien violent?

"I think that is for the best." I murmur my agreement and when I look up at Alex, I see regret flash across his features.

I can't help but look at Zander after learning this piece of information, but his expression is closed. I guess I half expected Zander to look pleased.

"I think it prudent for you to not drive your other vehicle." Zander states thoughtfully. "It would be just as easy for Seth to hack into that one, if that is what we find from the wreckage."

"She could get an older car that doesn't have the computer to hack." Grayson points out with an eager grin. "I know a guy who just tried to sell Lucien and I a 1969 Dodge Charger. It is in mint condition and would be reliable transportation."

"You and I can go and look at it together if that is alright." Zander suggests to Grayson. "I would like to have it looked over before she buys it, just to be safe."

"Of course." Grayson readily agrees.

"Should I be concerned that Lucien will hurt me?" I ask Grayson telepathically.

"He just needs time to get his head back on straight." Grayson answers me vaguely without really answering my question. Grayson is nervous at my question and I can feel his need to hide his reaction to my question. I drop the issue because I am obviously not ready to face that one yet.

Needing to retreat, I head towards the stairs only to

have Zander grab my wrist gently.

"When was the last time you ate?" He wants to know as he perceptively watches my expression. I blush and look away from him before shrugging. "Jac?"

"I had a beignet finger at the restaurant with Charlotte." I confess. "I'm not hungry."

"It is Wednesday afternoon." Zander pushes. "That was Monday morning. Relax on the sofa and I will make you something to eat."

Too tired to argue, I sit back down on the sofa and sip my coffee with a sigh. Alex takes his security team back outside and Grayson starts doing something on his phone. As I look out the window, I see Rune outside with Freya, showing each other affection.

Chapter Thirty-Three

The next two weeks pass by agonizingly slow for me. The only time I leave the house is with one of my armed security guards to see the doctor.

I never thought healing from a concussion would take so long. The dizziness and nausea are daily companions for the first eight days after which they start to slowly fade away. Fortunately, my eyesight was not damaged from the airbag and my headaches go away about the same time as my other symptoms.

Grayson encourages me to not answer Lucien's text messages yet won't explain to me why. I get pretty much the same response from Nicole and Victor when I ask them about Lucien.

I heard Victor and Nicole whispering that Lucien has been off of work this whole time and I can't understand why the scene at the hospital would mean he couldn't work. I honestly don't know if I miss Lucien or that I am just so terrified of him now that I am afraid to suddenly see him without warning.

Grandma, grandpa, and Aunt Kyna all come to visit me while I am recuperating from my concussion. They don't ask me about my time with Seth, but instead I hear them whispering with Grayson about it. I am not upset because I honestly don't want to talk about it anyways.

Charlotte comes down to stay for a couple days and finally gets to meet Grayson. They hit is off just as quickly and the three of us have become quite close, almost as if we had known each other our whole lives.

Zander has been more at my house than away from it. He is still working the case he just seems to be doing most of it while he helps to protect me. When he does sleep, he does it for short stretches out in the garage with the other guys.

It is discovered that there used to be a bathroom out there in the garage once upon a time so when the guys aren't working their security shift, they are putting in a bathroom. I pay for all of the materials they need and within just a couple days there is a large bathroom for them to use. I will be able to use it for guests when I have pool parties as well so people won't be tracking water all through the house. It is a smart investment.

Zander and Grayson went to look at the 1969 Dodge Charger. It passed Zander's inspection so I am now the proud new owner of my very own muscle car. Its color is called bright blue and I like the color very much. It also has a white top with matching blue leather interior. It reminds me of the black car that Vin Diesel drove in the first Fast and the Furious movie.

I call the head of my human resources department for the New Orleans branch of Delta Logistics to see if there is room for another employee in the accounting department. I explain to her about my cousin Charlotte and that I would like her interviewed for a paid internship while she continues to go to school.

There is indeed room for Charlotte so I message my cousin about it encouraging her to send in her resume and school transcripts to the head of my HR department.

Seth, of course, has gotten away with his abduction of me. The tire tracks from the shack led them to a stolen car and he has not returned to the apartment his parole officer has as his address.

My car's computer was hacked, which is no big surprise. Seth led me to that specific area by the shack and disabled my brakes which caused me to crash.

Zander went to The Absinthe House where Seth's mother used to work for so many years but all he was able to learn was that she had an affair with a married man. The women that used to work with Ava have either passed away or moved away.

Alex, my head of security, and I have grown quite close over the last couple weeks. He is in his fifties with short snowy white hair and beard, large muscled build and tan from being outdoors so much. He is nearly as tall as Grayson. He has really become like a father to me over a very short period of time and I couldn't imagine my life without him in it anymore.

He was married when he first went into the marines shortly after high school. He was sent overseas when his wife was just a few months pregnant. There were complications with the birth and he lost both wife and daughter.

I can feel he has a tenderness towards me and I think it is because he thinks his daughter would be like me. If I were to choose my own biological dad Alex would definitely be it.

He has bought me many things to show how much he cares in just the last couple weeks. I now wear this beautiful sterling silver bracelet that has a Celtic knot on it with a tracking device inside it. The bracelet fits me perfectly and needs a jeweler to remove it. He goes to buy me food from restaurants when I have a craving for something. He saw my coffee mug with the Burt family crest on it, that used to belong to my birth mother, so he ordered a thick fuzzy blanket made with that on it.

I cook for the guys all the time and I especially make Alex's favorite dishes all the time, going out of my way to learn to cook ones I don't know how to.

The first week in May arrives and I am officially cleared by the doctor to return to normal activities now that my concussion has healed.

"Don't shoot me down before hearing my entire idea." Zander tells me the evening after my last doctor appointment while we are sitting on the sofa.

"That really isn't a good way to start trying to convince me to do something." I state as I raise my eyebrow at him questioningly.

"I mentioned quite some time ago that I have a yacht at Island Marina and that we could take it out into the gulf." Zander begins. "Grayson said that it would be fun to snorkel at the coral reefs off of the coast of Texas, Flower Garden Banks. We could spend a few days just boating around the gulf. My yacht has enough bedrooms for the three of us. It would be good for the three of us to get away for a few days and just relax."

"I don't really want to snorkel." I state anxiously. The thought of even swimming in the gulf makes me shudder.

"You like boating though and there won't be any storms on the gulf that we will need to worry about. Alex has agreed to stay and watch things around here with Henry so the other guys can have a few days off. Rune and Freya will be taken care of while you take a much-needed vacation to just unwind." Zander encourages gently.

"You asked Grayson to come along knowing I would say yes that way." I state as I look into Zander's perceptive blue eyes.

"I did." He confesses as I watch those blue eyes darken seductively. "Is that a yes?"

I blush and look away from him feeling my body respond to the erotic expression on his face. I nod slightly and am surprised when Zander leans forward and kisses my cheek tenderly.

"We leave first thing tomorrow morning." He tells me, his voice husky, giving me goose bumps. "We are all free to be gone for seven days. I will have my satellite phone on the boat so we can stay in contact with people in addition to the radio on the yacht."

"Alright." I look up at him feel my breath catch at the desire plainly visible there. Rising from the sofa I step over to the windows quickly to hide the tear of confusion that trickles down my cheek.

Lucien.

Why won't anyone tell me where he is? Why won't they tell me what really happened to him in the emergency department two weeks ago?

My instincts tell me that had Lucien and I been alone in that room that he would have hurt me, intentionally or unintentionally. The violence radiating off of him was vast in its intensity. I don't honestly believe that it was directed at me but my disappearance did something to him that I am not understanding.

"Jac?" Zander says my name softly as he comes up behind me and places his hands on my shoulders softly. "Are you alright?"

"Yes." I murmur, trying to keep the sound of tears from my voice and failing.

"Don't lie for me, baby." Zander turns me around and

pulls me into his arms tenderly. "I know you are confused and no one is answering your questions. I know what you witnessed frightened you. It will be okay."

My emotions cannot be held back any longer and I finally begin sobbing uncontrollably while Zander picks me up to cradle me in his arms. I cling to him as if he were my lifeline and I sob over my new fear of Lucien, my terror for Seth, my growing attraction for Zander and my uncertainty of the future.

He holds me on his lap while rocking me gently on the sofa until my tears finally subside into hiccups.

Grayson steps into the house, returning from somewhere and stops in place when he finds Zander and I on the sofa together.

"You need to tell her Grayson." Zander states firmly as he continues to stroke my back soothingly. "She can't move on without knowing."

"Mom and Dad told me not to tell her yet." Grayson argues.

"She needs to know." Zander pushes the issue. "Look at her! She has been holding this in for the last two weeks and feeling like whatever happened is all her fault. Tell her, man!"

Grayson sighs before he sits down in one of the recliners across from the sofa.

"Dad brought Lucien to his psychiatrist that day at the emergency department." Grayson begins. "This isn't the only time Lucien has had an episode like that. When Tiffany, his high school sweetheart died, we eventually had to have Lucien hospitalized for a time. He had a psychotic break. He was hallucinating, hearing voices, and was convinced that he could still see Tiffany. Lucien was given some medication to help him through that episode after you were found, but he just continued to get worse. He is currently at a psychiatric facility."

"This is all my fault." I state in shock. "If I had only called Lucien to let him know I was going alone none of this would have happened."

"No, Jac." Grayson sighs regretfully. "None of us should have let you and Lucien grow close like you did with his past. We all just hoped that he would stay the Lucien we know and love. The psychiatrist says that anything could have caused him to snap. It's not your fault. That's why we didn't answer your questions about Lucien and we encouraged you to not text him back."

"Is there a family history of mental illness in the Devereaux family?" I ask curiously.

"Mom has a brother who is schizophrenic." Grayson confesses. "He has been institutionalized since he was in his early twenties."

"I don't know what to say." I whisper sadly. "All of my schooling and I never suspected that Lucien ever had anything wrong with him. He seemed so strong, so normal."

"He has been normal, pretty much, since he graduated from high school." Grayson shares. "The doctors said that we would know for sure if Lucien made it to his thirties without another episode. I am so sorry, Jack. We really had no idea. We thought; hoped, that he was fine."

"You are sure your fine with us going out on the yacht with Zander?" I ask Grayson, not caring at this point if I offend Zander or not.

"I am." Grayson nods firmly. "We all need to get away. Do something happy. Make new memories. Move on."

"Alright then." I nod as I wipe the tears from my cheeks.

"Give Zander a chance, Jac." Grayson blurts, obviously not caring that Zander is right there. "He has more than shown how much he cares for you. You guys have a lot in common and I have overheard things from your thoughts I wish I hadn't concerning your attraction for him. You deserve happiness too, sis."

"Grayson!" I exclaim, blushing furiously and hiding my face in Zander's chest.

"I will see you guys in the morning." Grayson says before kissing me on the head. "I love you Jac."

"I love you too, Grayson." I whisper sincerely.

Chapter Thirty-Four

I am up extra early due to the fact that I had nightmares most of the night. Zander is on the sofa sleeping when I tiptoe downstairs to make a pot of coffee and feed the wolves. Rune and Freya have been outside since Ted's friend completed the den for them about a week ago. Freya has accepted me and she will come up to me to get affection occasionally but she prefers to it to be just her and Rune.

I am still stunned over what I learned about Lucien. It feels like it is my fault that he is in the psychiatric hospital. Thinking back to what happened that day in the emergency department, I now know for certain that I never would have been able to trust him again. I felt the violence, I felt the rage and knew that if he had been able, I would have been physically hurt by it. Lucien was dealing with too much.

I take my coffee quietly out to the patio and sit to watch the sun come up. Henry nods at me as he walks by on his patrol of the yard. When I look over at the bowls of meat I filled for Rune and Freya I notice that they are still full. Where are they?

I gaze around the yard and in the far corner of the yard, closest to the den, I see them; mating. Freya must be in heat then. Ted will be glad to have wolves to relocate up north.

"Have you ever seen wolves' mate before?" Zander asks from right behind me.

"No." I blush when he sits down next to me and looks

at me with those seductive blue eyes.

"They weren't doing that yesterday so I am guessing Rune will be busy with her for the next couple weeks." Zander states thoughtfully.

"It sounded like he hurt her." I comment softly.

"I have heard that pain helps her to ovulate." Zander explains.

"Are you going to make go snorkeling?" I ask anxiously.

"No." He shakes his head. "I want you to overcome your fear, not be traumatized because I forced you to do something you weren't ready for."

"Are we going to be safe sleeping on your boat?" I continue as I twist my fingers together.

"Yes." Zander answers me patiently. "That is why I wanted to take my yacht because I have an alarm system that will wake me up if something gets within a certain distance."

"You know, just because Grayson told me to give you a chance doesn't mean I will be encouraging you in any way." I drop my gaze from Zander and curl into a ball in my chair.

"I wouldn't have it any other way, baby." Zander's husky voice washes over me, making my body respond in ways I wish it wouldn't. He laughs softly as he watches me squirm in my chair to ease the intensity taking hold.

"It's not fair, you know!" I exclaim furiously as I look up at him. "You read me better than I can read you, and I am the empath!"

"I have wondered about that because you call

everyone else around you out on what they are feeling or lying about but you have never done it to me." Zander's expression turns serious.

"I can't." I whisper uncomfortably.

"Grayson?" He asks and I shake my head. "That is part of why you are afraid of me."

"Yes." I breathe honestly.

"You could see it as a break from everyone's emotions overwhelming you all the time." He brings to my attention. "You don't have to be on guard around me, you can just relax."

"I *always* have to be on guard around you." I laugh sarcastically. "If I weren't, I probably would have lost my virginity to you long ago."

"You wound me, Jac." Zander murmurs with an impish smile. "I fully intend to make you beg me to take that from you."

"Zander." I scold him breathlessly as I blush a deep crimson and look away as my heart begins to race.

"Am I interrupting?" Grayson probes from the doorway uncertainly.

"No!" I exclaim vehemently while Zander just laughs.

"Just teasing your sister, Grayson." Zander responds honestly.

"She is never going to agree to date you if you keep doing that." Grayson points out logically.

"I am weakening her resolve." Zander states confidently.

"How did you sleep, Jac?" Grayson inquires seriously.

"I thought I heard you talking up there last night."

"Nightmares." I whisper uncomfortably.

"Seth?" Grayson questions softly and I nod quietly.

"You need to talk to someone about what happened." Zander pushes, again. He must have told me this a hundred times in the last two weeks.

"I can't." I shudder at the thought. "He's my biological father and I am having nightmares that he is trying to rape me."

"Why didn't you say anything?" Grayson exclaims angrily. "You don't have to suffer through that alone, you know!"

"Well, you can't sleep with me forever." I point out rationally.

"Then you need to do as Zander says." Grayson pushes firmly. "You know he is telling you the truth and when you start working in law enforcement you will have to tell victims the exact same thing, Jac!"

"I'm not a victim!" I scream furiously as I flee towards the house and run right into Alex who pulls me into his arms.

"You need to stop living in denial, Jacqueline." Alex whispers to me bluntly. "Henry checks on you several times throughout the night and has told me you have been having nightmares a lot. It's time that you do something about this."

"Alex!" I whimper as I cling to his shirt fighting tears.

"No, Jacqueline." Alex cups the back of my head tenderly. "I know a woman who you will feel comfortable talking to. This is not up for discussion. Do you understand me?"

"Yes, Alex." I reply obediently.

"That's my good girl." Alex kisses the top of my head before turning his attention to Zander. "I better never hear that you pushed Jac too far too soon. I understand what is going on between the two of you, but you also know how fragile she is. She needs a strong man in her life. One that will put her needs first. I might not be her real father, but Jac will never find one that loves her more than I do."

"Yes sir." Zander nods to Alex solemnly. "Duly noted and I won't disappoint you."

"Come on, let's go make some breakfast." Alex leads me towards the house. "I'm famished and you need to eat."

A tear trickles down my face at Alex's heartfelt words to Zander. My own adopted father, William, never declared or showed such love to me and I knew him my whole life.

I have a couple loaves of bread to use before leaving today so I decide to make a big batch of French toast with sausage links and scrambled eggs. Alex works on the sausages and scrambled eggs while I get out an electric griddle to start on the French toast.

We have breakfast ready in a half hour and all the guys crowd into the kitchen except for Henry who is out in the booth watching the camera feed. I make him a plate first, while it is still hot, to make sure he gets his fair share before everyone else inhales the rest.

Alex is waiting for me when I get back from bringing Henry his food and wordlessly points to the kitchen. Obediently, I make myself a small plate and join Alex outside at the patio table. He watches to make sure I eat enough because he knows that my stomach tightens up during stress.

"Zander and Grayson can clean up the kitchen." Alex orders before he turns to me. "Go on upstairs and take a long hot shower. You will feel better afterwards."

I nod and make my way up to my bathroom to do just that.

After my shower, I finish packing and carry my one suitcase downstairs. Zander and Grayson are already waiting on me so we can head over to the marina. I give Alex a big hug and kiss his cheek before following Grayson out to Zander's car.

Zander drives a Monte Carlo from the eighties that is completely restored. What is it with guys and their cars?

I stare out the window from back seat as we drive through New Orleans to get to the marina. Grayson and Zander are chatting in the front about snorkeling and the possibility of putting in at Galveston for dinner one night.

It has been so long since I have been out on my boat that I find myself getting excited to experience the Gulf of Mexico for the first time. I wonder what kind of a yacht Zander has and how he can afford such an expensive toy on a detective's salary. It would be rude to ask but if his is newer and larger than mine than that means it cost a lot, possibly millions.

Island Marina is a nice place to dock your boat. Zander insists on checking on mine to make sure there was no damage from its transport across the country. Everything is just as I left it and I am eager to take it out by myself sometime soon, after this situation when Seth is gone.

Zander's yacht is a Bandido 75 and looks like it may be about ten years old or so, but still probably cost him at least a million dollars. It has three staterooms, an open wide flybridge, and a comfortable salon providing ample space to enjoy long voyages. This yacht is definitely ocean worthy whereas I would never take mine out there with it only being forty-six feet and this one being seventy-seven feet.

The colors in the salon are white and taupe with glass accents. It is open and spacious with plenty of room for quite a few people. There are three decks in addition to the sleeping cabins, the galley and the head down below.

I am surprised to see that there is a large screen television in the salon as well as in the master cabin and even a washer and dryer. My adopted parent's yacht had all of these bells and whistles, but I am still surprised that Zander can afford all of this luxury.

Zander shows us to our staterooms, and I am not surprised when he puts Grayson in the one on the other side of the yacht from the one I will be sleeping in, right next to his. I unpack my suitcase and then join Zander up on the flybridge deck as we move out of the marina towards the gulf.

It is a beautiful day to be out on the water. The sun is shining, there is a light breeze blowing, and it is warm without being too hot. By midafternoon we are out in the gulf far enough that we can't see the shore. Zander lowers the anchor and Grayson excitedly jumps right into the water. Apparently, the thought of predators in the gulf does not make my brother nervous.

Zander stays on deck with me although I can guess he would like to go for a swim as well. I can see a few other boats out on the gulf as well but they are pretty far away and don't appear to be coming any closer to us.

I hadn't realized how much I missed Puget Sound

until just now. The abundance of whales and orcas up there were always a joy for me to be able to watch from the deck of my boat. The playful dolphins that would race the yacht and jump out of the water making their adorable noises. I could look out onto the shore and see all sorts of wildlife out there as well; moose, elk, bear and the occasional wolf. Bald eagles flew overhead, swooping down to scoop a fish from the water.

"It is rude of me to ask, but I am just too curious." I blurt before I lose my courage. "How can you afford a yacht like this being a detective?"

"It was handed down to me from an older cousin." Zander confesses. "He buys a new boat down here in the gulf every year. I got this one from him about seven years ago."

"Very generous." I shake my head with a laugh. "Here, have a two-million-dollar yacht."

"He would give me one every year if I let him, but I like this one." Zander confesses. "It is the first one he gave me for my twentieth birthday and I don't need a new one."

"You have never told me about your family." I state as I look at him, wishing I could read him.

"I really don't have much family." He shrugs. "My mom and dad live in California and we don't really stay in contact. My grandparents are all gone and my cousin is really the only one I talk to once in a while."

"You never wanted to have your own family?" I ask.

"Oh, sure." He nods. "I just haven't found the girl I want to settle down with. Most of the women I have seen over the years do not understand the demands of my job. They usually break up with me before it gets too serious because they don't feel like they are a priority."

"Being in law enforcement is an all-consuming career." I agree. "It isn't for everyone."

"That is part of the reason why you chose it." Zander shares with me honestly. "You never really felt close to your parents and didn't really have any friends growing up so you chose a career path that wouldn't leave room for loneliness."

"Your perceptiveness never ceases to amaze me." I exclaim uncomfortably.

"I bet you have wondered since meeting your twin whether or not you want to pursue the exact branch of law enforcement you were interested in prior." Zander continues. "Now, you want time for family and friends because you are suddenly surrounded by people that you connect with."

"You can quit now." I laugh. "I guess I am happy I don't have access to that mind of yours."

"You would definitely blush a lot more around me than you do presently." He chuckles huskily. As if on cue, I turn a light pink at the seductive teasing in his voice.

Chapter Thirty-Five

The first day passes pleasantly. Grayson spends most of his time in the water or tanning on the deck. Zander insists that I do no cooking since I am technically on vacation and I must confess that for a guy he is a pretty good cook.

I spend most of the day just enjoying the serenity of nature as dolphins play around the boat, seagulls fly overhead or just the sound of the water lapping against the boat.

Grayson turns in early after his day of swimming and tanning and I opt to just sit underneath the cloudless sky and enjoy the full moon. The darker it gets out the more the moon creates a silver path across the water that appears magical.

Zander is with me on deck, but he seems to enjoy the solitude as much as I do and we don't speak. I do catch him watching me thoughtfully from time to time, but I know better by now than to ask him what he is thinking. It will only make me blush.

To be honest, part of the reason that I am not retiring to my stateroom is because I am afraid to go to sleep. The nightmares I had last night were way to realistic for me to go through again.

Sometime later, I startle awake when Zander picks me up in his arms and I realize that I must have fallen asleep.

"I'm awake." I push against his chest, feeling near panic at the thought of going to bed.

"You fell asleep quite a while ago." He informs me as he carries me down below despite my protests. "I know why you are avoiding going to your room, Jac."

"Please Zander." I plead, though he ignores me and carries me into my stateroom where he places me on the bed.

"There is a connecting door between our rooms." He shares with me. "I gave you this room on purpose so I will hear you in the night. I am a light sleeper, baby."

"Alright." I nod reluctantly.

"Go ahead and open it after you get changed for bed." He strokes my cheek tenderly before he disappears through the connecting door into the master suite.

I change into a dark blue cotton nightgown that swirls around my knees in ruffles and then open up the door without looking inside his room.

I am so exhausted from staying awake too long that I slip right to sleep, but my tiredness doesn't keep the monster away.

I am back in the shack. I can hear the fire crackling in the wood stove and the rain pounding on the metal roof.
When I look around the small room, I pray I am here alone, but no such luck. Seth is tending the stove and turns when he notices I am awake.
"You came back to me, baby." Seth exclaims eagerly.
"No!" I shake my head and try to run for the door but he beats me there with a wicked grin.
"My Phemie!" Seth whispers, his expression looking manic.
"No! I'm not Phemie!" I protest but he tosses me down on the bed, pins my wrists above my head, parts my legs, and I scream,

and scream, and scream.

"Jac!"

I fight, scratch, kick, punch, and try to free myself from the monster trying to hold me down on the bed.

"It's Zander, Jac."

"I'm not Phemie!" I whimper. "I'm not Phemie!"

"Jac, wake up!"

Finally, I dare to open my eyes and I am confused when it isn't Seth holding me down on the bed, leering down at me, but it is Zander. He has bloody scratches on his face, bare chest, and arms; no doubt from me in the midst of my nightmare.

"Zander?" I whisper, guilt and shame rushing through me at how much I hurt him in my endeavor to escape Seth.

"Your safe now, baby." He croons to me, pulling me into the safety of his arms.

"I'm sorry!" I exclaim. "Did I do that to you?"

"I'm fine, Jac." He insists. "It's just a couple scratches. Tell me what happened."

I shake my head and try to push him away because the last thing I want to do is relive the horrible nightmare. He holds me gently yet firmly, not allowing me to escape him.

"Come on, baby." He continues to croon to me softly. "Tell me about it. Talk about it and let it go."

Knowing he will not relent until I do as he asks, I finally tell him the nightmare, every excruciating detail. He holds me tenderly while I sob, stroking my back soothingly and murmuring in my ear softly.

My tears eventually dry up and I hiccup until I finally calm down. Fatigued beyond memory, I yawn widely but struggle to stay awake still too scared to allow myself rest.

Zander rolls onto his back and pulls me into his embrace so I am lying on his chest. He has a light covering of hair on his chest with a thin trail leading down into his boxers. He is not as tall as Lucien but his shoulders are wider, his biceps are bigger and Lucien had no hair on his chest or stomach. Zander has a natural golden glow to his skin that most likely comes from an Italian heritage or perhaps Spanish.

I shouldn't be wrapped around another man so soon after Lucien, but I feel safe for the first time in a long time and can't force myself to move away.

"Sleep, baby." He kisses the top of my head. "I am not going anywhere. You're safe."

The bright morning sun shining in my face slowly rouses me from a deep dreamless sleep. I stretch languidly and suddenly realize that I am all wrapped around a nearly naked Zander, who is still sleeping soundly.

Gulping anxiously, I stare down at his strangely innocent face and wonder how I am going to get out of bed without waking him up. Just as I attempt to disentangle my limbs from his he opens those sexy blue eyes and smiles up at me.

"Good morning." His throaty rumble washes over me and affects me instantly.

"Good morning." I return, not recognizing the erotic sound of my own voice as I try to scramble off of the bed quickly.

With almost no effort, Zander smiles wickedly and rolls us over so I am on my back beneath him.

"Rushing away so soon?" He teases me as he caresses a lock of my hair off my face. I nod, speechless at the blunt sexuality on his face. I push on his biceps, hoping to put some space between us but he just chuckles deep in his chest as he nuzzles my neck.

My nipples pebble, I am breathing in pants, and I can feel that I am actually wet between my legs.

"Zander." I moan, my own voice husky with need.

He presses himself into my hip and instead of frightening me it just seems to pull me into his spell even further.

"Please?" I beg, although I don't know if it is to stop or continue.

Taking my wrists in one of his hands he pins them above my head as he gazes down at me, his blue eyes dark with his own desire. He is panting as well as he straddles my legs with his and leans down to dominantly claim my lips with his.

Lost.

I am lost.

I suckle his tongue into my mouth, no longer bashful, but acting on the overwhelming need coursing through me, my need, not his. He growls low and deep and kisses me roughly, possessing and claiming while I arch up into him, wanting; needing.

He lifts his head, breathing so hard it is like he is running a marathon, and gazes down at me. When I realize he isn't going to kiss me anymore I open my eyes and pout up at him as I try to rub against him.

"Jac!" He scolds me roughly as he parts my legs quickly and presses his engorged length against me. "I am near where I will not be able to stop and you are not ready yet."

My brain instantly registers that he feels much larger pressed against me than Lucien did and that acts like a dash of cold water. Flushing with shame, I struggle against his hold on my wrists as I realize just how quickly I proved Zander right. I would indeed beg him for it.

"Easy, baby." He whispers soothingly into my ear as he kisses my neck softly. "What was that look just now?"

I shake my head in horror at him knowing what I was thinking.

"Come on." He encourages me gently.

"I can't." I shake my head. "You don't want to hear my ignorant thoughts."

"Tell me, then you won't be ignorant." He nibbles on my earlobe, making me shiver. So easily he can rouse my desire with just a simple touch.

"You feel a lot bigger than Lucien felt when we were kissing in the hot tub." I confess as I turn my face away bashfully, unable to look into his eyes.

"Look at me, Jac." He tips up my chin. I can see that he is reading my expression to tell him why I said that. Flushing anxiously, I try to free my chin and look away but he just tightens his grip slightly.

"A lot of innocent girls are afraid of that." He states as he continues to search my face and then he suddenly nods to himself. "You are little, just like the other girls. Grayson told you about Annie." He perceptively connects the dots.

How does he do that? He is right every time!

Blushing furiously, I nod quietly and feel a tear trickle down into my hairline.

Zander rolls away into a sitting position with his back against the headboard and pulls me on his lap so I am straddling his hips.

"I will never hurt you." He vows solemnly. "Those girls were raped, Jac. There will be a lot of pain when that happens and yes, it is worse when they are tiny like that. All I have to do is look at you and you get wet for me. I will not be too big for you if we have sex."

"If?" I ask, noticing right away that he didn't arrogantly assume 'when' we will have sex.

"If." He nods as he traces a finger across my full lower lip.

"How do you know that I am wet?" I blurt before thinking. Zander laughs softly.

"You squirm your hips." He shares with me honestly. "It is not a familiar sensation for you yet."

I blush and glance away from him.

"Honestly, I don't know if I can let you be my boyfriend." I state.

"Why not?" His expression is amused.

"You told me after saving me from Seth that if I were your girlfriend you would blister my ass until I sobbed for you to stop." I point out in a huff.

"I would." He nods his head seriously, gazing at me intently. "You squirmed, baby."

"Excuse me?" I exclaim haughtily.

"In the car that day." He tells me earnestly. "Right after I told you that, you squirmed."

"Oh god!" I gasp as I realize he is right once more and try to scurry off of his lap. What is wrong with me?

He flips us over and pins me down gently.

"You aren't as afraid of me as much as you are afraid of how I make you feel." He tells me bluntly.

He leans down and kisses me forcefully until I am whimpering for more.

"Naughty and innocent and all mine." He whispers into my mouth before nibbling on my lower lip.

Chapter Thirty-Six

Zander takes a cold shower in his master bathroom while I put on a bikini and matching sarong before making a pot of coffee. Grayson groggily joins me up on deck with a mug of his own a few minutes later where I am enjoying the dolphins playing next to the yacht.

"You got more sleep than I did and yet you still look tired." I tell Grayson with a grin and he just grunts at me while sipping his coffee.

Zander doesn't come up on deck for some time and I am just wondering what he is doing when he pokes his head in the stairway.

"Breakfast." He yells before disappearing back down below. Grayson is apparently awake enough to charge down to the galley for breakfast. I laugh softly as I follow along more slowly.

Zander has made breakfast burritos complete with homemade salsa and pickled jalapeno peppers. I refill my coffee and can feel Zander staring holes into my back. I don't have to be an empath to feel that his lust from earlier this morning has not eased at all. This makes me feel strangely powerful and makes me want to be naughty as well. It is a good thing that Grayson is on this trip!

Speaking of which, my dear twin is wolfing down his breakfast as if he had not eaten at all yesterday. Shaking my head, I grab myself a couple burritos and spoon some salsa over the top before sitting down.

"Did you have any nightmares last night?" Grayson asks after pushing away his empty plate. I tense up and set my uneaten burrito down on my plate, no longer hungry. Zander shakes his head in irritation before he plucks me out of my chair and cradles me on his lap.

"Eat, baby." He encourages me softly before he turns to Grayson. "She did. I managed to hear her right away and it only took me a few seconds to wake her up. I made her tell me about it and then after a little while she actually went back to sleep because I stayed in her room."

"Seth?" Grayson's expression now reflects his helpless rage at my suffering. Zander nods.

"Come on, Jac." Zander's thumb strokes my stomach softly. "You need to eat."

I nibble on my burrito until my tension eases enough that I can finish all of my breakfast.

"What is the plan for today?" My brother wants to know as he gets up from the table to clean up our meal.

"I thought we would head closer to the coral reef." Zander shares. "It is still two days away or so."

"You didn't wear your swim suit yesterday." Grayson points out to me. "Planning on going into the water later?"

"Nope." I relax back in Zander's arms and gaze at my twin challengingly.

"I was just asking!" He exclaims. "No pressure! Someone's feisty this morning." Grayson grumbles as he turns his attention back to cleaning up.

"He has no idea!" Zander whispers into my ear softly.

"Telepathic brother over here!" Grayson yells in disgust.

"Then stay out of my head!" I yell back at him in frustration.

"I don't need to dig, remember?" He grouses. "Put up a mental barrier or something. You might as well be broadcasting what you guys did this morning."

Moaning in mortification, I hide my face in Zander's chest while he throws back his head and laughs long and hard.

"Sorry, man." Zander finally is able to say after he stops laughing. "I'm still not used to your abilities. You need to cut your sister some slack though. She is struggling with just me right now and I don't think she can multitask enough to block you out at the same time."

"Noted." Grayson sighs. "I will put up my own wall, thanks."

Most of the rest of the day passes with us speeding closer to the coral reef they want to snorkel around. I spend some time enjoying the sun while my sun block keeps my porcelain skin from burning. There are also the dolphins to watch as they swim alongside the yacht, leaping from the water.

Grayson lays out on the deck, his tan getting darker and I am jealous because as a red head I cannot get a deep tan like his. Zander can also get darker in the sun without looking like a lobster.

This is the least emotional overload I have had in a very long time. Since I cannot feel what Zander is feeling I never have to worry about overload and now that Grayson is blocking me, I can't feel him either. I can just relax.

We stop the yacht shortly before the sun goes down and Zander drops the anchor before making dinner. I have to admit that I am pretty impressed with how much work

Zander is doing on this trip. He has insisted that I need a vacation and so far, has not allowed me to lift a finger.

Within a short amount of time he has managed to make medium-rare ribeye steaks, baked sweet potatoes with a dinner salad. My stomach grumbles since I have not eaten since breakfast and I can feel my appetite returning to normal.

I can feel Zander's eyes on me as I practically inhale my food with gusto, the first time in a while.

"That was delicious, thank you." I tell Zander sincerely.

"That was the best steak I have ever had." Grayson exclaims. "I don't know what your secret is, but whatever it is you should have your own restaurant."

"My Italian grandmother showed me how to cook." Zander shares proudly.

"Well, you will make some woman very happy someday." Grayson jokes.

"I sincerely hope so." Zander strokes my thigh under the table.

I really try not to blush but fail miserably. Luckily, Grayson doesn't even look over at me as he continues to clean up.

The next two days pretty much pass in a routine. We spend the daylight hours moving closer to the coral reef and spend the evenings talking as we look at the sky or listen to the whales beneath the boat.

I have not had a nightmare the last couple days and I admit to feeling more rested during the day. Zander hasn't kissed me again either, but instead watches me perceptively and gives me the distance he seems to think I need.

My thoughts still return to Lucien. I only knew him for a few short weeks but I thought we connected pretty quickly. The fact that I didn't go all the way with him is a blessing because I would definitely be regretting it.

I want to move slowly with Zander, if I decide to move at all, but my bodies reaction to him is so intense I fear I will just throw myself at him in a moment of passion.

We are above the coral reef on the fourth day and Grayson is eager to go snorkeling. There are a few other boats in the vicinity and Zander doesn't want to leave me alone on the yacht.

"Come sit down here with your feet in the water." Zander encourages me. "The water is clear and you will see something long before it is close to you. Grayson and I will stay close. If you need us just tell Grayson mentally."

I am anxious but since I am sitting on the boat and he is right, the water is clear enough for me to see through I can talk myself into being calm. There are a few other people snorkeling nearby when Zander and Grayson slip into the water.

Zander is true to his word and they stay pretty close to the yacht. A pod of dolphins even gets curious and come to play with the people snorkeling near the reef. One swims right up to me while I sit there and makes its noise at me playfully.

The day passes wonderfully and I have to admit that this trip was exactly what I needed right now.

Zander actually lets me help him make dinner. He has chicken alfredo planned with broccoli and he lets me slice up and sauté the chicken while he takes care of the rest. He makes his own alfredo sauce and watching him in the kitchen is really quite impressive. It is obvious that he knows what he is doing and is very good at it.

After dinner, Zander pours me a glass of wine to enjoy while we stargaze with Grayson. The peace and solitude of a night on the water is a wonderful experience. The wine is a sweet white and I find that I like it very much. I sip it slowly because the few times I had alcohol to drink it went right to my head.

I am slowly sipping my way through the second glass when I hear a voice in my head.

"Good evening, my daughter." Seth's voice slides through my thoughts.

I accidently drop my wine glass on the deck as his voice causes me to instantly feel terrified. Jumping to my feet my first instinct is to run away, but there is no way to run away from his telepathy. Grayson and Zander are both on their feet with me but are looking at the panic on my face with confusion. Looking at Grayson without saying anything, I point to my head as I begin to cry.

"I hope you are enjoying the Gulf of Mexico." Seth continues. *"I can't wait for us to see each other again."*

I watch the shock on Grayson's face as he hears Seth's last statement to me in my thoughts. He shares with Zander what is going on and I see Zander's face tighten with rage.

Raising my hands questioningly at Grayson I quietly try to ask him what I should do. Grayson makes a motion with his hand of keeping my mouth shut so I do not respond to Seth but instead curl up on Zander's lap where I hide my head under his chin.

"Alright, Jacqueline." Seth murmurs happily mentally. *"We will see one another very soon. You can't hide*

from me for long."

I am so rattled by Seth speaking to me inside my head, miles away from me, that I am starting to feel nauseous and I can't stop trembling violently. Grayson softly repeats what Seth is telling me in my head and I can feel Zander's anger in his tension.

"*Oh!*" Seth's voice continues suddenly. "*Don't be a naughty girl with Detective Cody. Save it for me, Jacqueline.*"

I am off of Zander's lap and vomiting violently over the side of the yacht until I dry heave, Seth's laughter ringing through my head manically.

"It's time to go home." Zander states ferociously as he picks me up and hands me to Grayson who cradles me in his arms. "I need to call your dad."

After a long satellite call with Victor, Zander joins us back on the deck where Grayson is holding me tenderly on his lap.

"Anything else?" Zander asks. I shake my head, still trembling violently from knowing Seth has been somehow listening in to my head without my knowledge.

"How did I not feel him listening?" I whimper. "I always feel you Grayson."

"I don't know, sis." He hugs me tighter. "I can only guess that he has really worked hard at it over the years."

"We will head for home at first light." Zander informs us. "Your dad will meet us with an armed escort at the marina."

He gently takes me from Grayson and brings me down to his stateroom instead of mine where he lies me down on the bed. Slipping into my stateroom he grabs my nightgown off of the bed to bring it back to me. I change in his bathroom before climbing into his king-size bed, still shaking like a leaf.

After he strips down to his boxers, he climbs in bed with me and pulls me into his arms.

"I will keep you safe, baby." He vows.

I cling to him as if he were my last lifeline and bite my lip to keep the tears at bay.

Chapter Thirty-Seven

The three days it takes us to reach Island Marina pass in a daze for me. I have withdrawn inside myself to a little spot in my head where no one can reach me, not even Seth. It is safe here. No one can hurt me here.

Having my most dreaded fears confirmed by the monster who shares my DNA was too much for me to bear. I eat when Zander or Grayson hold me on their lap and make me, otherwise, I stare out at the water unresponsive.

Frigidly cold water all over me suddenly brings me back to reality and I find myself in Alex's arms as he gazes at me anxiously. I look around and discover I somehow made it home from our trip to the gulf without realizing it.

"There's my girl." Alex wraps me in a towel and hands me off to Zander so he can change into dry clothes. Apparently, when nothing else worked Alex turned on the icy cold water in the shower and doused us both to shock me out of my stupor.

My house is full of people. Nicole, Victor, grandma, grandpa, aunt Kyna, Charlotte, all of my security guards, plus a bunch of armed guys I have never seen before.

"What is it?" I ask anxiously as I can feel everyone holding back their fear about something, something I am not supposed to know.

Alex comes back into the house wearing dry clothes and takes me from Zander before sitting down on the sofa with me on his lap.

"Seth contacted the police." Alex tells me while a lot of those gathered around us gasp in shock. "He has had a little girl for the last three weeks and no one realized she was missing. It was assumed that she ran away again. She is from a local foster home. He has told Zander's team that he will release the girl alive if we trade you."

"Seth hasn't been the one to kill the girls." I point out. "Why would he start killing them now?"

"Because now he wants you." Zander states. "My guess is that he will do anything to get his hands on you, including killing the girls himself."

"We have had no leads as to where he is holding them." Victor sighs in frustration. "After all this time."

"I think I might know where he is keeping them." Charlotte speaks up uncertainly. "My grandmother used to live on a large property out by river road and when she passed away, she left it in trust to her daughter's children; me and Seth. I haven't been out there since before my mom died. The property is in my grandmother's maiden name; Schmidt."

"Do you remember how to find it?" Zander asks her hopefully.

"It is down around a corner from the Destrehan plantation." Charlotte explains. "There is a dirt road that looks like a two-track just a mile or so down the road. Take that and there will be another two-track that goes off to the left, that is the driveway. It is pretty long. The house really isn't all that livable but I would guess he keeps the girl in the old bunker that's behind the old carriage house."

"I will call in for a helicopter it is quicker and we may be able to surprise him that way." Zander says.

I don't feel Seth picking his way through my

thoughts but that doesn't mean he isn't doing just that. Using all of my mental strength, I slam up a mental barrier against my mind and reach for the pad of paper on that table next to me.

I look up at Grayson and he has his head cocked to the side as he wonders what I am doing. I point to my head, at him, and then shake my head no.

In big letters on the paper I write;

SETH

Grayson nods that he understands as I continue to write.

Seth has been listening in to my thoughts and he may very well have listened to us discussing raiding his grandmother's property. You must be prepared that he already knows of your impending arrival.

I hand the paper to Zander as I struggle to keep my wall up in my head against Seth. Victor and Zander step outside where I cannot hear their conversation.

"Your attorney has been trying to get a hold of you." Alex informs me as I curl up on his lap with my head on his chest.

"Did he say what he wanted?" I ask, not wanting to move from his embrace. This is the safest I have felt in days.

"No. He made me promise to have you call him as soon as you got home." Alex explains.

Henry hands me my cell phone that has been sitting in the kitchen during my trip to the gulf. I turn it on and then call Mr. Sorenson wondering if it is something serious. He tells me right away, without small talk, that the audit for Delta Logistics has been completed. John has been embezzling billions from the company for years. My adopted father's assistant shared that before he went missing my father and John had had several heated arguments. John has gone missing.

They are working on returning the money he routed into several off shore accounts back to the company. The board requires my immediate presence as they need to vote in a new chief executive officer. John has been officially terminated from the company and his shares have been added to mine. Technically, this means that I am the new CEO of the company but I am truly not interested.

"I need to fly to Seattle." I state as I grudgingly get off of Alex's lap with a sigh. I explain to Alex what has happened and why my presence is required.

"Me, Henry, Chris, and Daniel will accompany you." Alex states.

"I will call Trevor, my adopted father's old assistant." I explain. "He can have the company jet here in New Orleans ready for us and I will have him book us a suite at the Four Seasons up there. The security there should be acceptable."

Alex follows me upstairs while I pack and call to make our travel arrangements. I step into my bathroom and change into a business suit; a knee length skirt, silk blouse, and matching suit jacket. My hair goes up in a French knot, I apply tasteful makeup and jewelry, and wear heels.

I step out of the bathroom and watch Alex's eyes go wide at my appearance.

"You look all grown up, Jac." He whispers.

"They are expecting a woman not a little girl." I explain as I laugh softly. "I really have no interest in running the company. I fully intend to encourage the board to vote in Joseph Faust to the position of CEO. He was close with William almost the entire time my father ran the company."

Alex grabs my suitcase and follows me back downstairs. Zander whistles when he sees me step into the living room.

"What's going on?" He asks, surprised. "Where are you going?"

"The CEO of my company, John Van Asselt, has been embezzling from the company." I explain and watch Zander's face pale for some reason. "Since I am now the major shareholder, I am needed in Seattle to meet with the board so we can vote in a new CEO to replace John."

"You aren't going alone." Zander states, not asks. I step up to him with a sardonic smile.

"No, I am not going alone." I murmur as I nuzzle his cheek. "Alex, Henry, Chris, and Daniel are coming with me. The company jet is waiting to take us to Seattle where we will be staying at the Four Seasons."

Zander has changed clothes and looks the detective again. My fingers brush his badge that is attached to his belt and I am instantly drawn into a brief vision. Zander falling to the floor, bleeding and unconscious. That's it.

I back away from him my face paling to a sickly gray color. Thankfully my grandparents and aunt Kyna are outside on the patio as they are not aware of my abilities.

"Baby?" Zander questions uncertainly as he stays where he is standing. I look up at Grayson who is watching me anxiously.

"What did you see, Jack?" He prompts me softly.

"Zander. I didn't see what happened to him but when you guys go on this raid you fall bleeding and unconscious to the floor. I didn't see what happened to you or who does it but I can only assume it is Seth." I whisper, feeling suddenly sick.

Are all the people I care about doomed to be hurt or die?

Zander steps up to me and pulls me into his arms. He kisses the top of my head gently.

"You warned me, baby." His husky voice washes over me confidently. "I will be expecting this and will be prepared, alright?"

"Helicopter is ready and waiting." Victor states.

Zander tips up my chin and kisses me possessively right in front of everyone before he strides out the door without a word.

"I want you to stay here while I am gone." I turn to Charlotte seriously. "Seth is not above using you as leverage to get to me and my security can keep you safe here. Promise me you will stay here with Grayson?"

"I promise." She pulls me into a hug and squeezes me tightly.

"Good. Feel free to use my bedroom while I am gone." I kiss her cheek. "I am sure you will appreciate the privacy. Grayson can really get on a girls' nerves." I tease my brother.

"Hey!" He exclaims as he hugs me too. "I love you. Come home safe."

"I will." I nod seriously. "I will have my laptop with me on the plane. If you hear anything about the raid, I need you to email me right away. Don't hide anything from me, please."

"I will let you know as soon as I hear anything." Grayson tells me solemnly.

Alex leads me outside and places my suitcases into the back of his suburban where the guys have already thrown their duffel bags. I sit in the back, of course, with Daniel on one side and Henry on the other. Chris sits shotgun in the front while Alex drives. The windows of the suburban are tinted so dark that people outside cannot see in.

Delta Logistics has their own hanger at the airport and Alex parks right inside. I am escorted onto the waiting jet with my men. The plane taxies down the runway to take off as soon as we are buckled.

I have never flown in the company jet before and I am surprised at the luxury. The white leather captains' chairs are soft as butter, the blonde wood tables have drink holders and other slots to hold cell phones or grooves for laptops and tablets. There is a flat screen television on one wall.

Alex sits right next to me and tells me to tell him about Seattle. He keeps me talking the entire flight so that I cannot concentrate on my worry for Zander. By the time the jet lands in Seattle, Alex pretty much knows about my childhood, everything I know about Delta Logistics, John Van Asselt, and anything else I think he may need to know.

Unfortunately, by the time we land in Seattle I have not heard anything about Zander from Grayson. There is a possibility that Victor will not tell Grayson anything because he is protecting me.

Alex seems to have connections here in Seattle because we are met at the airport by a couple guys with a black suburban for us to use while we are here. I am ushered into the back seat and the guys take the same seats as we had previously.

Traffic at this time of the day is gridlock and it takes us over an hour to reach the hotel. Daniel parks the suburban, while the other three escort me inside. Alex walks at my side with his hand gently on my arm and Chris and Henry a couple steps behind.

I can feel the surprise and curiosity of the people we pass in the lobby as they watch the young woman flanked by a security detail. No doubt, they are wondering who I am why I don't look familiar.

Trevor has reserved one of the four suites on the top floor because you have to have a key to access that floor on the elevator. The woman at the desk checks us in without batting an eye and is coolly professional.

Daniel joins us at the elevator and the four of us take the long ride up together. Alex stands with me outside the suite door while the other three do a sweep of the rooms to make sure I am safe to enter.

I step into my bedroom where I hang up my business suits, put away my clothes, and freshen up from the flight. Out in the living room of the suite I call Trevor to inform him that I have landed and will be headed to Delta Logistics shortly. He lets me know that the board is waiting on my arrival.

Chapter Thirty-Eight

It feels strange to be in my dad's office building after so long. I haven't had a reason to come here since he went missing. I just let Uncle John take care of everything since he was Dad's business partner.

The security guard at the desk in the lobby, of course, does not recognize me but is instantly at attention when I show him my identification. He quickly makes me my ID badge as well as temporary passes for Alex, Chris, Henry, and Daniel.

We take the elevator up to the twelfth floor where the large boardroom is located. Trevor meets me right outside the elevator and escorts me and my guards into the large room where everyone is already gathered in groups chatting together.

As soon as I step up to the head of the table and set down my briefcase the room goes silent as they all turn to look at me curiously. Alex, Daniel, and Chris stand behind me at attention, not taking any chances.

Mr. Sorenson, even though he is not directly connected with Delta Logistics, is present to my left since he is my personal attorney. I use him for his knowledge and trust him implicitly because my adopted father, William, did also.

"I want to call this meeting to order and ask that everyone take their seats, please." I state in a loud professional voice.

"I want to apologize for my delay in arriving. Unfortunately, I was unreachable for the last couple days." I begin sincerely. "I know everyone is concerned in light of recent events and I want to put everyone's minds at ease. Yes, John Van Asselt is missing but I have been assured that some of the money that was embezzled has been located and will be returned to the company. We will bounce back from this."

"I know that everyone wants to know my thoughts on the new Chief Executive Officer. No one should be surprised that I defer to my father, William's, thoughts on this. Joseph Faust has been at my father's right hand almost since the beginning. Joseph has always managed to balance putting the company's interest first while at the same time protecting the jobs of our employees. We have always been a family-oriented company because we care about those who work so hard for us. Just like my father, Joseph has given himself a pay cut when times were hard in order to allow more of our people to keep their jobs because they desperately needed them. We are family and under Joseph Faust we will stay a family. Our employees work hard because we value them, because they are important to us, because we take care of them. Let us continue this tradition and vote in Joseph Faust for Chief Executive Officer."

The board applauds my speech and I can feel that my three guards are quite impressed as well, having never seen this side of me before. My phone vibrates in my briefcase and when I take it out, I see that it is Grayson. I hand the phone to Alex and point to the hallway. He steps out of the meeting to talk to Grayson since I cannot.

I can feel that at least ninety-five percent of my board members agree with my choice of choosing Joseph Faust for CEO. The other five percent are being persuaded by those around the table who wholeheartedly agree with my choice. Once the conversations die down an anonymous vote is cast on the iPad's in front of every board member on the table.

The tablet in front of me pings when the vote is complete and I am pleased to see that only one person voted against Joseph. He has become the new Chief Executive Officer and I know he will make my father's memory proud.

Joseph comes up to shake my hand and thank me for the recommendation. He is in his early forties with a wife and three boys. He looks the typical business man type in his expensive suite, well-trimmed hair, manicured hands, and impeccable manners.

"Thank you, Jacqueline." He smiles at me affectionately. "I almost didn't recognize you."

"I suppose it is time I grew up." I laugh softly. "There is no need to thank me Joe. I merely did what William would have wanted me to do."

"I am really sorry about your parents, Jacqueline." Joe exclaims sincerely. "I heard that John hid from you how they really died. I hope you have found some happiness with your birth family in New Orleans."

"I have, thank you, Joe." I smile at him sadly. "I can only guess that their deaths were somehow connected to the embezzlement. I have discovered that I have a twin brother and we have become very close. My birth mothers' parents, an aunt and a cousin on my birth father's side. William and Zacari were wonderful parents and will always be remembered with love."

"I have your contact information if I come across any issues that I need to consult you about." Joseph states. "Now that you are the sole owner of Delta Logistics everything will have to be ultimately approved by you."

"We can have virtual meetings any time you have the need Joe." I assure him. "I know William really wanted me to take over for him one day but I confess that my true love lies in forensic psychology. I should be done with my masters in just a couple more years."

"What do you intend to do once that is completed?" He asks curiously.

"I am not sure what branch of law enforcement, whether it be just the police department or the FBI, but I want to help catch criminals." I share with him.

"How long will you be in Seattle?" He inquires politely.

"I will probably fly back tomorrow morning." I reply. "I have a lot going on right now. My attorney will be having all of John's belongings removed from his office because the police want it for their investigation. The office, obviously, is now yours. Please make yourself at home."

"Thank you again Jacqueline." Joe states before hurrying away.

Alex steps up to me his expression grave now that I am alone.

"Zander." I whisper and Alex nods.

"He was stabbed during the raid. He is in surgery right now and they won't know anything until he gets out. The girl didn't survive. Seth must have known that you wouldn't give yourself up. The medical examiner said that she had been dead for a couple hours before police arrived."

"This is my fault." I breathe sadly.

"You know that is not true." Daniel steps up to me,

his voice no-nonsense. "She was already dead before you had the chance to go to him."

"I know that you probably want to fly right home, but Zander is in surgery and our hurrying home right now will make no difference to how this turns out." Alex states. "Seth is on the run and he is aware that Zander is in the hospital. He will be waiting for you to show up there to check on Zander. Our first priority is to keep you safe, Jac."

"You are right." I nod as I wipe away a tear. "I have been selfish in my decisions lately and way too impulsive. Zander wouldn't want me there if it meant I was in danger."

"Let's get you back to the hotel." Daniel suggests with a warm smile.

I shake hands with all of the board members on my way out and reassure them that I will be in constant contact with Joseph. Most of them offer their condolences on the passing of my parents, which touches me deeply.

Alex drives the suburban up to the door and I am ushered into the back seat between Henry and Daniel while Chris sits in the front passenger seat. At the hotel, it is the same routine. Chris parks the suburban while Alex, Henry, and Daniel escort me up to the suite in the elevator. An older couple tries to share the elevator with us but Daniel scares them away with a simple glare.

"That wasn't very nice you know." I tease Daniel. "You could have just spoke to them. Words work just as well."

"Daniel doesn't like words." Alex remarks sarcastically. "You should feel honored if he feels the need to speak to you instead of a grunt or glare."

"Well then, I do indeed feel honored." I state sardonically and Daniel just grunts at us.

The guys discuss what to order for room service and by the time everyone has chosen what they want to eat a virtual buffet is delivered to the room. Alex surprisingly pours me a glass of wine with my dinner.

"You are letting me drink?" I ask incredulously.

"It will relax you enough that I am hoping you will actually eat something." He replies bluntly. Daniel and Henry both laugh at his response while Chris toasts me with his glass of Coke. None of the guys will drink when they are on duty so I am the only one to drink a whole bottle of wine apparently.

I ordered a simple mushroom burger with sweet potato waffle fries for my dinner. I swear the guys each ordered two entrees a piece and I watch as they inhale everything quickly. True to his word, I manage to eat a lot more thanks to the wine, just like Alex suggested.

"Did you and Zander talk about his family yet." Henry asks me as he watches me closely. He is one of my younger bodyguards and is only in his early thirties. He really is quite attractive in a bad boy sort of way with the bandana he wears on his head, the tattoos, the earrings, and his nearly scraggly beard.

"He said he learned to cook from his Italian grandmother." I reply uncertainly. "He mentioned that a cousin had given him the yacht. He said his cousin buys a new one every year and that this one was a gift for his twentieth birthday."

As I look around at my bodyguards, they are all gauging my reaction to this conversation closely. Whatever I am going to learn I am not going to like.

"John Van Asselt is the cousin that bought Zander the boat." Henry states softly as he watches my face apprehensively. I feel all color drain from my face at this new piece of information.

"How long have you guys known this?" I want to know, trying really hard not to explode with the rage surging through me suddenly.

"The same day Zander saved you from the shack." Henry fills me in honestly. "We were waiting for him to tell you himself."

"Was Zander watching me for John?" I ask, my fury getting the better of me. "If John is somehow responsible for my adopted parent's death, is Zander only around because he was asked to?"

"John and Zander have had absolutely no contact since long before you flew down to New Orleans the first time." Daniel tells me. "We made sure of it before we allowed you to go with him on the gulf."

"I don't understand!" I exclaim angrily. "This is just a coincidence?"

"I am guessing that Zander was afraid to tell you because it would cause you to distance yourself from him." Chris brings up logically. "Zander has been doing his own digging and he had to have discovered your relationship with John and your feelings for your business partner."

"Why would he be afraid of me?" I voice, my low self-esteem showing. "He is confident and attractive enough he could have any woman he wanted."

"When you meet *her* you just know." Alex explains thoughtfully. "If Lucien wouldn't have had his schizophrenic break him and Zander would still be fighting over you."

"I'm not special." I shake my head. "I'm just an

ignorant girl who has never dated before I came to New Orleans."

"You are definitely special." Daniel murmurs. "You have this intriguing blend of seductive innocence that is just driving those two boys crazy; add in your curiosity and feistiness that shows up unexpectedly and they are hooked."

I blush a deep pink, not expecting this from Daniel who is always so quiet. The rest of the guys nod their agreement with his perception.

"You notice more than I give you credit for." I whisper bashfully.

"It's the quiet ones you have to worry about." Henry discloses sarcastically.

"Fuck you, Bennett." Daniel returns as he throws a pillow at Henry's head.

My phone rings and when I look down at it, I see that it is Grayson, with an update on Zander, no doubt. Alex reaches over and answers the phone putting it on speaker.

"Hey Grayson, I put you on speaker." Alex states simply.

"Zander is out of surgery. He will survive the stabbing just fine. Seth missed anything vital by just a breath. Unfortunately, he suffered a traumatic brain injury and is in a medically induced coma. They haven't done surgery on his brain yet because they say at this point, he might be fine with a diuretic and rest. Only time will tell."

"Thank you, Grayson." I reply woodenly.

"Stop blaming yourself, sis." He exclaims emphatically. "You warned Zander something was going to happen to him. He survived the stabbing because he was expecting it. The doctor said the brain injury could be much worse."

"Zander is related to my Uncle John, Gray." I share, still unsure how I feel about this.

"Give him the benefit of the doubt, Jac." My brother reassures me. "Let him tell you his side of the story."

"Your dad is alright?" I ask. "No one else was hurt?"

"Dad is fine." Gray tells me. "Seth was stabbed with the same knife he attacked Zander with. So far, he hasn't gone anywhere for treatment. I will call you if there is any change. Good night, sis."

"Good night Grayson." I declare.

I finish my second glass of wine and Alex pours me another with a grin.

"I think I am very nearly already intoxicated." I slur, trying to sound prim and proper and failing miserably. All four of them throw their heads back and laugh at my buzzed state.

"So, what's your deal with Zander anyway?" Daniel asks me bluntly. "You made out with Lucien in the hot tub but keep Zander an arm's length at all times."

"Wow." I frown at him, feeling slightly less inhibited because of the alcohol. "Zander says I just pretend to be innocent, that I am really just a naughty girl waiting to come out."

The other three guys are avidly watching this exchange between us, just waiting to see what I will say.

"Are you naughty?" Daniel asks, his tone of voice definitely candid.

"He said something that shocked you but you

reacted to in a way that frightened you." Daniel continues when I don't answer his question. I nod and color slightly.

"He got angry at me when he got me back in the car after finding me at the shack." I confess uncertainly. "He told me that I was lucky I didn't pull that stunt if I were his girlfriend because he would put me over his knee and blister my ass until I sobbed for him to stop."

Daniel chuckles at my reply and leans forward so he is closer to me.

"The reason you are holding him away is because one; that pissed you off that he would say such a thing and two; a part of you was curious and turned on by his threat." Daniel tells me, his voice now soft and soothing. "You might be feisty at times, Jac, but you are a meek girl who really is just looking for a strong man who can step up and take care of her. You are attracted to Zander because he is a man's man who won't take your crap. Why do you think you and Alex have connected so strongly?"

I shrug and shake my head because I hadn't really thought about it.

"Alex is a strict father figure." Daniel explains. "You could say he is an alpha male, just like Zander and the rest of your bodyguards are. You run right over Grayson and did over Lucien too because they allow you to. Alex puts his foot down and has no problem showing you your place."

The truth of his statement resonates inside me and I flush uncomfortably.

"Why are you telling me this?" I ask him, keeping my gaze averted to the floor.

Daniel kneels in front of me and tips up my chin, forcing me to look at him. His expression is warm and kind.

"Because we are grown men with experience." He explains tenderly. "Zander has been so straightforward with you that he has nearly scared you away. You can be a good girl who enjoys being naughty. We checked out Zander. John is his only skeleton in the closet. He has no mental illness in his family tree, he has dated enough for us to know he is never violent or abusive. He is a good guy, Jac. You can trust him."

"What about Lucien?" I ask anxiously.

"Lucien is schizophrenic." Daniel tells me honestly. "You didn't fall in love with Lucien. He was a hot guy who was safe for you because he was your twin's brother. Lucien allowed you to control him. He was safe."

"What if Zander doesn't make it?" I look into Daniel's dark eyes imploringly.

"Grayson gave you good news." He reaches up and strokes my cheek softly. "You saved his life by warning him otherwise Seth would have probably sunk that knife in his heart. He has a head injury that the doctors don't think needs surgery, just rest."

Chapter Thirty-Nine

"Come on, Jac." Someone whispers into my ear persistently for probably the tenth time. When I attempt to roll away from this annoying voice I am scooped out of bed and carried out to the living room where I hear several chuckles.

Moaning against the horrible headache I hide my face under the chin of whoever is carrying me, to protect my eyes from the bright sunlight that is just killing my head.

"I think our girl has a wee bit of a hangover." I hear Henry exclaim in amusement.

"Maybe only a half a bottle of wine next time, Alex." Chris laughs.

"Do you have a headache, angel?" Daniel murmurs to me gently. I nod, keeping my face under his chin. "Want some breakfast?" He asks. My stomach rebels at the thought and is instantly queasy so I shake my head in the negative.

"You are going to have to eat at least a piece of toast, little girl." Alex states in his commanding tone. "We can give you something for the headache but you need food in your stomach first."

"Okay." I whisper grudgingly, knowing better than to argue with Alex.

Henry makes a call down for room service and orders tons of food while my stomach roils at the thought of smelling it all. I pray I won't be sick when it all arrives. Daniel helps me to sip some water while we wait for breakfast to arrive.

Daniel holds off on eating his breakfast and instead encourages me to eat a piece of toast before washing down a handful of vitamins.

Only after he is certain I will not be throwing up does he set me next to him on the sofa and eat his own meal.

It really surprises me that Daniel has been taking care of me so compassionately these last couple days. He hasn't been one of my bodyguards for long but he has been extremely quiet and he always feels intimidating. I was uncomfortable just greeting him at first.

My headache eases somewhat and my stomach ache as well so I make my way into my room to shower and dress. The hot water feels like heaven and really goes a long way in making me feel better.

I put on another one of my business suits for the flight home, twisting my hair up into a French twist with very sophisticated makeup and jewelry. When I step back into the living room, I look a lot better than I feel and I get nods of approval from my guys.

Breakfast is already gone and they are waiting on me to check out. I have already called to have the jet ready as we take the elevator to the lobby. Check out is smooth and soon we are driving through gridlock traffic to the jet.

It is nearly noon by the time we board the company jet and take off for New Orleans. I buckle myself in with a moan of misery, I am never drinking again.

"Nightmares last night?" Alex asks me pointedly.

"No. I think I was dead last night." I reply softly, holding my head gingerly. "I don't think I have ever slept that deeply."

"That is the only reason I encouraged you to drink the wine." He explains. "I, of course, didn't mean for you to drink quite so much, but you were very anxious and you suffer nightmares more under those circumstances."

"I appreciate the lack of nightmares, truly; however, my headache doesn't thank you. I think you have cured me of having any wild partying tendencies." I share, keeping my voice quiet.

"Good." Alex nods proudly. "My plan was a success then." He laughs.

I manage to sleep a little on the flight and by the time we arrive in New Orleans I am almost feeling somewhat human.

Stepping into my living room, I sigh with happiness and sink down on the sofa with my head on one of the cushions. It feels so good to be home.

"You are back sooner than I thought." Grayson comes into the living room from the stairs. He must have been working out.

"They only needed my vote for the new Chief Executive Officer." I reply with a smile and bolt upright anxiously when Lucien appears next to Grayson.

I am instantly terrified as I remember the violent, out of control Lucien at the hospital a few weeks ago. Daniel and Alex instantly place themselves between Lucien and I protectively.

"You deserve an explanation." Lucien states calmly. I can feel the guilt and shame rolling off of him.

"He isn't schizophrenic like the doctors had originally thought." Grayson interjects. "I don't think that what happened in the ER was his fault."

I look between the two of them in confusion. How could it not be his fault?

"I started hearing a strange voice in my head after I realized that you were missing." Lucien confesses. "It continued the entire time you were gone and was so loud and insistent at the hospital I guess I just cracked from trying to ignore it." Lucien explains.

"That is a symptom of schizophrenia." I enlighten him softly.

"It is." Lucien agrees. "The doctors have put me through a battery of tests these last few weeks and realized that I am not schizophrenic. They cannot explain the voice I heard but can only tell me it is not the result of a mental condition. It was assumed since my maternal uncle is schizophrenic that I must be also. I am sorry about what happened and I understand why you are afraid of me."

"I believe it was Seth." Grayson states hesitantly. "I have been hearing him as well. I think Seth is trying to separate you from all the men trying to protect you to make it easier to get his hands on you."

I look up at my bodyguards and they are all giving each other a look that instantly tells me they are suffering the same thing.

"Can a telepathic really communicate with people who are not gifted?" I ask curiously.

"Yes." Charlotte steps into the living room from upstairs. "My grandmother was a very powerful psychic. She was able to strengthen her abilities over the years by practice. She was just an empath when she was a young girl. She was also able to have visions, move objects with her mind, and be telepathic with everyone by the time she died. I remember if I was doing something naughty when I was at her house, I would hear what sounded like my conscience encouraging me to behave myself. It wasn't until after she died that my mother told me about it. If my grandmother could make me think that the voice in my head was mine after years of practice then Seth is much more powerful than all of you probably realize. The extent of his abilities could be endless."

"I think I need to talk to Lucien, alone." I express hesitantly. "Please."

"Why don't we step into your office?" Lucien suggests. I nod and follow him into my office, closing the door behind me.

I step over to the window and gaze out as I attempt to gain the courage to say what I must. My stomach hurts with the anxiety rushing through me.

"You are going to tell me we can't be together anymore." Lucien beats me to the punch.

"Yes." I whisper as I turn around with tears streaming down my cheeks. Lucien's need to hold me washes over me but he keeps his distance. "I can't deny that I found you attractive. I knew instantly that the main reason I allowed us to get to know each other in that way was because you were safe. You are my twin's brother. What I didn't consider was what happens if things don't work out between us? That puts Grayson and your parents in an uncomfortable position. I don't want that. I like that we are all family. Grayson loves you very much and he loves me very much too. It isn't fair for us to put him in a position where he has to have negative thoughts about either one of us. I will not force him to take sides between us."

"I agree." He nods his head solemnly. "I had actually thought about the same thing but was afraid to say something with everything that was going on. You needed me and I couldn't hurt you during all of this."

"I'm sorry." I look away from him shamefully.

"You don't need to be sorry, Jac." Lucien steps up to me and tips up my chin. He smiles down at me as strokes my cheek softly. "This was a mutual decision and it is early enough that we can still be close friends without any uncomfortable feelings. I know it is none of my business but are you going to give Zander a chance?"

"I don't know!" I exclaim as I look up at him nervously. "It just seems wrong to talk to you about this."

"I have worked closely with Zander for a few years now and he is really a great guy." Lucien confesses. "He is one of the best detectives we have in the sex crimes unit. I can't see him using you. Grayson told me about your trip on the Gulf of Mexico. It sounds to me that Zander intends on taking things slow with you and that is just what you need. I have never known him to be this serious about a woman before. It's been kind of joke around the precinct that he is a Casanova. That means you are pretty special."

"Uncle John is Zander's cousin." I state uncertainly. "My bodyguards say that they haven't been in contact with each other since before I flew down here to meet Grayson. It really makes me nervous though because John was just caught embezzling billions from Delta Logistics and is missing."

"Let Zander tell you his side of things." Lucien repeats what everyone else has told me.

"Well, since that seems to be everyone's general

consensus then I will do that." I agree. "I see you have met Charlotte."

"She's a great girl." Lucien states as he suddenly feels nervous. I raise my eyebrow at him questioningly and he actually blushes.

"Tell me how you really feel." I laugh at him sincerely. "Please, feel free. We all deserve happiness. If you can make Charlie happy after all her loss and loneliness than I am behind you one hundred percent. I am guessing she feels the same interest in you?"

"Yes." Lucien says hesitantly. "She said it goes nowhere until you and I talk first."

"Let's go tell her the good news then." I pull him towards the living room. He must have really fallen hard for Charlie because he is still blushing and seems uncertain.

My bodyguards are having a pow wow in the kitchen when I step back into the great room while Grayson chats with Charlie.

"You don't mind if I steal her for a second do you?" I ask Grayson with a mischievous grin. Grayson looks up at Lucien questioningly as I pull Charlie aside so I can whisper in her ear privately.

"Not that you need my blessing with Lucien, but I am giving it nonetheless." I tell her so only she can hear. I am not surprised to see my quiet cousin blush a pretty pink color as she gazes down at the floor shyly. I know without her telling me that she hasn't dated either because of her ability to move objects with her mind and the resulting fear of rejection. I catch the look her and Lucien give each other and it warms my heart to know that I made the right decision.

"Any word on Zander?" I ask Grayson, trying not to worry.

"He is out of the coma." Grayson explains. "I just got off the phone with Dad who is up at the hospital. The diuretic reduced the fluid on the brain and he was awake briefly. He asked about you and then told Dad he didn't want you risking your safety by coming to see him. He made Dad promise to tell you that his threat after he found you at the shack still stands should you think of disobeying him."

Daniel and Alex both roar with laughter at Grayson's words because they know what Zander's threat is. The thought of being spanked like a naughty child makes me color with embarrassment.

Grayson raises his eyebrow at me questioningly and I shake my head at him.

"Don't ask because I am not telling you." I exclaim tightly. "Enough people know about it as it is."

Chapter Forty

The next couple of weeks pass slowly with me not leaving the house for any reason. Seth is still at large with no clues as to where he may have gone and due to that fact, my bodyguards are on high alert. Grayson and my guys continue to hear a voice in their heads trying to get them to do as Seth wants. Grayson has been teaching them how to block Seth out with some success.

Charlotte is still here at my insistence. I had a couple of my bodyguards take her back to Baton Rouge so she could pack more of her things from her apartment. I just don't trust that Seth will leave her alone. There is a chance that he will use my new relationship with my cousin to try and force me to come to him.

Lucien spends a lot of time at the house so he and Charlotte can get to know each other. Charlotte has moved into my office and sleeps on the pull-out sofa sleeper now that she will be here longer.

Everyone wants to throw Grayson and I a birthday party but I finally convince everyone to put it off at least until Zander is out of the hospital. Ultimately, I would rather celebrate my nineteenth birthday with Seth and John behind bars.

May 30th, our birthday, comes and goes with only a special dinner at the house with my bodyguards, Grayson, Charlotte, our grandparents, aunt Kyna, Lucien, Nicole, and Victor. I managed to buy a building for Grayson so he can open up his fitness center without having to rent one. He accepts it grudgingly at first then gets excited because he can open his business that much sooner.

Grayson has taken all of the home movies our grandparents had of our mother and put them all on one disc for me to enjoy.

My grandparents give me my mother's journals that she kept over the years. Aunt Kyna gives me a beautiful black opal necklace. Nicole and Victor give Grayson and I an oil painting of our mother that they had done from a photograph. It is large enough for us to put above the mantle of the fireplace. My bodyguards have all gone together and given me a certificate for scuba diving lessons. When I protest rather vehemently Alex explains that all of the lessons are given in a pool until I feel confident enough in moving on. Trust my bodyguards to push me to grow somehow. Charlotte hands me a computer disc and when I look at it in confusion, she explains that she has been working on our family tree for the last couple weeks. She has been working with someone online to create a family tree from my DNA matches. I am touched that she spent so much of her time making me such a thoughtful gift. She very proudly tells me that she has the family tree traced back to the sixteenth century.

Zander is released from the hospital, but since he lives alone the doctor only releases him with the understanding that he stays with family. In preparation for Zander coming to stay I have had the workout equipment from the third bedroom moved out into the garage and turned it into a guest room.

I purchased a queen size bed, chest of drawers, bed side tables, bedding, and anything else one would need for a bedroom. I made the mistake of having Lucien sleep in my bed too soon, even though we were never intimate I am not ready to invite Zander there.

Zander is released after two weeks in the hospital. It is a hot June day when Victor brings him over after he is discharged. I am stunned at how pale and tired he looks.

"Do you want me to help you upstairs?" I ask Zander anxiously. "You can rest better up there away from all of the noise."

"No, baby." He smiles at me affectionately. "I think noise is just what I need after being cooped up in the hospital for more than two weeks."

I bring a pillow and a blanket out to the sofa that way he can recline if he feels tired.

"Can I get you anything? Are you hungry or thirsty?" I probe softly.

"You can sit here next to me, Jac." He insists.

"I was afraid I lost you." I state tentatively. "I can't even make up my mind if I want to make our relationship official or not."

"I think that is my fault for messing with your head while you were with Lucien." Zander confesses with a sigh. "I was a jerk. I wanted you for myself and had no problem competing for you. I used your attraction for me against you and that was wrong. Not to mention, my spanking threat is what is most likely keeping you from making a commitment. I'm sorry, Jac."

"Why would you be sorry about the spanking threat?" I point out logically. "You meant it."

"I'm sorry because it has frightened you away from me." He reasons with me.

"I brought Alex, Daniel, Henry, and Chris with me to Seattle and they had a little something to say about you." I share with him, glazing down at my fingers nervously.

Zander tips up my chin with a tender smile.

"Do I want to know?" He asks seriously. I nod and wonder how in the world I am going to find the courage to tell him what they said.

"They checked you out and told me you really have no skeletons in your closet I need to worry about, aside from John Van Asselt being your cousin." I share with him, but hold up my hand when he opens his mouth to speak. "Let me finish. I will hear your side, just please let me say this before I lose my nerve. They brought to my attention that even though I am feisty I crave a stronger man in my life, not one that I can just walk all over. They said that is why I have grown so close to Alex so fast. He has become like a father to me, but he is what they called an alpha male, like you and the rest of my bodyguards are. That is why I crave spending time with him and am so comfortable with all of you. I tend to act impulsively and get myself into trouble. They said that I wouldn't be happy with someone who just lets me get away with whatever I want."

"You appreciate it that I am an alpha male." He states, not questioning me. I nod.

"They know about what you told me when we were leaving the shack." I confess. "They say I am trying to deny the truth to myself. That I think it makes me a bad girl for how I reacted to it."

"And?" He prompts me gently.

"Daniel told me that I can still be a good girl. He said it is ok for me to be a good girl who enjoys being naughty." I whisper, looking away from his perceptiveness.

"Well. That is not what I expected to hear from them." Zander chuckles as he leans forward and nuzzles my neck. "I will need some time to heal before I will have the stamina to spank you being naughty, however."

"Zander." I color a deep red at his teasing.

"I missed you, baby." He nibbles on my earlobe. "I'm glad you stayed home and didn't put yourself at risk."

"I missed you too." I lean into his caress.

"Does this mean I can finally tell people that you are mine?" He whispers into my ear, his husky voice driving me crazy.

"Yes." I reply breathlessly.

"Oh, baby." He croons. "You have made me a happy man."

"I admit I was very upset to learn that you were related to John and didn't tell me." I share, after our intimate moment passes. "Everyone told me to let you tell me your side. The guys told me that you haven't been in contact with him since before I even came down here to New Orleans."

"I found out you shared ownership of Delta Logistics not long after we met at the park that day." He tells me. "At that time, I didn't think it was important to tell you that I knew and then we started to get to know each other, sparks were flying between us and it got to be a question of when to tell you. I heard about how your relationship with him took a turn for the worse. John and I have never really been close. My grandmother and his mother were sisters. The extent of our relationship was to get together and have dinner a couple times a year when he was working out of the New Orleans office. Neither him nor I have any other close family so we stay in contact out of obligation, I guess."

"I was so upset when I found out he lied to me about

how my adopted parents died." I tell him. "I guess those feelings were just transferred to you because you are his family. John didn't tell me that they were murdered before they went down in their yacht. Then to find out he had been embezzling billions from the company all of these years. He was trying to keep me under his thumb and got quite upset with me when I wanted to stay with Grayson's family instead of with him. My first thought was that John was using you to keep tabs on me and I was furious."

"Victor shared a lot of that with me while I was in the hospital." Zander says. "I wish I could tell you where he would go to hide, but our family doesn't have a piece of property like Seth's does. He more than likely is traveling under an alias. I can talk to whoever is in charge of the investigation if you want. I am sure I have enough information about him that it may help them."

"I will let my attorney know." I nod. "He will know who is in charge."

"I would think that John wanted to keep control of you because if he controlled you then in effect, he controlled your shares of the company as well." Zander tells me. "He didn't want you discovering his secret."

"No, I am sure he would have liked nothing better than to continue to steal money from his own personal bank." I exclaim sarcastically.

"So, what happened up in Seattle? I never heard." He asks curiously.

"The board gave me John's shares of the company so I am the sole owner of Delta Logistics. I only want minimal involvement so I encouraged the board to vote in someone that worked with my adopted father, William, for years, as the new CEO. He will take good care of the company's interests."

"I'm sure John is furious." Zander states thoughtfully. "Do you have any new ideas you want to incorporate into the company?"

"I do actually." I share with him excitedly. "We are losing out on some excellent employees because they can't afford the schooling. I have created an internship program throughout the different departments, both paid and unpaid, where Delta will pay for these people to get their degrees in order to continue to work for us, at least for a certain time period. They will be required to work for our company by contract. Once that contract is completed, they would be free to look elsewhere to work or continue with us. My cousin Charlotte is the first to be able to enjoy this internship and scholarship program."

"Have you thought about that property that was left to Charlotte?" Zander asks. "Maybe there is a legal loophole that could be used to make it only hers."

"I have actually." I sigh. "Charlotte is proud, though, and I don't think she would allow me to fix it up. I would have to put a lot of money into it just to make it livable for her."

"Compromise with her." Zander tells me. "Fix only what is absolutely necessary and then let her do it here and there when she can afford it. It will give her something that is hers and make it easy to pay you back later. Let her keep her pride."

"I hadn't thought of that." I nod eagerly. "She just might allow me to do that for her."

"Allow you to do what?" Charlie asks as she comes in from outside.

"Come on over and have a seat." I offer with a smile.

"You have done a lot for me already with the

internship and the scholarship for my master's degree." Charlie informs me firmly.

"I have been thinking of your grandmother's property." I share with her honestly. "I would like you to allow my attorney to look over the will in the hopes we can find a loophole allowing the property to be solely yours. Obviously, you and Seth cannot share it. If we can accomplish that much, I would like you to allow me to fix just what is necessary to make it livable. Then you can finish it as you have time and resources and it is all yours. You can always pay me back later."

"That is still awfully generous, Jac." Charlie argues.

"I know how important family is to you, Charlie." I point out logically. "You have a lot of happy memories there and I would love for you to be able to make your own memories there with your own children and grandchildren. I am not trying to offend you, really. We are family and my relationship with you is a dream come true for me. I never had a close girlfriend growing up, not until I met you. I can share everything with you. I grew up not being allowed to have anything and I understand how important it is to pull your own weight. I don't want you upset with me, I just want to convince you to let me be generous."

"Jac!" Charlie protests and I can feel her weakening.

"Charlie!" I exclaim with a laugh.

"Okay." She sighs. "Nothing is done without my express approval. All plans go through me first."

"Obviously." I state sarcastically. "It's your house not mine."

I stand up excitedly and pull her into my arms for a hug.

"Yay!" I exclaim joyfully. "You know, I will have my attorney look into any grants you can get since it is considered a historical piece of property. It is practically right next door to one of those plantations people tour all the time."

Chapter Forty-One

My home has become overfull with all of the people that are living here currently so I come up with a plan to build a second story to the garage. The garage is large enough that a second story will be plenty of room for a small apartment. If I allow the builders to add on to the garage the second story will be that much bigger. The downfall to this is that my bodyguards will have to sleep inside the house during construction.

Charlie moves into a guest room at Lucien's house so that opens up my office for someone to sleep in. I am really not comfortable with her leaving the safety of my bodyguards but Lucien insists she will be safe. It is more comfortable for everyone that Lucien and Charlie spend more time alone at this point. I don't know about Lucien, but it is still weird for me to see him with someone else.

Nicole's crew promises me that they can get the garage project done in a couple weeks if they work around the clock. Of course, this includes putting in plumbing, electrical, a whole new roof, and the list goes on.

Alex has told me that once Seth is caught, I will still need a couple bodyguards considering I am the owner of such a large company. That in itself warrants security. I agree with him because I can't see a future without my Alex in it. I have grown close with Daniel and Henry too.

Three cots can fit in my office so the others are just folded up to be used in the living room on an as needed basis. It is easier for three of them to sleep at a time in the office since that room can be shut against noise.

So, during the garage construction, my bodyguards switch to a three on three off shift in order for them to be able to sleep peacefully. Alex screens all of the people working on the construction project and has me there to be sure they are being honest with him and not hiding anything important. Only after they pass this security screening are they allowed to start working. No one is allowed on the property unless they have been vetted.

My attorney, Mr. Sorenson, has informed me that there was indeed a loophole that allows the property to be passed directly on to Charlotte with Seth having no legal rights. Charlotte is thrilled with this news and I send Nicole and Victor out there with her to decide what needs to be done before she can move in.

After connecting with Lucien, Charlotte has had her summer classes moved down here to Tulane University so she doesn't have to drive back and forth to Baton Rouge.

It has been weeks and there has been no word about either Seth or John. No more little girls have gone missing and although this makes me very happy it also frightens me because I think it means Seth is more interested in me.

Even though nothing has happened lately, Alex refuses me to resume a normal life. I only leave the house if two bodyguards accompany me and only for something important. Alex and Daniel have taken over grocery shopping and buying whatever is necessary for the house. If I need something personal, I have taken to buying it online.

Apparently, Freya got pregnant while we were gone in the Gulf of Mexico. This puts her due date sometime around the seventh of July which is just a few weeks away. She is getting quite big and tends to stay back by the den in the back corner of the yard with Rune. Rune doesn't spend much time with me after getting him Freya, which is alright. He is happy with his mate and hopefully bringing them together will help increase wild numbers of the Mackenzie Valley Wolf.

With Seth still on the loose, I have canceled any classes at the college where I would actually have to be on campus. I will see if that is allowable for winter semester when we get close to that time period.

Alex, Henry, and Daniel have taken it upon themselves to spar with me every day, weather permitting. They expound on what I already know, having me improve what skills I already know and teaching me new ones.

I swim laps in the pool every day, I lift weights and I run on the treadmill which has found its way into my bedroom.

Zander gets stronger every day and the doctor has finally told him he can resume getting in shape with weights. He is still off work because of the stab wound. He has to be in a certain physical shape to be allowed to return.

He has refused to go back home now that the doctor says he is allowed to and instead insists that I need the extra protection. I am getting used to having him in the house all the time. We spend a lot of time together; swimming in the pool, lifting weights together, cuddled on the sofa watching television, playing cards, or just talking and getting to know each other better.

Victor calls him every day and they talk about Seth. So far there is really nothing new to disclose, but they brainstorm new ideas daily. Zander has also started sparring with the bodyguards in his preparation to go back to work. I watch with fascination because it honestly looks like they are trying to kill each other. I have a hard time fighting for real with my bodyguards because I am afraid of hurting them. What happens if I really drive their nose into their brain? What if I manage to slam my foot on their knee and break their leg? I know I am small but I have been taught how to protect myself and I cannot help but fear hurting them or worse. The know the only way to get me to fight for real is if they make me very angry. They know exactly what to say to make my rage rise to the surface.

July arrives and the heat and humidity down here is nearly too much for me to bear. I already miss the cold winters up north. This heat just sucks all of the energy right out of me.

I am making breakfast one morning, just days before Freya is due to have her litter, when the house phone rings. The only one who usually calls the house phone is grandma. I smile as I pick it up and greet her happily but soon find myself crying.

Grandpa died from a heart attack late last night. It was sudden and there was nothing that the doctors could do. Poor Grayson is beside himself with grief because they had been working out together these last few months and had grown very close. I was always closer to grandma but it makes me sad that I will never see him smile at me with that loving expression on his face again. My presence in his life helped him to move on with the loss of Phemie.

Grandma tells me that she is hoping to have the funeral in just a couple days and have him interred next to Phemie in the family crypt.

"He is my grandfather!" I exclaim when Alex initially tells me it is not safe for me to attend the funeral.

"It is the perfect opportunity for Seth to get his hands on you." Daniel states firmly. "We understand it is your grandpa, angel."

"This is exactly why I have a security detail." I point out logically. "Protect me while I pay my respects at the funeral. My grandma will need me with her and I want to be there for her."

Alex sighs in frustration but finally nods his agreement.

"You will have all six of us at your side at all times." Alex reiterates. "You are not allowed to walk away without us at any time. If you go to the bathroom, we will make sure it is safe before you step into the room. You will be surrounded by us at all times. Do I make myself clear?"

"Yes." I agree with him meekly.

"Seven of us." Zander states as he steps into the room. "Once your grandma tells you what church it is at a couple of us should go there ahead of time to check it out. Make sure we know where all the exits and entrances are, locate any potential hiding places. I will talk to Victor and see if PD can use this as a trap to catch Seth. He will no doubt attempt to use this to his advantage. If we have plain clothes officers strategically placed maybe we can catch him."

"That sounds like a good idea, Zander, but our first priority is to protect our girl." Alex states angrily. "I will not use my little girl as bait."

"That isn't what I am suggesting." Zander states with a chuckle. "I would not use her as bait either, but you have allowed her to go. Seth will use this situation to try and get his hands on her. He has no choice because she isn't allowed to leave the property. You know as well as I that he will be there regardless of whether or not we want him there."

I leave the men to debate over how to handle the

funeral and I step outside, breakfast forgotten to grieve for my grandfather. He was only fifty-five years old and much too young to die of a heart attack. Apparently, his health was too far gone for Grayson's workouts and diet changes to help soon enough. I wish I had been able to get to know him better, but my life has been one drama after another since my arrival in New Orleans just a few short months ago. I am grateful that he had a chance to get close to Grayson. That was good for the both of them.

He is with Phemie now. Daddy is with his girl once more.

Grayson does not appear for the rest of the day and instead stays in his room, trying to deal with this sudden loss. He won't even allow me to comfort him. Lucien and Charlie come over and thankfully, Grayson speaks to his older brother. They are in there for a long-time leaving Charlotte time to fill me in on how it is going with her and Lucien.

She gushes over how wonderful he is. He is always putting her first and is so romantic. He is helping her make decisions at her grandmother's property and works right alongside all of the workers. Nicole and Victor have accepted her as one of the family, insisting that she call them Mom and Dad.

I am so happy for her. She really needed someone in her life to make it complete.

The morning of the funeral arrives and when I step downstairs wearing my black dress, I am stunned to see all of my bodyguards wearing black suits. They all looks so dashing. Zander is also wearing an expensive black suit that looks like it was tailored to fit him. My heart races seeing him like this. He, of course, notices my reaction to him and his eyes darken seductively. I blush and look away bashfully. We haven't made out since we were on the boat and it didn't take me long to feel shy around him again.

Alex's suburban seats eight people so all of us are able to ride together, which pleases the guys completely. The funeral is in St. Louis Cathedral, the one everyone tours when they come to New Orleans. It is huge and I am surprised that three of my bodyguards were able to walk through it already this morning.

Victor has a couple dozen officers attending the funeral in plain clothes in hopes of catching Seth. We are early since he was my grandfather. I step right up to grandma and give her a big hug. She looks pretty well considering and I am guessing she has done all of her crying already while she was alone.

I stay in the main part of the church and help grandma greet people and thank them for their condolences. Many of those attending remember my mother and I hear from them how much I look like her.

Grayson is riding with Lucien and Charlotte. He is still struggling over the loss and can't seem to work his way past it at all. He has been with grandpa almost every day for the last few months.

Now that I am here, I feel exposed and too terrified to move. Just knowing that I am probably being stalked by a monster right now almost makes me wish I had stayed home. Alex, Daniel and Zander circle me wherever I am with my other bodyguards creating another protective circle.

The service takes about an hour and from there most of those in attendance will walk the fifteen minutes to the cemetery where grandpa will be interred. I am completely surrounded by my bodyguards and Zander on the walk to the cemetery. I see Lucien, Charlotte, and Grayson walking close by as well as many of the plain clothes police officers.

My anxiety when we enter the cemetery skyrockets because I remember one of the little girls Seth took disappeared from a cemetery. I have a death grip on Zander's arm and I can feel the tension just radiating off of my bodyguards as they try to keep me safe.

I want to run, back home where I am safe. I don't know if my abilities are screaming at me because I know something is going to happen or if it is just because I am scared. The procession stops at the Burt family crypt where grandpa is placed in the middle where my mother once sat. Grandpa will stay there in the middle until another Burt family member passes away.

The priest says a few more words before inviting everyone to return to the church for a light luncheon. Grandma doesn't want to leave grandpa behind and it breaks my heart to pull her along with us back towards the church.

Chapter Forty-Two

Alex leads us down Basin Street towards St Peter, which will lead us back to the church. Many of the other people are taking a different route than we are. We are approaching the corner where we will turn right and I see a park right up ahead with trees when I suddenly hear a loud buzzing overhead like a hive of bees or something followed by a loud popping sound. People's screams and panic fill the air as Alex pushes us into the shelter of the trees.

I cannot see anything being surrounded by my bodyguard and Zander as I am, but the terrified emotions of the people around me are making it hard for me to try and stay calm. Alex and the guys are yelling now too and when I look around, I see Henry on the ground staring sightlessly up at me. When I attempt to feel him, I get nothing. Henry has been killed. Anguish rushes through me and I try to squat down to him but I am yanked roughly to my feet. Many of my bodyguards are lying on the ground not moving and I do not understand what has happened so quickly.

Alex and Zander place me between them protectively and try to rush me towards safety somewhere. We only manage to move a couple of feet before suddenly Alex and Zander are no longer there. When I pivot in a panicked circle, I see them lying on the ground as well. My ears are ringing and I all I hear is people screaming and chaos. Before I can run more than a foot I am grabbed from behind.

"*Daddy's girl.*" Seth's voice whispers through my thoughts right before he wraps his arm around my neck.

"*Seth has me.*" I manage to shout telepathically to Grayson before everything goes dark.

I come awake sometime later and find myself on the small deck of my yacht. Seth is unaware that I am awake yet as he unties the small yacht preparing it to leave the marina. Carefully I put up a mental block so he won't feel me and I call out to Grayson once more.

"*Seth has me on my yacht. I am unhurt. I don't know how long before threatens me not to talk to you this way.*" I send to Grayson mentally. "*Please tell me someone is left alive?*"

"*Lucien, Zander, Dad, Alex, and Daniel are on their way.*" Grayson relays to me. "*Henry didn't make it. Chris, Tony, and Cooper are at the hospital. Hang in there, sis.*"

"*Seth is just untying the boat. We haven't left the marina yet.*" I share with my brother helpfully before I go quiet.

Too soon the yacht is heading out of the marina and I can only assume Seth is taking me out onto the Gulf of Mexico somewhere. Thankfully, he will be too busy trying to escape to hurt me just yet and I pray that I am saved before I lose my virginity to this monster.

I keep my eyes closed when I feel his attention switch to me and I keep my mental block up so he doesn't feel anything going on inside my head. Hopefully he will think I am still unconscious.

Time passes and we make it out onto the gulf and I can't stop the panic from rushing through me. I am getting too far away and am afraid it will be too late by the time someone gets close enough to save me.

Looking down at the Celtic knot bracelet Alex gave me I feel a tear trickle down into my hair as I pray the tracking device in it will lead them to me. I had forgotten about the bracelet in all of the chaos and I am grateful that Seth is unaware of it.

My heart races with hope when I hear a boat nearby and especially when it comes up right alongside us. I am confused though because Seth seems to not be upset about this and actually calls the person on board.

"What have you done this time, Seth?" A voice, that I recognize and have not heard in some time, speaks.

"She is my daughter, John." Seth explains as if that makes all the sense in the world. I open my eyes just a slit and see Uncle John standing there only a few feet from me talking with Seth as if he knows him!

"You have every law enforcement agency on the lookout for you." John states furiously. "I am tired of cleaning up your messes, brother."

Brother?

My brain starts to make sense of this new information and so many details start to click together.

Oh my god!

Betrayal overwhelms me and I can't stop the sob that escapes my throat.

John sending my book to Seth while he was in prison.

John killing the girls after Seth was done playing with them so he wouldn't get caught.

John must have known my mother was pregnant with Grayson and I. John is the one who must have arranged my adoption.

Did John kill my adopted parents because William discovered the embezzlement?

Did he have something to do with the disappearance of their daughter Wilhelmina?

"Well, well." John looks over at me and notices that I am awake. "Hello princess."

"There won't be any more messes, as you call them." Seth tells John arrogantly. "Jacqueline is all I need. She is daddy's girl."

I watch in stunned amazement as John very calmly takes a straight razor and attempts to slice Seth's throat. A struggle ensues between them ending with Seth lying on the floor wounded to the point that he cannot stand up.

Unable to move because I am pretty much hogtied, I can only stare at him helplessly.

"Oh god!" I telepathically scream to Grayson in a panic when I see John stepping towards me with a hypodermic needle. *"John Van Asselt just stabbed Seth. He is Seth's brother. He is the connection. He killed all the girls. He has a hypodermic needle Grayson and I don't know if he means to kill me or put me to sleep."*

"My princess." John murmurs manically as he sinks the needle into my thigh quickly before swinging me up into his arms to carry me onto his larger yacht. Whatever was in the needle seems to be working slowly as he carries me down below, strips me naked, and ties me to one of the beds.

"Lucien knows." Grayson tells me on our mental connection. *"They say they are gaining on your location. Your bracelet is close to them. Do you still have it on?"*

"Yes." I manage to whimper as I feel myself slipping

away from consciousness. *"I don't want to die Grayson."*

"Jac!" Grayson's scream echoes through my head as darkness claims me.

I am groggy and my head hurts as I struggle to wake up. My adrenaline is rushing full speed making me writhe to free myself from the person who is holding me.

"Easy baby, you're safe." A husky voice that makes me feel safe washes over me, but it confuses me. Is this a trick?

"Please." I whimper, too scared to believe that I am truly safe. Is Seth really dead? Is this just him using his psychic abilities to fool me?

"Open your eyes Jac." That husky voice again. It takes a lot of effort but I finally manage to open my eyes to find Zander gazing down at me anxiously.

"Zander?" I sob as I reach up to touch his face to ensure he is real.

"It's me baby." He nuzzles my cheek with his. "We got you."

"Henry!" I exclaim. Alex appears above me with a sad expression on his face.

"We lost Henry." Alex tells me as he brushes a lock of my hair off my face tenderly. "He would be happy to know his death wasn't in vain. You're safe now little girl."

I relax back against Zander and close my eyes at the nausea that looking around is causing. I cry softly as everything washes over me suddenly. All those times that I spent the night with Uncle John. Wonderful, compassionate, giving Uncle John. Uncle John who spoiled me every chance he got. Taking me places and buying me things that my parents wouldn't allow me to have.

He killed all of those innocent girls. Girls who just wanted to go home to their families after the horror they suffered. He covered for Seth all those years, why? Why did he arrange my adoption? Is he really the one responsible for killing my adopted parents?

The straight razor! He killed Seth with it and it may very well be the same blade used on all of the girls and my adopted parents. I am sure they will test it for DNA.

Is Seth dead? What happened to John, did they arrest him? Am I safe now?

Made in the USA
Middletown, DE
21 July 2022